LANDS END

LANDS END

THE FORENSIC GEOLOGY SERIES
BOOK 6

TONI DWIGGINS

—— To be notified of new releases, sign up for my mailing list:

https://eepurl.com/GtdZn

—— Contact me at:

Website: tonidwiggins.com

Facebook: facebook.com/ToniDwigginsBooks

San Francisco is 49 square miles of city wrapped on three sides by water, edged at its northwestern corner by the wild and rocky stretch known as LANDS END.

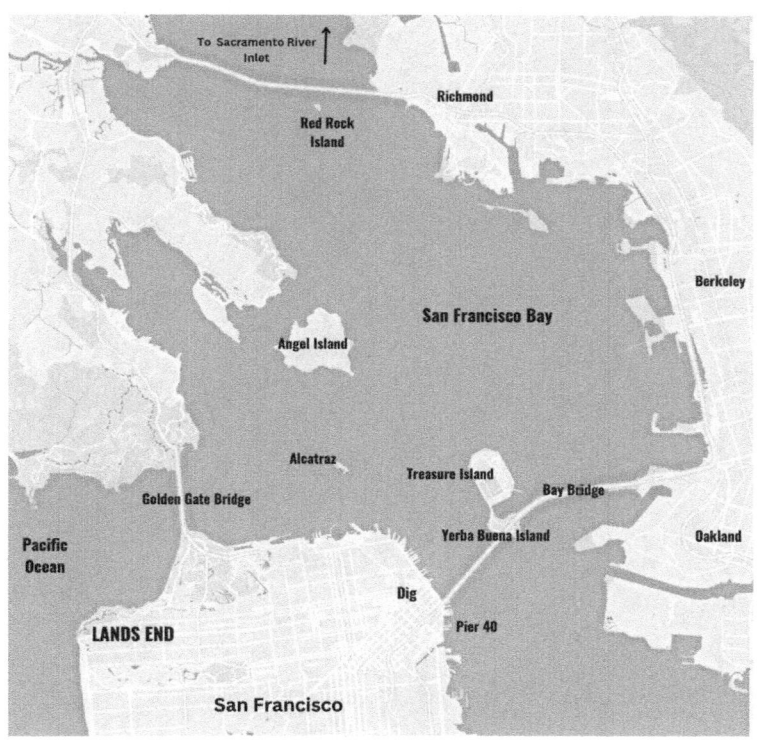

1

DURING THE LONG drive from our forensics lab in the eastern Sierra foothills to the city by the bay, my partner and I discussed the case we'd just signed onto, and the implication of the note pinned to the murder victim's shirt.

The note was four short words: *we will bury you.*

The San Francisco detective who'd phoned yesterday to explain the situation and request our services gave a grim laugh when I asked, "*Will*, future tense?" I didn't inquire about the other three words. We were between jobs and the case sounded intriguing. Our work is geoforensics--analyzing earth evidence at scenes of crimes and crises--and serendipitously we each had a past in San Francisco. We knew the geology.

This job was right up our alley.

We arrived early enough for lunch, found a parking garage near the waterfront, winced at the exorbitant fee, and headed off--Walter to pick up sandwiches at the Ferry Building food court, me to stake out a spot at the end of the adjacent pier.

Pier 14 jutted like a probe into San Francisco Bay, whose blue-green waters stretched far and wide. To my right, the lofty Bay Bridge reached across the water to the eastern shoreline by way of a hilly island in the middle of the bay. My view from the pier was unobstructed. I took a seat in the metal swivel chair that was bolted to the concrete, got the binoculars from my pack, and trained the lenses on that island. Eleven years ago I'd camped there--up from UCLA with a grad-school group to learn how to measure sea-level rise. It was my first field trip and I was dead set on proving myself. What I got was a lesson in monitoring tide gauges with an elevated heart rate when an earthquake shook my narrow beach and pebbles rained down from the facing cliff.

"Is it there?" Walter asked, settling into the metal chair beside me, paper bag in hand, mission accomplished.

He knew the story of my memorable beach. There was no sign of it now. Perhaps rising waters had erased it. I stowed the binocs. "It's gone."

"The nature of the past," he said. "We keep losing pieces of it."

Yeah, I kept learning that lesson. The past addressed, I asked my partner, "What's for lunch?"

He opened the paper bag and withdrew two bottled lemonades and two long sandwiches, then passed one of each to me. I unwrapped my sandwich and peeked inside the crusty sourdough baguette. The filling was some kind of goat cheese, layered with some kind of chutney. Vegetation curled out the sides. Arugula. Very San Francisco.

Walter bit into his sandwich. "Oh my."

I tasted mine. Oh yes.

"It's good to be back in the Bay Area," he said, around a mouthful.

Thirty-some years ago he'd completed his graduate work at UC Berkeley, across the bay, then set out on the path to a career in geoforensics, settling in a Sierra town where the geology tickled his fancy. It was my hometown, and that's where we met.

As a kid I got a job in his lab doing scutwork; as an adult I joined him as partner.

And now here we were with our grad-school geology in hand.

"Yes," I said, "good to be back."

Walter swiveled his seat to face the stupendous view.

I followed suit.

The air was crisp, the sun was warm on my back, and the bay water was sparkling. I relaxed and worked on my sandwich.

Lunch finished, we turned our backs on the bay and walked up the pier toward the city.

Ahead, the towers of the Financial District were gilded by the sun. The city's neighborhoods were known as 'districts' and right now this one looked the appropriate color. Golden.

We came to the end of the pier and exited onto the Embarcadero, a waterfront roadway and promenade that ran along a three-mile seawall on the city's edge. Its name came from the Spanish *embarcar*—meaning the place to embark, inspired by long-ago ships embarking from the port of San Francisco into the bay, and thence out through the narrow strait between two headlands known as the golden gate, and into the sea beyond.

A project to upgrade the seawall was underway to protect the city's edge from rising waters, so I'd read. San Francisco was nothing if not getting ready.

We turned left on the Embarcadero and threaded our way among the walkers and runners and scooters and cyclists and skaters and kid-packed strollers and tourist-toting pedicabs.

We passed a woman wrapped in a worn blanket huddled against the sun-warmed concrete seawall.

"Cassie, you have any cash?" Walter asked.

Not nearly enough to make a difference but I rummaged in my wallet and passed him a twenty. Our sandwiches had cost more than that. He placed the bill in the Starbucks cup beside her.

We continued in silence a few dozen yards and then, at the green light, crossed the wide roadway.

On the other side of the street, we entered the Financial District.

The district was San Francisco's flattest land, in a city known for its steep hills. This downtown area--along with most of the city's eastern and northern flanks--was built on landfill. These lands did not exist in the mid-nineteenth century. These lands used to be water. When I was here on that field trip we visited the area and took a walk inland through the district's high-rise canyons. When the sidewalk was no longer horizontal and we started heading uphill, we knew we had reached the original shoreline.

I thought about the land beneath our feet.

I thought about the note pinned to the victim's body, about the third word.

Bury.

2

"*THAT'S NOT RIGHT.*"

The shout carried in the still air across the giant pit.

When Walter and I had arrived at the excavated site and looked down into it, we'd gotten a bird's eye perspective. The pit was about the size of a football field, a rectangle dug some twenty feet below street level.

Now that we were down inside, our view was grounded. We peered across the pit, wondering what was not right. At the far end, diggers were huddling to examine some archaeological artifact that we couldn't see from here.

We weren't the only ones looking. The cop tending the yellow crime-scene tape that enclosed our end of the pit was staring, as well.

"You must be my geologists!"

We turned.

And she was our detective, Debra Talon--I recognized her from the photo on the SFPD website. Mid-forties I thought, tall and thin, buzz-cut blonde hair untouched by gray, angular face touched by lines at the mouth and the brow. She wore aviator sunglasses, even though the pit was mostly in shade. She wore a dark gray blazer over a black T-shirt, over gray slacks, gold badge pinned to her belt. Her black sneakers were dusted with gray silt.

You couldn't take two steps down here without stirring up silt unless you used the planking laid down like old-west walkways in muddy towns.

I'd strayed from the walkway and already acquired a dusting of my own. I wore my standard field gear, low boots and khaki pants and shirt. Silt didn't much change the look. Walter dressed similarly. We could have modeled for *Field Geology Today*.

Indeed, we both bore marks of the field. Walter was in his mid-sixties, weathered by the decades on the job, but when he smiled he lost a good ten years. I was heading for my mid-thirties, feeling the weight of the job more with each passing year, fighting the weathering with hats and sunscreen. When I smiled, it was not at the mirror.

I smiled now, along with Walter, and we said our hellos.

Detective Talon shook our hands. "Glad you got yourselves down here. I apologize for the delay but I had to work my way through the crowd." She pointed up top. "This place is a zoo."

I looked. We'd worked our own way through ten minutes ago but already the crowd had grown. Up top, people lined the chain-link fence that blocked off the dig. Suits, dresses, shorts, sweats, jeans. Kids on shoulders. An ice cream vendor. A drummer. Chattering. Jostling. My attention caught on the figure in jeans and blue hoodie who we'd passed to reach the wooden ramp that led from street level down to the pit. She'd turned to watch us, then. She watched us, now. *She*, I thought, given the drape of the hoodie.

"I'm told there are regulars," the detective continued, "and they call themselves Fencies. Feeling like a regular, myself. And before I get caught without this..." She had a helmet in one hand; she clamped it over the buzz cut. "I hate these things."

Everybody down here--diggers, cops, us, and now the detective--wore the white hard hats. There was a box of them at the entrance, like party favors.

"Before we get down to business," she said, "let's get names out of the way. People hear my last name, Talon, and think sharp nails on a bird of prey. When I first joined the department my colleagues gave me hassle and nicknamed me Raptor. Suits me-- I dive into a case like a bird of prey and don't come out until I've got my talons into the perp." She lifted a hand, showing her black-tipped French manicure. "Think Raptor if you like but please do call me Debra, out loud. So that's me. Now let's talk you, Cassie Oldfield and Walter Shaws, with your impressive credentials--which is why I'm glad to have you on the case--so tell me if you prefer titles or last names or first names."

I waited to be sure she'd finished. I said, "First names work fine."

Walter said, "If I had a nickname like yours, Debra, I'd guard it jealously. Pleased to meet you in person. I'm Walter."

"All right," she said, "good all around! And let me repeat what I told you on the phone yesterday--thank you for taking the job on short notice."

As she'd explained yesterday, the SFPD crime lab did not have geology expertise, and the outside lab the department used wasn't available because they were up to their ears in a case. But they recommended us.

I glanced again at the activity at the far end of the pit, and at the people up above watching.

"The zoo." Debra shook her head, and gestured at the dig. "This place has been a 'destination' ever since that was found. And then our victim Roger Forster turns up here and that brings out the ghouls. Fourteen years in homicide and I've never seen anything like it. Still, I get the job done and I expect you're the same."

I caught Walter's smile of approval.

"So," she said, "let's talk dirt."

While waiting for Debra, we'd had a quick-and-dirty look around. The surficial soil was a silty clay, with interbeds of sand. Where the sun reached the ground in the deep pit, it was dry. Elsewhere, it was damp and gave off a scent of wet soil.

She began, "There was no dirt in the victim's orifices. My techs did find soil in the clothing--socks, pants, shirt, jacket, wool cap--and they set the clothing aside for you. The boots have mud compacted in the waffle soles, but my techs didn't excavate that. They said you'd appreciate it."

"Indeed we do," Walter said.

"I'll let them know. So, all that's in sealed evidence containers at the department. We'll do the chain-of-custody transfer when we get to your lab." She added, "You won't believe the lab space I've got for you."

"We look forward to it."

"Good. Now, let me give you the run-down--some of this I told you on the phone, a lot is new, so I'll go over all of it. Medical examiner's preliminary results say cause of death was asphyxia. The means, strangulation--the victim was throttled around the neck from behind. The body was found here..." she pointed to a shallow indentation in the damp soil, "around seven yesterday morning. The ME got to it ASAP. She's estimating time of death the afternoon before, a two-to-six p.m. window. It turned chilly early evening, which complicates estimations as I'm sure you know, yada yada yada, but one thing she did nail down was that the body had been moved. There were fibers consistent with a vehicle trunk liner on the right side of the clothing. Vic was jammed up on his side when found here-- rigor and lividity were fixed. So he would have been in rigor when transferred from the car down here to his final resting place."

Walter said, "That wouldn't be trivial. Are you thinking more than one perp?"

"Makes sense."

"We'll assume it was after dark?"

"We will--late enough and dark enough that there were no witnesses. Gate up top gets padlocked at the end of the day. Padlock was severed. Bolt cutters. Security camera at the bottom of the ramp was ripped off its post. Gone."

"Footprints?"

"Nothing identifiable. Some dirt on the planking but that was scuffed."

"We'll take a sample."

"One more fun fact," she said. "The vic's car was found in a parking garage nearby, the entrance time-stamped nine-eighteen a.m. the day before he was found *here*. The morning of the day he died. Ran up quite a charge. Not that it matters to our vic, but maybe it'll help catch his killer. It tells us our vic got here fairly early. Tells us he didn't use the car again."

"Any idea why he came here?" Walter asked. "A zoo regular?"

"Yes, according to his cousin. He lived with the cousin."

"So he began his last day there?"

"So his cousin says."

"We'll want to examine the soils there."

"All right, sure. We'll pay a visit after you're done here."

I said, "Given that the victim drove from home to the dig, parked nearby, and ended his day here, is that why you're thinking the murder is connected to all this?"

"Can't help but wonder. As to where he was killed..." She regarded us. "You two can find out where he'd been?"

"The geology should have something to say."

"May it talk as much as I do."

I smiled. You had to like her. "If it were me, I wouldn't have left those dirty clothes and muddy boots on the body."

"People think dirt is just dirt."

"Their mistake."

She gave me a thumbs-up.

"Let's think about transport," Walter said. "The victim's car being in the garage, wherever he went from here, he didn't drive. He walked or took a bus or called an Uber or, if the motive lies here, perhaps he caught a ride with the perp."

"That covers it," she said. "But nix on the Uber--we checked his phone records. And FYI, phone wasn't found on his body, or at his place. We tried pinging it, no joy, it's not in service. Could be he removed the battery."

"Could be the killer trashed the phone."

"That's on the could-be list. Now, how do you two want to proceed with the dirt?"

"We'll want to do some sampling. Certainly, some of the soil your techs found on the victim originated here. Possibly, we can learn if he was down here before he left that morning."

She nodded.

He glanced across the pit. "And we'll want to sample the dig itself, given that the vic was dumped next to it."

"Makes sense, but the archaeologist is a touchy sort. You'll need an introduction. I'll take you over there."

I put up a hand. "First, about that note found on the body..."

She flashed a grin. "You mean the question I dodged on the phone yesterday."

"Yes, that."

"The note's cut and paste, words from a newspaper, old-fashioned. No prints. Smart perp. Wore gloves."

"Might we break it down?"

"As in?"

"Word by word. *We will bury you.*"

"Let's do it."

"Starting with the *we*. Plural."

"As we agreed, more than one perp makes sense, to move him. There's your plural."

I nodded. "Next word--the one I asked about on the phone. *Will.* Warns of another killing?"

"Not necessarily. The note could refer specifically to this vic."

"True."

"Or," she said, "it could be the way you read it."

"Which way do you read it?"

"Depends if I want to be optimistic or pessimistic."

I waited.

"Pessimistic." She put her hands on her hips and her blazer flapped open, revealing the badge and holstered gun on her belt. "I'm a homicide detective."

Okay, then.

She said, "Go on."

"Third word. *Bury.*"

"Could refer to this vic. Not literally, of course. Metaphorically buried here."

All three of us glanced around the pit. Twenty feet below street level. Some burying had sure occurred here. Past and, metaphorically, present.

"Taken literally," I said, "I'm wondering if the note refers to burial, somewhere, in the future. A future victim."

The detective grimaced.

Goes with the homicide territory, I thought. Gives you lines around the mouth.

I said, "And the fourth word. *You.*"

"Could mean Roger Forster and nobody else," she said. " Optimistically speaking."

"If the threat referred solely to this homicide."

"Yes. If."

"And if not," I said, "the question is, who is *you*?"

Future tense.

3

THE DETECTIVE TOOK THE LEAD, striding across the pit, calling out, "Hey Burt, what'd you all discover that's *not right*? Anything to do with my vic?"

I hadn't realized she'd heard the shout, on her way down the ramp from the zoo. Clearly, she had. As we drew up, a man turned to watch us. Burt, evidently. He didn't answer her question.

I scanned the dig. I couldn't tell what was *not right*, aside from the fact of a hundred-foot sailing vessel buried beneath the San Francisco streets. The three diggers were still huddled around something at the stern.

"Burt," Debra said, "meet the geologists consulting on my case, Cassie Oldfield and Walter Shaws. Cassie, Walter, meet archaeologist Burt Zhang. First names all around, good to go."

I switched my focus from the ship to the man. He had a slight stubble and his black hair bristled from beneath his white hard hat. He was muscular and deeply tanned and looked like he belonged in the field. I couldn't judge his age. Younger than Walter's mid-sixties, and older than my mid-thirties. He wore jeans and a red T-shirt with jagged black lettering: *Don't blame me, it's San Andreas's fault.*

That would be the infamous San Andreas Fault, the rift zone that caused the big 1906 San Francisco earthquake, and other less calamitous quakes over subsequent decades. Most recently, about a year ago, the fault unleashed a modest quake that gave the city a shake--and that led to a resurgence of seismic retrofitting. And *that* doomed the building that had stood on this spot, an aging office tower. The owner decided retrofitting wasn't cost-effective and so had the building demolished, intending to sell the lot. First though, according to preservation laws, an archaeological assessment had to be done. One of the drilling boreholes produced evidence of an oaken ship's keel.

Hence, this dig.

Walter and I smiled and said our hellos.

"Howdy," Burt said. His voice was canyon-deep.

"Burt," the detective said, "my geologists need to do some soil sampling. We want to find out if my victim might have poked around your dig on the day he died."

"You asked me that two days ago."

"And you told me no. Since then, I've learned he was a regular visitor."

"I'm aware. He was all over the place, talking to reporters, handing out books his cousin wrote."

Debra said to us, "I'll explain later." She turned back to Burt, "Then you *did* see him?"

"Off and on. It's always busy here."

"So might he have boarded your ship?"

"If he tried I would have had him drawn and quartered."

Walter's eyebrows lifted.

"Don't worry," Debra said to us, "Burt has a unique sense of humor. He told me having the SFPD as a neighbor to his dig should be a criminal offense. He told me he was joking. I told him my vic is more time-sensitive than his old vic. No joke."

Walter's interest stirred. "You have a victim here, Burt?"

"Evidence of."

"Perhaps that could shed light on our victim's burial nearby."

"The past always sheds light."

"Then please do."

"For that, you'll need to fathom the scene."

Did we? The scene, I thought, was clear enough. There was the giant pit, reinforced with wood retaining walls that were reinforced by piles of excavated dirt. The dig itself occupied about a third of the pit. Here, there were the bones of the nineteenth-century ship. And then there were the archaeology trappings: the yellow string gridding the site, the tools, the brushes, the trowels, the picks, the shovels, the buckets, the break-time folding camp chairs, and, sitting on a makeshift ledge of old bricks, the plastic bins labeled *artifacts*. On another brick ledge was a splintered wooden crate with lettering engraved on its side, the name of the ship I assumed: *Dawn*.

I'd been told of San Francisco's buried ships back when my field team was learning about the landfill underlying the city's downtown. Yesterday, when Debra phoned us, she'd given a brief overview. Walter and I had read up on the subject before our westward journey.

I said, "We're familiar with the situation."

The archaeologist gave me a long look.

I added, "Somewhat."

"You have gold fever."

"I...what?"

"There's a gold rush in California," he continued, in that deep-canyon voice, "and you live elsewhere and the fastest way to get to the gold fields is to sail to San Francisco. Its bay has a deep cove, a natural port. You disembark and join the hordes.

The passengers, the crew--you all abandon your vessel and catch a smaller ship, which ferries you up the bay to the inlet of the Sacramento River, then up the river to Sacramento, where you strike out overland. You head for the hills, aflame with gold fever."

Walter leaned in closer. He was the history buff in our partnership.

Burt swiveled to Walter. "And *you*. While she and her shipmates have run off to the gold fields, you're left with a problem. You're the mayor of San Francisco. You've got a waterfront teeming with newcomers, a city bursting at its seams. You've got a cove clogged with abandoned ships. Some burn in the fires that sweep the wooden wharves. Some rot in place. Some are taken for salvage. Some are re-purposed as saloons and jails and churches and brothels and boarding houses. And *still* your city is overrun. You need more land. So you make it. You scuttle the derelict ships, you have sand brought in from nearby dunes, you add trash and debris, and you fill in the shallow cove where the ships lay. Year after year, decade after decade, your city expands, your waterfront creeps outward, until you fill in the entire cove. And then there is no more Yerba Buena Cove. All is buried."

Walter listened with a half-smile. I thought, he's enjoying the fantasy of being a gold-rush mayor.

The archaeologist pointed toward the Embarcadero. "And eventually, a seawall is built to protect your created land."

Reflexively, I glanced up, although the waterfront was several blocks away and twenty feet higher than our pit. And I caught sight of the blue hoodie. She'd moved, away from the ramp. She was pressed against the fence, fingers laced through the chain links, watching us.

I shifted focus back where it belonged, to our little group.

Burt continued, "And your legacy today, Walter?"

Walter cocked his head.

"A ghost fleet buried beneath our streets. Forty-five ships, to
be precise."

Walter let out a soft whistle.

"Dozens more suspected, going by historical records."

"Was *this* ship recorded?"

"It's not on a list. This one's a ghost."

"A pity," Walter said. "Still, all in all, I created quite a legacy."

"You'll do."

"For what?"

"For entry to my dig."

I didn't know if the archaeologist was joking. Or if we'd just
been put to a test, and passed. If so, I understood, being overprotective myself when it came to rocks and soils at crime
scenes. Respect the evidence.

The evidence here being one hundred and eighty-some
years old.

"All right," Debra said, "does any of this relate to my vic?"

Burt swiveled to face the detective. "And *you*. You're the
captain of this ship, one of the few to return to your vessel. You
come back from the gold fields along with some of your shipmates. Passengers or crew or maybe a mix. To collect belongings.
To sail back home. To ferry more gold hunters here. But you
never leave the cove. You all fall into discord. A fight.
Doubtlessly over gold, because you are all still aflame with the
fever." He cocked a finger. "And you're armed, doubtlessly with
the popular Colt percussion revolvers. 'Sixguns,' in the parlance
of the day."

Debra said, "My service weapon is a Glock."

"My victim was shot with a Colt." Burt released the trigger
finger. "Where did you go, I wonder, after the shooting?"

"Thanks for not casting me as the vic."

I stifled a grin.

Walter said, "Burt, you mentioned evidence?"

"His boot."

"His?"

"Judging by the size."

"Where did you find it?"

"At the bow. Behind some crates. Buried in the mud."

I asked, "How do you know he was shot?"

"The evidence."

"You're going to make me ask?"

"You're experiencing how an archaeologist uncovers the past. Piece by hard-won piece."

"Thank you for the lesson." Again.

"A 36-caliber round lead projectile is embedded in the boot heel. A 'ball,' in the parlance of the day. There are two holes in the upper boot, entry and exit." He smiled. "Evidence."

Walter indicated the remains of the ship. "It's lucky the evidence survived."

"Happenstance. After she was abandoned, the *Dawn* was hauled up onto the mudflats by salvagers. We found ship-breaking tools scattered around. Fortunately, the salvagers didn't finish the job. Ran out of money, or labor. So she was left half-gutted, and eventually buried along with the rest."

I glanced at the broken ship, the front and mid-sections gutted to the waterline, the nearly intact stern rising from the mud like a bird on the wing.

"A point of historical interest," the archaeologist added, "the salvagers who reaped the profit hired others to do the grunt work. Those ill-paid ship-breakers were Chinese."

Walter said, "I didn't know that. I knew Chinese immigrants did a lot of the grunt work in the gold fields."

Burt folded his arms. "Not all of us. Some of us sailed from China seeking *gold mountain*--in the parlance of the immigrants--and worked claims abandoned by the whites. Those of us who evaded mistreatment."

Us? I thought.

Walter said, "Thank you for reading me into the history."

"Not many ask."

I said, "Then these ships aren't just history for you, Burt?"

He gave me one of his long looks. "I'm old San Francisco."

One of the workers at the stern shouted, "And now *you're* breaking up ships."

Burt shot back, "As my field tech, *you're* breaking up the ship. As archaeologist, *I'm* deciding what's worth saving."

I asked, carefully, "What's worth saving?"

"Whatever tells the story."

Walter asked, "Such as that boot evidence?"

Burt swiveled. "Would you like to see it?"

I watched my partner. Does the Earth turn? Yes, he'd like to see the evidence.

"All right gang," Debra said, "here's how it's going to go down. Burt is going to explain anything that could relate to the choice of this pit as a dumping ground for my vic. Starting with what, in his professional estimation, is *not right*--because it sounds like you all found something new. Then we'll get to the shot-up boot."

"Wrong order," the archaeologist said. "We're going to see the boot first, to familiarize you with the situation, because what you heard needs context."

She put up her hands. "Your dig. Your rules."

We headed for the artifact bins on the brick ledge.

I got a glimpse inside one bin: rusted nails and stoneware bottles and unidentifiable ship's hardware.

Burt opened another bin. Inside was the boot.

It looked, I thought in surprise, remarkably wearable. Grimed, of course. But intact. The upper was about eight inches tall, leather, cracked and worn and muddied, heavy-looking, a boot made for rugged conditions. There were tabs at the top, to help pull the boot on and off. The heel was stacked, made from several leather layers. The boot was slightly canted in the bin so that the bottom of the sole was just visible. It too was made of layers of leather, which were pinned to one another and to the upper by what looked to be square wooden pegs--which were visible because the top layer of the sole had slightly separated from the boot's upper.

The space was filled by pebbly mud.

Walter sucked in a breath. "You have some nice geology there."

Burt looked at him with interest.

Walter pointed to the leather upper, which was deeply abraded and gouged. "Looks as though there was a scuffle."

"And a shooting." Burt lifted the boot from the bin, holding it up by the pull tabs, rotating it like a salesman displaying footwear to a buyer.

We got a good long look.

A shooting, all right. The evidence said the wearer was hit twice.

One shot had hit the back of the stacked heel. A lead-gray ball was lodged there, burrowed partway into the layered leather. It looked like a ball bearing, only not shiny, not smooth. Dull. Roughened.

Another shot had hit the boot's upper. As Burt rotated the boot to and fro, I saw the holes, front and back, lining up. Shot through the leg, in and out.

In the back, out the front, most likely--given that the shot to the boot had hit the back of the heel.

The boot-guy had been shot while walking away. Or, likely, running.

I'd once slammed my bare foot into a concrete step. I'd gone nauseated from the pain. Now, I stared at the boot and winced. A lead ball had torn through boot-guy's leg. In the back, out the front. The vic must have howled from the pain. The ball probably didn't hit the femoral artery because if it had, the victim would not likely have been able to grasp those pull tabs and remove the boot. He would have bled out.

But he got the boot off.

And then what?

Well, he'd crawled behind some crates because that's where the boot was found. So he hides there. Probably binds up the leg wound with whatever is at hand. His shirt would do. And then? Maybe the shooter finds him hiding and finishes the job. Or maybe boot-guy escapes, jumping overboard.

Or maybe someone else removed the shot-up boot. Trying to help?

I glanced up at the fence and saw the hoodie still watching. I wondered if she could make out the bullet holes in the boot, as Burt held it up for our inspection.

Burt said, "Do you care to reconstruct?"

I returned my attention to the scene at hand. Burt was addressing Walter, not me.

"I can give it a try," my partner said. "Given that the boot wearer was shot, I'd say that the mud-pebble stratum and the gouges to the upper resulted from a scuffle. The attack took place on land, where the mud and pebbles were acquired. Logically, the shooting followed the scuffle. The shooting could have taken place on land--or, more likely, since the victim ended up aboard the ship, he tried to take refuge but was ambushed there. After that, at some point, the boot was removed."

Burt said, "You'll do."

Walter cocked his head.

"You may take a sample of the evidence." The archaeologist placed the boot on the brick ledge. "On the condition you provide a full report on your analysis."

Walter glanced at Debra.

"Long as you keep my vic on the front burner."

Walter smiled. He got his phone and photographed the boot. He opened his field kit and retrieved tweezers and a specimen dish, then carefully tweezed out several pebbles, depositing them in the dish. They were rough, coated in mud, pretty much unidentifiable.

I said, "The boot-guy could have survived, right?"

Burt turned to me. "You get shot. The ball goes through your leg, tearing up the flesh. You either get to a doctor or you die of gangrene. We'll say you find a doctor. In the city, there are plenty with experience treating gunshots. When you recover you have a choice. Catch a ship, go back where you came from--but with what money? If you found gold on your quest, it was no doubt stolen in the attack. You would be wise to worry about the brigand who shot you, who might learn you're still alive. So you disappear into the wilds of San Francisco. You don't leave a record. If the *Dawn*'s manifest is found, you don't want your name revealed. This is a dangerous city. It's known as the Barbary Coast." Burt eyed me. "Yes, you could have survived, although you might have lost your leg."

I said, "My foot's too small for that boot. But thanks for not casting me as the shooter." In truth, I wasn't wild about being cast as the vic, instead. Burt's saga did, though, lead to a question that had been vexing me. "How do you know the fight occurred after they returned from the gold fields? Why not before?"

"It could have been before. But after makes a better story."

"Then finish it," Debra said. "Show us what's *not right*."

4

BURT ZHANG STROLLED to the ship, lifting a hand, crooking a follow-me finger.

We boarded the vessel, entering at the bow, identifiable primarily by its tapered shape. We carefully stepped over the low edge, where the nineteenth-century Chinese ship-breakers had cut the hull down to waterline. Heavy labor. Ill-paid. The ship's ribs--the frame--looked like a row of tree stumps. Here at the bow it was a ghost of a ship, the barest outline, but still, once inside, walking along the gut of the *Dawn*, it was possible to imagine walking into the past. As though I'd returned from the gold fields, aflame with the fever, and boarded my ship to... To do what? Was I crew? Passenger? Shooter? Vic? I shrugged. I was here to do the forensics on a murder that may or may not be connected to this relic with its surprise waiting ahead at the stern. As I walked upon the dried mud that coated whatever was left of a deck layer, I had to give Burt his due. He'd put me in the story.

We passed through the mid-ship section and then entered the unbroken stern, the sides of the ship rising to flank us.

Ahead, three people were at work, reaching up to take

measurements, take photos, and scrape mud from a spot higher on the inner hull.

As we drew close, Burt said, "Can you give us the ship?"

The workers turned. Two women, one man, faces grimed, safety glasses grimed. They pulled off masks. They backed away from the hull, the man raising his excavation brush at Burt like a middle finger--the joker who'd teased him, I figured--and then they passed us by, heading for the bow and then climbing over the tree stumps to the camp chairs near the brick ledge.

We took their places.

I had to look up.

It took me a moment to see what they'd been measuring, photographing, brushing clean.

And then I saw.

Mud had been scraped from a section of the inner hull.

Silvery-gray balls dotted the wood like tiny moons.

I didn't get it.

As it turned out, I did not know enough to understand the situation.

Debra said, "A Colt?"

"A number of Colts," the archaeologist replied.

She nodded. "Sixguns. Six balls per load."

Walter said, "I'm unfamiliar with the layout of the ship's decking. Where the decking would have been. Where are we standing?"

"The mud hasn't been fully dug out," Burt said, "not all the way down to keel level. We're standing somewhere below the upper deck."

"Where the upper deck would have been."

"Correct."

We were standing, I estimated, about four feet below, looking up. The balls were embedded up there on the hull, below the ship's railing--where the ship's railing would have been.

Walter said, "So the shooters would have been standing on the upper deck."

"Correct. The straight-on entry angles indicate that."

"Burt," Debra said, "you know your ballistics."

"I know my geometry."

"How accurate were the revolvers?"

"At short-range, accurate enough."

She regarded the shot-up hull. "So they hit what they were aiming at."

Burt waited.

I spoke up. "If the boot-guy was standing here at the hull, they could have killed him. But he was shot in the heel and back of the leg. Which suggests he was running away."

"Hard to hit a running target. They were lucky to hit him at all. Still, with sixguns, they could squeeze off a good number of shots." He cocked that finger again. "And get two wild hits."

I turned and stared along the length of the ship, to the bow-- to the tree-stump perimeter, where the crates had stood, where the boot had been found. "So he got to safety and removed the boot. But why didn't the shooters chase him down? Finish what they started."

"You're getting there. The context."

Was I?

I looked up at the hull. "You're saying...they were interrupted. They were shooting at this, instead."

Burt gave me a slow nod.

Debra snorted. "Forget the boot-guy. What the hell's up with *this*?"

Walter moved closer to the hull, looking up, lifting a forefinger, counting the silver moons.

"The sheathing is pine," Burt said. "Soft enough that the lead balls lodged there."

I watched my partner count.

"Fifty-one," he said.

"Don't try the math," Burt said. "The number of balls might not tell you the number of shooters. It wasn't uncommon to carry a set of revolvers. Some shooters could have been firing two at a time. Others, just one."

I gaped at the silver moons, and I accepted Burt's math lesson, and I trusted Walter's counting, and the sum of it gave me a shiver.

I blurted, "But that's not what matters--not how many *shooters*. Why not just one or two, reloading? Or a couple of dozen, some with two pistols? Or fifty-one, everybody fires just once? The number that matters is how many *shots* were fired. Fifty-one balls fired into the side of the ship, all pretty much clustered in one area. I mean, they had to be firing at close range, right? I don't care how accurate the guns were, or weren't, or if they were marksmen, or weren't, it makes no sense they'd miss their targets so often, and continue firing."

"Now you see," Burt said.

"I see they were shooting into the hull of their ship."

Walter said, softly, "That's not right."

Yeah.

"*I* don't see," Debra said. She took off her shades, as if that might help.

Her eyes were startling--pale green, almost translucent, color of the mineral olivine.

"Burt," she said, "you're the archaeologist, so you tell me. I assume they weren't trying to sink their ship, since they were anchored near land, according to Walter's clever reconstruction-- and could they even *sink* a ship with a bunch of sixguns?--and I assume they weren't target-practicing since that makes no sense, and I assume they weren't carrying out some sort of execution since the balls ended up in the wood and not bodies, and I assume they weren't shooting at a pirate ship because they'd have shot over the top and not into the hull. Burt, what the hell were they shooting at?"

"That's the question."

Something spooked them, I thought. And they started shooting. And didn't stop.

I SHIVERED.

In the fifteen minutes or so since everyone else had abandoned ship, the angle of the sun had shifted and shadow crept farther across the pit.

The archaeologist was checking in with his team, the detective had returned to the crime scene to pace and talk on her cell, and my partner was grid-sampling the soil at Roger Forster's 'grave' site.

Meanwhile, I had the ship to myself--solitary commander of the *Dawn*.

I had already collected soil around the ship. Now I was preparing to sample the muddy deck of the ship itself, perhaps learn if Roger Forster had been poking around here before he left the giant excavation pit for parts currently unknown.

I knelt to the deck--where the deck must have been.

A saying came to me: six feet under. Meaning dead and buried--six feet being the traditional depth of a grave.

This ship had been buried a whole lot deeper.

Nevertheless, buried.

Sunk.

Marooned.

Gone to the bottom.

Resurfaced here, for a very short while. In a few weeks, the dig would be finished and the ship and artifacts removed, or reburied, and the site released to the owner.

I laid out my tools: specimen dishes, plastic scoops, scalpel with stainless-steel blade so as not to contaminate the sample with trace metals. I placed an L-shaped ruler on the working site, for dimensional reference, then got my phone and took photos. Then I set to work, using the scalpel to carve out a slice of the compacted layer of muddy silty sand and dark gritty clay. Given that this site was once at shoreline, I assumed this came from the mudflats of Yerba Buena Cove, where the ship had been hauled onto shore for salvaging.

Something screamed. I looked up and saw a seagull.

Below the gull, at street level, Debra's zoo still lined the fence. The crowd had thinned, perhaps chilled by the encroaching shadows cast by neighboring office towers. But the hoodie remained, fingers laced through the chain links. Best I could recall her earlier position, she hadn't moved.

I stifled the urge to wave.

Instead, I secured the cove mud in a specimen dish, took two more samples, and then moved from bow to stern to sample there.

It was not until I'd done the first slice at the stern that I allowed myself to look up again.

I blinked.

There was a second hoodie at the fence.

They multiplying?

Maybe the second had been there all along, and just now moved into my line of sight. They both wore jeans and hooded sweatshirts--the first navy blue, the second deep purple, color of grape jelly. And they were staring down at the ship with such intensity that I wondered if it was my work that held their attention. Could be. They might well have heard the shout a while ago from the diggers--*that's not right*. And then they'd seen Burt showing the hull to Walter and Debra and me. And now here I was with my scalpel. If they were waiting for me to dig out a bullet, they were going to be disappointed. The archaeologist would have my head.

I shifted focus back to the job and sliced into the mud of the vanished deck, where Roger Forster had conceivably walked. He was the regular who mattered and everyone else in the zoo was peripheral. Not my problem. And yet, once I'd extracted this mud sample and secured it in a dish, and prepared to make the next collection, I could not resist another look up at the fence.

Still there. They were nothing if not patient. Possibly regulars, day-in day-out dedicated Fencies.

Okay, time to break the spell. I waved.

After a very long moment, the purple hoodie waved back.

The blue remained immobile, fingers embedded in the weave of the fence.

6

"YOU'RE NOT GOING to believe this place," the detective said.

At the moment, I could not believe her driving. She knew how to navigate the city and was taking us the back way to dodge traffic, snaking through narrow streets, rollercoastering up and down steep San Francisco hills, all the while giving us a backgrounder on the Forster family, and when she reached the end of that narrative, telling us once again we weren't going to believe the lab space she'd secured for us.

First, though, we were en route to the Forster place to collect soil samples.

We had finished at the dig, having spent a good hour or so doing the geology. During that period the two hoodies held their spot at the fence. I'd mentioned them to Walter and Debra. Walter shrugged. Debra said, "It's a zoo." And I'd figured that's that.

Now, I followed our route on my Google map, trying to keep my bearings in this head-snapping city. Debra swerved around a double-parked car blocking half the road and I gave up on the map.

Walter, from the back seat, asked where Debra had acquired her driving skills.

"Here," she said. "Grew up in the city." She launched into the story of her teenage years.

And then we came to the northwestern edge of the city and entered the neighborhood known as Sea Cliff.

There could be no other name for the parade of estates that lined the sheer cliff edge, with front-row seats to the spectacle of the sea.

The Golden Gate Bridge soared in the distance.

We passed what I took to be a French chateau and then an English manor and then an iconic San Francisco Victorian, and then I ran out of recognizable styles, and then Debra parked in front of a terracotta-colored estate that was fringed in palm trees. Mediterranean, I decided.

Tall privacy hedges bordered the property on both sides, ramparts between this estate and the neighboring estates.

Walter and I grabbed our packs and got out, following Debra to the slate-tiled driveway. She gave us a moment to gawk. The place looked like huge boxes stacked atop one another, each level slightly offset, each level roofed with Spanish tiles. Bold. In-your-face. I thought it looked like something Picasso might have imagined.

The box directly in front of us, at the head of the driveway, with the white-paneled doors, was no doubt the garage--I assumed Roger Forster's car had been moved from the public garage near the dig back to this one.

"You're about to meet the cousin," Debra said, "and one thing about this guy--just to avoid the hassle--is how to address him. His name is Gregory Forster but he likes to be called Forster. No first name needed, like he's the only Forster who could possibly matter." She laughed. "Names again, right? I gave you a sermon on my nickname, poor you. And poor *us*, if we get into it with Gregory here. So call him Forster and don't smile when you do."

She led us to a slate-paved pathway that arrowed past a side door into the garage, past ornamental shrubs, past the scaled trunks of palm trees, to a white front door flanked by tall narrow wavy-glass windows.

A man stood at the right-hand window, peering out at us. Through the distortion of the glass, he appeared to be underwater.

Debra said, "Wait for it."

The door opened.

The man stood with feet planted wide, one hand on the doorknob, the other tucked into the pocket of his white linen pants, ragged and unhemmed. His gold silk long-sleeve T-shirt was torn at one shoulder. Pricey shabby chic. He wore soft-soled deck shoes without socks. He was medium height with a trim build. His hair was quartz white, neatly combed. His eyes were a warm golden-brown, his nose was strong, and his face was square. He was very tan.

Who wouldn't be tan, I thought, with the sea as your backyard.

Debra said, "Forster, hello again. These are the geologists I mentioned on the phone, Cassie Oldfield and Walter Shaws. They prefer first names, as I do."

Forster said, "Hello." Using no names.

Walter said, "May we extend our condolences on the death of your cousin."

"Yes," I echoed.

"Thank you. It was a shock."

"We'll keep our business brief," Walter said. "We're trying to track his steps."

"Here?"

"I understand he lived with you."

"That's right. I have plenty of room. Empty-nester, widower--no condolences required. A few months ago the condo Roger rented was sold, so he moved in here. It was supposed to be temporary."

Walter gave a sympathetic smile, then moved on. "Is there any place here he would have picked up soil in his boots?"

"As you may have noticed, the grounds are manicured. Or hardscaped."

I pointed in the direction of the sea. "How about out there?"

He took a moment. "Come on through the house." He stepped aside, opening the door wide, his eyes flicking downward.

Oh. There was a woven doormat monogrammed with an 'F'. There had been a doormat by the side door to the garage, although not monogrammed. Either way, this guy was serious about not tracking around dirt.

We wiped our feet.

Inside, the four of us walked side by side into the cavernous living room. Forster moved quickly and we kept up and I got fleeting impressions--as if passing through a landscape on an express train--of staircases and Persian throw rugs on the dark planked floor and low-slung formal sofas and deep chairs and shelves full of books that looked handled, read, and everywhere potted plants and abstract animal sculptures. A chunk of polished tan limestone with sleek lines hinted at mountain lion. A twig creature of loops and bends on a bleached wood stump suggested cormorant.

I paused at a lacquered-white side table to look at a photo: two men stood on the deck of a sleek cabin cruiser named *Maverick*, according to the black lettering on the white hull. One man was Gregory Forster. The other was shorter and so slim he looked like a boy, with curly brown hair and big ears and a big grin that made me think puppy.

"That's Roger," Forster said.

"Your boat?"

"Roger's." Forster added, "Mine now, I suppose."

He urged us onward, marching to the sliding glass door that windowed the sea. He put a hand on the latch. "By the way, I didn't see Roger on the day he died. I left for a meeting, early. As I previously explained to the detective."

"Forster," Debra said, "we're just doing our jobs."

"Then do it. Find Roger's killer. The sooner the better."

I thought, he's a little edgy--understandable, given the situation. Or maybe that was his nature.

Debra said, "Then let's put my geologists to work."

He unhooked the latch and slid the door open and held out an upturned palm to guide us outside.

There was another 'F' monogrammed doormat and beyond that, cascading slate patios with rattan furniture and terracotta planters that bristled with greenery, but all of that was secondary. All of that was backdrop for the sea. From open ocean to the headlands that formed the entrance to the bay--the golden gate and its namesake bridge--the sea was the main event. I could have stood rooted for an hour and not taken it all in, but Forster moved us onward in our express-train tour, saying, "Down below is some dirt for you," and we descended two patios and then turned a tight corner and came to a third, which abutted the cliff edge.

Our tour halted there.

I stared in surprise.

A statue faced us, another abstract only this wasn't an animal but a metal-limbed man. He was a miner with a pickaxe on his shoulder, one foot resting on a gray-green chunk of serpentine, which was appropriate since the rock can be found in association with gold deposits. The sculptor knew his mineralogy.

The surprise was not the statue but the orange traffic cone perched on his head like a warped hard hat.

"Roger gifted me the prospector," Forster said. "I added the hat."

"A bit of an insult?" Walter asked.

"A critique. My cousin and I had a difference of opinion about celebrating our family roots."

"I understand your family dates back to gold-rush days."

"It does."

Small world, I thought. Archaeologist Burt Zhang's family dates back to gold-rush days, as well. Of course, San Francisco expanded its shoreline and its population back then and who knows how many put down roots. Including, perhaps, boot-guy--if he survived the shooting on the *Dawn*.

"Forster," Debra said, "I gave them a backgrounder, including your statement that your family has no link to the ship being dug up."

"That is still the case, detective."

She smiled. "We detectives like to reexamine details, on the chance that recollections change. You've had the chance to process the shock of your cousin's death, and now that a couple of days have passed I wonder if you recall anything else, relevant to that threatening note. Some connection that might explain why your cousin's body was placed at the dig."

"Let me elaborate--my ancestors did *not* arrive in San Francisco on that ship, or any ship. They migrated from Los Angeles, *overland*, in 1848, because of the gold rush, yes, but they made their living selling goods in the waterfront district for many years. After that, they migrated to the western edge of the city, and eventually bought land here, in the early affordable days."

"I see." She considered the statue. "I would have been interested to see this, last time I was here. Why *did* you and your cousin clash over this? Given your family's roots."

"Because my cousin loved the idea of some gold-rush-era Forsters joining the hordes and finding gold."

"You didn't love the idea?"

"I found it fantasy."

"Then what led you to write about the gold rush?"

"My agent pitched it." Forster turned to Walter and me. "I'm an author. Eight of the books on those bookshelves inside are mine. My first was a history of the period. The lawless waterfront area was called, with some truth, the Barbary Coast."

I recalled Burt Zhang describing it as such.

Debra said, "I filled them in."

She'd filled us in during a rollercoaster descent, explaining more about Roger Forster's book-pitching antics at the dig. I had thought, as my stomach lurched, well well.

Forster said, "Did you fill them in on Roger's contribution?"

"You didn't fill *me* in on it during our first chat. But no problem. We detectives like to investigate. I investigated."

He shrugged. "It's no secret. I made the mistake of enlisting Roger, who'd been in advertising, to promote *Barbary Coast*. He labeled it a rip-roaring page-turner and spun the family's roots. The book was a bestseller." Forster gave a thin laugh. "Critics called it Barbary Boast."

Debra said, "But you didn't fire Roger."

"Family ties. And he was a good researcher."

"All right, fast-forward to a couple of months ago, when the ship was unearthed. You told me Roger was intrigued--no surprise--and that he often went to the site in the weeks before he was killed."

"Nothing new now."

"Oh, but there is. One more thing I turned up after we last

spoke. I asked around and learned that your cousin kept busy, talking to reporters, pitching your books."

Forster expelled a long breath. "The interviews."

"Worked for you, though? Sales-wise?"

He said, evenly, "Yes, detective, *Barbary*'s had a bump in sales."

"No doubt. Readers love the sensational. Congratulations." She added, "How about your Sutro book?"

"You *have* been following my work."

"Only since your cousin's murder. I read the blurbs on Amazon. Gotta say, the Barbary Coast is a sexier subject than Adolph Sutro."

Forster sighed and turned to us. "Adolph Sutro was San Francisco's mayor in the late eighteen-hundreds. I wrote his bio--did the detective fill you in on that, too?"

I nodded. She'd filled us in on everything.

She continued, "Why *did* you switch from sexy to biography?"

"My publisher wanted another San Francisco book, drafting on *Barbary*'s success. He came up with Sutro as a subject."

"Was that book a success?"

"Not in comparison to *Barbary*."

"Is that why Roger pitched them both at the dig? *Barbary* lifts *Sutro*?"

"He was playing the history angle. The ship made it hot."

"But you disapproved?"

"Roger got us some bad press, 'highjacking' the dig."

The detective nodded. "I read some of it. Your cousin certainly drew attention--maybe the wrong kind."

"Christ," Forster said, "you think *that* got him killed?"

"I think about every angle that presents itself."

"Then let me know if I need to be worried. That bury-you

note--am I a target? I have a black belt in karate but I'm damned if I want to end up needing it."

"Better yet," Debra said, "let's move on to dirt and boots. I'm talking about those trendy Timberlands your cousin wore. The boots on his feet when his body was found."

"And?"

"Did he wear them often?"

"Now and then. But I civilized him--he learned to wipe his feet. So anything he picked up here..." Forster shrugged.

Walter cut in, "Nevertheless, we'd like to see."

Forster pointed toward the far end of the patio. "There's some landscaping. Not much in the way of bare earth, but help yourself."

I asked, "Any place else?"

"Yes, but... Yes." He jerked a thumb. "Down the cliff."

7

WALTER SET off to check out the patio landscaping, Debra moved aside to take a call, and I followed Forster to the adobe wall at the edge of the cliff.

It was another gobsmacking view. I wondered if he ever got inured to it, if the neighbors with their estates dug into this precipitous cliff grew inured to it, ever grew a little nervous about hanging on the edge high above the rocks and the waves--what with sea-level rise and stronger storms creating bigger and higher waves, eating at the cliff--but I guessed they could afford underpinning, driving steel pilings deep into the bedrock to anchor themselves. Get rich enough to pay for good enough geo-tech engineering and the laws of gravity are thwarted.

The waves boomed and the air was salt-rich and the sun warmed Forster's estate.

He stood waiting.

I braced my forearms on the sun-warmed adobe and leaned further over.

There was more to be seen below--more cascading stairs zigzagging down the cliff face, like switchbacks on a steep mountainside.

And there was something else.

On a small landing between the zigzags, a green webbed lawn chair sat slightly askew. Its lack of firm footing was clearly due to the fact that it sat upon a small plot of earth.

I said, "Spectacular place to sit and watch the sea go by."

"No question."

"Whose chair?"

"Roger's."

"Did he go down there often?"

"I couldn't say. I didn't bell him."

"If this were my place I'd go down every morning with a cup of coffee."

"You want to wait while I brew one for you?"

I smiled. "Too late for caffeine, thanks anyway. What I want is to go sample that piece of earth."

"Be sure to watch your step."

I planned to. I took note that there was no railing, that there was a paver with a large crack.

"I'll come along," Forster said, "in case I can be of assistance."

He moved to the gate in the wall, opened the latch, then stood aside.

I started down the stairs, which proved stable enough, although the cracked paver had a wobble, and so I descended mindfully, watching the rock-rimmed cove below where the stairs ended. I glanced, once, over my shoulder. Forster was three steps behind, matching my pace.

We reached the little landing.

"If this were my place," I said, "I'd get that cracked paver repaired."

"It's on the to-do list."

"Steps competent all the way down?"

He nodded.

I headed down to the cove, Forster following.

The cove was sheltered by the tall arms of the cliff. The water frothed, foaming a thin strip of sand. I did a photo, got the field kit, did the sampling.

"You're wasting your time," Forster said. "There's never enough beach to spread a towel, and Roger wasn't a swimmer."

"What about you?"

"I swim it. Don't recommend it for amateurs."

Such as Roger.

When I finished we climbed back up to the landing, and I turned my attention to the sitting area.

Up close, the lawn chair looked well-used. Its webbing was fraying here and there but the aluminum frame appeared competent. I touched the seat. My hand came away gritty with sea salt. I wondered how long it took to precipitate out from the air. Not long, I hazarded, on this terrace overhanging the ocean.

The cliff face backing the terrace was dominated by massive lumpy beds of a dark gritty sandstone, graywacke, known as 'dirty sandstone' because it's rich in silt and clay and volcanic fragments. It's part of the quintessential San Francisco rock unit, the Franciscan Complex--as I recalled from my grad-school field trip--born in the oceanic subduction zone where one tectonic plate slid beneath another. Maker of earthquakes.

"I've often wished," Forster said, "that my cliff was prettier rock than this."

"It holds up your house."

He laughed. "Still, it's unlovely."

The man wants designer rock. I shrugged. Opened the field kit, set up the ruler, photographed the site. Forster leaned against the cliff wall, watching. I knelt to the plot of earth. The soil was compacted around the edges but in the middle of the landing, where the chair sat, where feet scuffed, the top layer was gritty decomposed graywacke. If there had been footprints, they'd been scuffed away. I considered the soil. Walk around and the loose stuff embeds in waffle soles. Gets compressed and adheres, especially if it is wetted by fog or sea spray. Right now, the top layer was sun-warmed and dry. Not only that, it was speckled, here and there, with green bits of webbing from the frayed chair. I used the plastic scoop and secured the sample in a specimen dish.

Forster said, "What's the point?"

I looked up. He loomed, from my angle looking elongated, like one of his abstract sculptures.

I said, "The point is to find out where the soils from his clothing and boots originated."

"I already told you he sometimes came down here."

"You did. I'll still need a forensic ID."

"You do know there's dozens of places he could've walked in this kind of dirt."

"Yup, graywacke is found in a good number of places. I'll be hoping for something unique in *this* soil--that's why I'll need that ID."

"When are you going to get it?"

"When we get to a microscope." When Walter and I get to the unbelievable lab space Debra promised.

"And then what?"

"And then--once we've analyzed all the soils and reconstructed enough of your cousin's journey--we track it in the field."

"When is *that* going to be?"

"In the next day or so."

"That will make it..." Forster calculated. "At least three *days* since he was murdered."

It was awkward, looking up at him. I got to my feet. "You want it fast, or you want it right?"

"Both."

"Don't worry, we'll be putting in the hours."

"I do worry--about being a target myself." He pushed away from the cliff face, coming a little closer to me.

I took a step back.

He said, "You're wasting time here."

"No," I said, "I'm not."

"Well, Roger sure as hell didn't die *here*. His car was found in a garage near that dig. So...what? Somebody grabbed him there and drove him back here? Killed him *here*? And then carried his body *up this*?" Forster gestured at the stairway. "And then drove back to the dig and dumped the body there? Get real."

I said, "Give me space, Forster."

"Give me a break. Stop wasting time. Go use that microscope for something useful and find out what in *holy hell* happened to my cousin."

Adrenaline spiked. I took another step back, claiming my space. When I could trust my voice, I said, icily, "My partner and I are collecting samples here because Roger lived here. And we can't fully reconstruct the journey-history of his footwear on the day of his death without *identifying* the soil in that footwear. If anything matches what I just collected, then we know it came from here, even if we don't know when Roger acquired it. But we can ID it, and move on. And I fully agree that it's highly unlikely the forensic event occurred here. Rather, I suspect any soil Roger picked up here was in a pre-forensic event. Walking here. Possibly, the morning of the day he died--before he drove to the dig." I took a deep breath. "Is that clear enough?"

His own breathing roughened. "*Forensic event*? You mean my cousin's murder." His chest heaved, beneath the gold silk T-shirt. He lifted his palms. Then looked away, at the edge of the landing where the cliff dropped down to the rocky cove. And when he turned back to face me, he had gained control. He no longer quaked. He said, voice tight, "I want the killer caught. I want the killer rotting in hell."

I snatched up the field kit. "*This* is how he gets caught."

"That a guarantee?"

No, that was bravado, based on ire, but long experience said finding out where the victim last walked increased the odds of catching the killer. I had no desire to slice and dice that for him right now so I just stowed the kit and shouldered the pack and started up the steps. Kept my focus tight on the cracked paver ahead. Didn't look back. But he was right behind me when I reached the top.

We joined Walter and Debra, who waited near the miner statute.

"I'm afraid I found nothing useful," Walter told me. "Did you have any luck?"

I nodded.

Debra said, "Then we're done here."

Forster led us back to the house, pausing at the patio door to wipe his shoes on the monogrammed doormat. We followed suit.

Inside, before we speed-trained through the room, Walter paused at a bookshelf. "Ah, here they are. Your books."

Forster was forced to stop.

"I see you have copies of each. Might I borrow *Barbary* and *Sutro*?"

"You have spare time for reading?"

"Now and then. I find spare time for meals, too." Walter smiled.

"Fine." Forster strode over to the bookshelf. "Just those two?"

"Just those. The books your cousin pitched at the dig."

8

I SAID, "WHOA."

Walter looked up from his worktable. "Whoa, what?"

"Roger Forster went wading."

Walter's eyebrows lifted. He looked out the window at the water.

San Francisco was surrounded on three sides by water. The Pacific Ocean bordered the city's western and northwestern flanks. The bay bordered its northern and eastern flanks.

The lab window faced a slice of the eastern bay.

Our lab was a mobile office trailer parked within a cavernous warehouse that took up nearly the entirety of Pier 40. The pier jutted into the bay. Our office window jutted against one of the warehouse windows, giving us a view of the bayfront marina and its forest of masts.

We weren't the only occupants of the warehouse. There were other mobile offices and sheds housing maritime businesses from kayak and motorboat rentals to a club for disabled sailors. And now us, the non-maritime outliers.

Debra had spoken truly: *you won't believe this place.*

After we'd left Forster's Sea Cliff estate we'd returned to the dig site to pick up Walter's Subaru Crosstrek, and from there we followed Debra to the apartment she'd arranged for our stay, where we unloaded our luggage. And then we caravanned the few dozen yards across the street to the pier, where we parked. And then she helped schlep our field equipment from the Subaru to the lab. And then an officer showed up to deliver the evidence containers to us, and we signed the chain-of-custody transfer.

By that time it was late afternoon.

We had a full suite of evidence to analyze so we set straight to work, later breaking for a trip to a nearby place to grab sandwiches. Sandwiches for lunch, sandwiches for dinner--that kind of day.

Then back to it.

Our mobile office was all white--gypsum ceiling, vinyl paneling and flooring, and plastic modular components. Fluorescent lights bathed everything. It was bright as an operating theater, which set the mood.

We'd rearranged the modulars into workspaces and stashed our scopes and analyzers and other field tools on the built-in white shelves.

The specimen dish of pebbles from Burt Zhang's boot-guy was set aside. We'd get to it sooner or later, if only to complete the story.

Right now we were busy with the job at hand.

Walter was tackling the mud in Roger Forster's boot soles, a painstaking effort.

I took on the rest.

I'd already identified dig soils from his clothing, acquired where he'd lain on his side in the makeshift grave--still in full rigor, 'jammed up' from his time in the car trunk.

Next, I focused on the non-dig stuff. He'd certainly gotten dirty; in fact, it looked as though he'd gone adventuring.

There were reddish iron-oxide smears on the knees of the pants, which were going to merit a deeper look.

More immediately telling were the grains of sand in the clothing. At that point, I started thinking *beach*. And then I lensed the pant legs below the knees and found crystals embedded in bands, down to the hems. The nylon material was lightly stained and gave off a faint briny smell. And thus I'd had my wading epiphany.

Now, I said to my partner, "Seems at some point Roger sat on a beach, took off his boots and socks, rolled up his pants, and went wading." I explained the salt crystals.

Walter thought that over. "There's a good number of beaches in San Francisco, and in the nearby areas."

"I'm assuming he didn't go much farther afield than that. I mean, his car was found in the dig parking garage, and our working hypothesis has him leaving that area--by some means-- and going to a site or sites unknown, so the travel time to and from the dig limits the range."

"It won't have escaped your attention that there are a couple of beaches near the Forster place."

"It didn't. There's also that little cove at the bottom of the stairway." I added, "Forster said Roger never went down there. Of course, Forster also said I was wasting my time."

Walter said, "The man was out of line."

I smiled. My protective partner. I'd ranted about Forster to Walter and Debra after we'd left Sea Cliff. I said, now, "To be fair, I got territorial with him, and clearly the guy didn't understand how we work. And he's something of an arrogant..." I shrugged. "Which isn't a crime."

"You've calmed down about it."

Took awhile. "To be even fairer, there's the bury-you note. I get why he'd think that's aimed at him. Why he tried to hurry me up."

"You're being overly fair."

"You drilled *fair* into me along with how to read the rocks."

He sighed. "So I did." He turned back to his work. "Let's find out where Roger went."

"Let's."

I returned to my work, characterizing the sand from Forster's cove, and then I focused on the sand from Roger's pants. I extracted what looked to be quartz grains and bits of shell. I was about to begin a deeper dive with the nifty X-ray diffractometer, hoping to identify trace minerals, when something flickered at the edge of my field of view. A shadow. I turned to the trailer window, which gave a view out of the corresponding warehouse window. Just outside the warehouse was a walkway. In the hours we'd been working I'd noticed a few people strolling by. It was summertime, late nightfall, with that melancholy light that comes as evening strolls into dark.

Getting chilly.

And the shadow that had just passed wore, I was certain, a hoodie--color nondescript in the gloom.

I thought about alerting Walter, about going outside to look, but we'd already run that drill an hour ago when I thought I saw a hoodie go by. By the time we'd walked the length of the warehouse to reach an exit, there was nobody in sight. The walkway wrapped around the pier. Someone passing our window could round the pier and return to the street without coming back our way.

And if it was the hoodie? Which one? Maybe both, one earlier, one now. And how did they find their way here? I supposed they could have hung out at the dig until we'd returned with Debra to pick up Walter's Subaru. Then followed us. I had no idea *why*, or who they were, or what they wanted. I thought about dashing out again to see if I could find this hour's hoodie. And ask, whassup?

Instead, I returned to my sand.

Half an hour later, Walter said, "I've made progress on the boot soil."

I came over to his workstation and had a look. He'd started on the right boot, working in the arch area where sediments were likely to be retained in the deeply recessed waffle indentations. Good. Should be able to build a profile of where Roger walked--the journey-history.

"Take a gander at these plugs," Walter said.

I took a gander. He'd extracted several plugs of compacted mud, neatly as an operating-room surgeon. The plugs in the specimen dishes were intact but their story was going to be anything but neat. "Looks like some mixing went on."

He agreed. "A somewhat shredded layer cake."

Layer-cake geology was the way Walter taught me when I was a kid hanging around his lab. Layers of rocks and soils, when neatly divided by time of deposition, look like layers of a cake. We still talk cake--and Oreo cookies, for that matter--when talking layers.

Yup, this cake looked mashed.

Walter selected a dish with a somewhat segmented plug. "I can differentiate four layers, using the term loosely. Starting at the top--the largest portion--we have a glop of mixed soil. That's layer one. Below that, layers two and three and four are more distinct."

I nodded. I saw.

"I have a preliminary ID on layer four. Graywacke, with telling inclusions--filaments of green plastic which I'd wager are from that fraying lawn chair. There's no telling when he acquired the soil, but it does establish our base."

"Guess I wasn't wasting my time."

He raised a hand, and we high-fived.

"Anything else?" I asked.

"Nothing from the dig, so it would seem he didn't walk down there that morning. Nothing from the ship, either."

I shrugged. Unlike the two fence-haunting hoodies, I wasn't invested in the ship.

"One more preliminary," he said. "In that top mixed layer, I found grains of quartz and feldspar and graywacke and bits of crab shell--your beach sand. From precisely *which* beach, to be determined."

"Whichever, I hope he enjoyed it."

"It's nice to think so."

Yeah. Given how his day ended.

It was later--we were wearier, the walkway outside the window was darker, emptier--when Walter let out a grunt.

I knew that grunt. It's the sound he makes when he's found something of particular interest. Possibly exciting.

"I'm just finishing the arch area of the left boot, and..." he paused, for effect, "I've found two unique clues."

I came alert. "And?"

"One involves your beach."

"Roger's beach," I corrected. "And...?"

He held out his hand. In his palm was a large multi-colored pebble. "It was caught in the top layer of a plug."

"It's lovely," I said. "What's its name and address?"

"The name is *melange*." He passed me the pebble.

I had a close look. Oh yeah, the different colors meant fragments of different rocks. No doubt they'd be Franciscan Complex rocks, ground up by tectonic subduction, the frags being survivors of the grinding. And that dark waxy-looking clay matrix cemented them. The whole concoction being known as a melange.

I returned the pebble. "The neighborhood?"

"Go take a gander at the map."

I pushed back from my workstation and moved to the modular unit we'd named a table, where our geologic map was laid out. It was a depiction of the various rock and soil units to be found in San Francisco.

He said, "You might as well fold it to show just the northwestern quadrangle."

I folded the map to quarter-size. One area was instantly familiar. Small world. "Sea Cliff's in that quadrangle."

"Yes it is. But scan further west."

I scanned until I hit the edge of the continent and ran into its name: Lands End. I said, "Apt name."

"Yes, it is. And the melange zone slices through its heart."

"Dazzling neighborhood."

"Do you see that promontory sticking out?"

Couldn't miss it. It jutted into the sea like the prow of a ship.

"You see that it's flanked by two beaches?"

I saw.

"I'll wager that my pebble came from one of them. And I'll wager that Roger went wading, from one of them."

I looked up. "Spectacular work, partner."

"Thank you. But now it gets puzzling. My other clue is a curious shale."

I started to look at the map again.

He stopped me. "You won't find it."

I sat back. "Then..."

"Then we have a mystery. According to the map, my curious shale is simply not to be found at Lands End."

9

I woke with a start--Walter was hammering on my door.

I untangled myself from the bedsheet and sat up, gazing in a stupor at the painting on the wall of some naval battle, somewhere in the past. The clock, adjacent, said eight-ten a.m.

Another knock, loud.

I found my voice. "Just a minute!"

"*Hurry.* You're not going to believe this!"

He sounded like Debra. This better be good.

I found my robe in the jumbled clothing I'd dumped on the floor last night--well past midnight by the time we'd locked the lab and made our way across the street to the apartment and thoroughly wiped our boots on the doormat and found the door key and, stumbling inside, found the light switches. I'd been too tired to do more than grab a shower and collapse into bed.

I vowed to properly unpack later. There was an imposing armoire, beneath the naval battle, in which to stow my stuff.

This apartment, this 'vacation rental' that Debra found for us, was fancier than we required but it had two ensuite bedrooms and a generous living room and kitchen and--especially appreciated last night--it was directly opposite Pier 40 and our warehouse lab. It was also pricier than we'd anticipated, but prices in San Francisco were an order of magnitude higher than prices in our Sierra Nevada mountain hometown of Bishop. Fortunately, Debra negotiated a discount with the rental agency. All in all, Walter our finance-man was satisfied.

Now, he shouted. "Cassie!"

I opened the door.

Walter was at the black-tiled breakfast bar with his laptop open. His back was to me.

I headed over. The black-tiled floor was cold. I nearly retreated to the bedroom to hunt for slippers. But I smelled coffee. "What won't I believe?"

He swiveled the breakfast-bar chair to face me. He wore his plaid flannel robe and a huge grin. His thinning hair was askew, his blue eyes were red-rimmed, and his bushy eyebrows needed smoothing.

I asked, "How much sleep did you get?"

"Enough. I was up late with Forster's Sutro book."

I saw it then--wedged between the laptop and the bowl of complimentary mangoes and kiwis--the biography of nine-teenth-century San Francisco mayor Adolph Sutro. Some kind of weird synchronicity: Burt Zhang had cast Walter as the fantasy-mayor of the gold-rush city, and here was the biography of his real-life successor.

Walter's coffee mug sat on top of Sutro's bewhiskered face.

My mouth quilted. I looked toward the French press.

"I'll *get* it," Walter said. "You have a look at my laptop."

Walter headed for the kitchen and I took his chair, swiveling to face the screen.

A Google satellite map showed a cliff face bordering a beach.

I didn't know what was unbelievable about the image on the screen but I knew my partner. He must have found something worth gloating about. I stared at the cliff without getting the point and then moved Walter's mug and picked up the book and saw a napkin inserted as a bookmark.

"I'll let you read it for yourself." His voice was honeyed.

"Okay."

He passed me a mug of coffee.

I breathed in the aroma, then took a sip. Nectar of the gods.

"You really aren't going to believe this."

"All right." I put down the coffee and opened the book at the napkin.

He said, "Left-hand page, top."

I was expecting to read about some mayoral scandal, maybe even some revelation about Gregory Forster's forebears, that they were distant cousins of Adolph Sutro or some such, but I didn't get how that would connect to the cliff face onscreen.

I didn't need to read beyond the second paragraph to learn that my expectation was way off the mark.

I looked up to find my partner watching closely.

"Whoa," I said. "Okay, I do actually believe this, because why would Forster make it up? But yeah, on the Debra believability scale, I am well and truly gobsmacked."

"Now the laptop."

I set aside the book and shifted my focus again to the image on the screen.

He said, "Welcome to the wild and untamed corner of the city."

"This?"

"Zoom in."

I zoomed in.

At first, I couldn't see the details, and then I could. "You've got to be kidding."

Walter said, "We're going to get wet."

10

"At some point," I said, "Roger Forster should have been afraid."

"Not down there," Walter said. "Or he wouldn't have continued his journey."

Down there, at the edge of the sea, his Lands End journey had most likely begun.

He'd continued it all the way to that alarming cliff I'd seen on Walter's laptop screen earlier this morning. To that place Walter had marked in Gregory Forster's bio of Adolph Sutro.

That place lay far ahead.

What lay below was a more public slice of Sutro history.

Walter and I sat on the low stone wall at the edge of the parking lot overlooking the sea, with the geologic map spread between us, our phones in hand, geo-marking every stop we'd identified of Roger's final journey, every stop we intended to make. The ragged mud layers from his boots had given us a rough chronology of his journey. The map corroborated it.

There was only one way to go.

It was a good day for a hike. Visibility was excellent--a squint-bright morning with cloudless skies that turned the Pacific Ocean crayon blue. No limits to what we could see.

I stirred. "Shall we?"

Walter folded the map and stashed it in his pack. He glanced at mine. "You did get the sandwiches?"

Another sandwich day. We'd breakfasted on mangoes and kiwis and energy bars in the apartment, then headed for the lab to complete the examination of the left boot arch area, and then we'd driven across the city to Lands End and parked at the visitor center, where we'd picked up several brochures, and lunch, and then we transferred the gear from the car into our packs. I'd stashed the sandwiches. Walter's pack was bulkier, with the big coiled rope. Lunch was safer in mine.

I confirmed, "I got the sandwiches."

We put on our hats and abandoned the wall and set off, starting down the long steep wooden stairway to the skeletal remains of Adolph Sutro's grand showpiece.

The stairway bottomed out at a wide marine terrace. Here, there had once been a glass-arched structure that covered three acres and housed promenades and swimming pools and slides and springboards and trapezes. The pools had been fed by the sea. It was an engineering marvel. It was a playground for rich and poor alike, but not for all. 'Whites Only' signs had hung in the building, according to the Golden Gate Parks Conservancy brochure I'd picked up in the visitor center.

Sutro Baths was now a gridwork of rotting stone foundations and broken walls and twisted steel supports, framing the watery reminders of the vanished pools. They were still being filled by the tides. At some point, the rising sea would bury these remains.

Three days ago, Roger Forster had walked here.

"Notable," I said, "Roger spending his last day in Sutro country."

Walter nodded. "I want to know why."

Layer by layer, we planned to find out.

We'd kept the same nomenclature Walter first used in the lab: layer four was Sea Cliff landing soil; layer three, we expected, came from Sutro Baths, here; layer two would be the trail beyond the Baths; and layer one indicated Roger's final destination, and ours.

The first thing that caught our attention at the Baths was the decaying remains of a brick retaining wall. This morning Walter had found brick grains in layers three and one, and I had identified brick as the likely source of the iron-oxide smears on the pant legs. This wouldn't be the only brick we would encounter today, but it was the first. We set up, photographed, collected a few brick grains, and then sampled the sandy soil.

The real prize--from this morning's X-ray diffractometer work--was to be found at the northern end of the ruins where a tunnel entered a high cliff.

We headed that way.

There were a number of people poking around, tightrope-walking the unstable walls, dipping hands into dark waters, venturing into the tunnel.

It wasn't crowded, unlike Debra's zoo at the dig, but it was clearly a tourist attraction. I said, "Maybe Roger came to pitch the Sutro book."

Walter eyed two teenagers playing chicken on a wall. "I doubt he'd find an audience here."

"You sound like a curmudgeon."

"I am a curmudgeon."

Ha. If nobody was around, Walter would be up on that wall, himself.

"More to the point," he said, "I wonder if the wrong kind of attention followed him here from the dig."

"Or brought him."

We came to the mouth of the tunnel.

Here was the prize. The rough cliff face was interbedded

with exposures of beige sandstone and black shale, the hard sandstone ridging out from the soft shale. Sandstone and shale were homeboys of the Franciscan Complex, but *this* sandstone was different. It contained a variety of feldspar rich in potassium, a difference that marked this place as the start of Roger's journey.

We ran the drill, sampling both the rock face and the ground below where the cliff had shed bits and pieces of itself. When a man in a hooded sweatshirt exited the tunnel I thought, hoodies everywhere.

And then we entered the tunnel's throat and the temperature dropped and we paused to add jackets and if mine had a hood, I would have raised it.

Not just cold, but dank and muddy in here. And dark. We donned headlamps.

Rock excavated from this tunnel had been used for the construction of the Baths. We intended to put the sandy residue to a different use. We muddied the knees of our hiking pants, sampling.

Then moved along for more.

The footing was uneven and we dodged rocks and puddles and I stepped wrong once and viscous mud like a hand grabbed my left boot and joined the soils already lodged there.

Someone hooted.

Ahead, at the end of the long tunnel, the exit to daylight terminated at a low gate. Two people were silhouetted there. They were making woo-woo ghost sounds, which echoed back our way.

"The place is supposed to be haunted," Walter said.

"Any place like this is supposed to be haunted."

We sampled again, and moved on.

Midway along the tunnel another sound came our way, not ghostly but hissing, swelling into booms, a sound that signaled caution. We came to a small cavern that pouched off the tunnel's side, that opened to the sea, and a booming wave crested and spat seawater inside.

I wiped the briny mist from my face.

We continued to the tunnel's end, passing the returning ghost-hunters. At the terminus, we did the forensic collection and then leaned against the low gate for a view outside. Below, waves crashed on jagged rocks.

"It strikes me," I said, "that one push by Roger's killers could have done the job here."

"And yet they didn't."

No, or Roger would not have continued his journey. And the evidence said that he did. In the lab, we'd come up with two scenarios. The first: Roger came here on his own, by bus perhaps, and journeyed alone until the end, when he was met by his killers. Second scenario: the killers accompanied him. Two second-scenario options: they were with him from the get-go, driving him from the dig. Or, they joined him at some point on his Lands End journey.

"Cassie," Walter said, "what are you getting at?"

"This tunnel. *If* they were with him, why not seize this opportunity? Why wait?"

"You have a thought, I take it."

"First, the obvious, they wanted a less public place to kill him and this place is too touristed."

"Agreed. You have another?"

I had a stab in the dark. "They were drawing it out. He knew them, he trusted them--or came to--and they were enjoying the deception. What they planned. Taking their time, continuing the journey. Savoring it."

"Vengeful."

"And, or, maybe they were trying to learn something from him along the way."

Walter considered. "And that something explains Lands End."

"It sure needs explaining."

"It does. The easier course would have been to kill him at the dig, given that they took his body there." He added, "As we discussed in the lab."

We'd made a start there, getting into some hows and whys.

"Yeah, but there's nothing like going to the field. Experiencing it--fresh eyes and all that. As you taught me a long time ago."

"Still true."

I glanced down at the perilous scene below. This place did the trick, putting me in the scene.

We turned to head back through the tunnel. If I believed in ghosts I'd conjure up Roger with his big puppy-dog ears, tramping through the mud alongside us.

And I'd say, you should have been afraid.

11

WE CONTINUED THE JOURNEY.

The stairway from the Baths took us back up to the parking area. From there, we found the start of the Coastal Trail, which would lead us to the wildest corner of the city.

As it had led Roger Forster.

The trail began wide and tame. Several yards in, we selected a place to sample.

Walter grunted. "Almost looks paved."

He liked his trails dirty. I thought this looked pretty natural, as intended. According to the report we'd found online, the erosion-resistant surface was an aggregate of crushed stone mixed with polymers and tree resins. It felt like compacted earth underfoot, with a satisfying crunch.

In the lab, Walter had found this stuff in Roger's boot soles and assigned it to layer two.

Here in the field, it told us we were on the right track.

We set to work.

A group of silver-head hikers skirted us, eyeing Walter on his knees scooping a helping of aggregate.

He glanced up. "I do sand art."

They gaped.

I hid a grin.

Before anyone else could come upon us, Walter packed up and we moved along.

The trail gently climbed, winding through scattered Cypress and sage-smelling brush, with the sea off to our left far below. I wondered if Roger had appreciated these pines and this view and the dappling sunlight three days ago. He'd certainly had sunshine for his journey, as we'd learned when checking weather records. He likely came late morning or midday, as we'd surmised when checking tide tables. We started a little later in the day because low tide came later in the day. Otherwise, same journey for us, more or less, albeit with a safer ending.

Easy to be lulled here. The peppery scent of the trees and the briny whiff of the sea and the mid-morning sun all did their work on me. I found myself hiking this glorious trail as if it were recreation.

Walter wore a smile and lifted his chin as though he did not want to miss a thing.

We were newcomers to Lands End. When Walter was at Berkeley he'd visited San Francisco now and then but didn't venture beyond the lively downtown. His student fieldwork took him elsewhere. My brief San Francisco field trip had been restricted to the island and the city's northern waterfront.

The trail climbed and wound its gentle way to a straighter stretch, where taller trees filled in the woods, their canopy filtering the sun, their branches limiting views of the sea.

We hiked in easy silence and nodded at everyone sharing the trail. It wasn't crowded, on this weekday morning.

Now and then, we paused to collect. More aggregate.

And then we passed a sign that warned *DANGER: Hazardous Cliffs* and within a few yards the trail took a sharp bend and headed cliff-ward. An overlook bumped out from the trail.

"Let's stop there," Walter said. "I want to get my bearings."

We veered off-trail and took in the killer views. There was an interpretive sign describing the twenty-some shipwrecks along this volatile coastline, out there in the not-so-peaceful Pacific Ocean.

Walter let out a low whistle.

I shifted my view northward, where he was looking. "Yeah, wow, there's the bridge."

I'd been mesmerized by the view of the rust-orange Golden Gate Bridge from the patio at Forster's Sea Cliff mansion, but this was different. A different angle, farther away, the bridge looking smaller on the horizon. Or perhaps the difference I felt was relief, that there was no Forster here to throw me off-balance.

Walter said, "I meant my promontory."

Ah. Yes. Lands End Point. His discovery, uniquely positioned between the two beaches with the melange addresses. I'd admired it on the geologic map. Seeing it in the field was a show-stopper. Even at this distance, the promontory commanded attention, jutting proud from the cliffs.

I wondered if Roger had stopped here to gape. He surely must have come this way more than once--at the least, years ago, to gather material for his cousin's Sutro book. And on *this* journey, his final, if he was doing another trek to prepare a new pitch, did he stop here for another gape? Because the promontory was an unmistakable landmark on the way to the beach where he had to have gone wading, on the way to that mind-blowing stop beyond.

And the question remained: was Roger alone at this point? Or did his killers pause here along with him to admire the view?

Either way, this journey sure looked like a tour of Sutro country.

According to Forster's book--relayed to me by Walter--much

of this trail followed the path of a now-vanished railroad that
Adolph Sutro had built to bring city-dwellers to the outdoors.
And, not incidentally, to his grand Baths. In fact, the man who
would become San Francisco mayor owned most of the land
along the city's rugged northwestern edge.

I said to my partner, "I'm trying to wrap my mind around this
Sutro link."

"You and me both."

We moved on.

The trail strayed back into the trees, dipping and climbing,
and then trended back toward the cliff edge, and then swerved
away yet again. I eased back into my rhythm. Nodding at
passers-by. Thinking, spectacular Lands End still brings people
to the wild.

We sampled the trail surface twice.

When we came to a deeply shaded heavily vegetated marshy
stretch, I thought I caught the scent of fresh water. There must
be a spring. Amidst the lush greenery, stalky calla lilies
popped up.

We continued.

And soon enough we came to a sign that read *Mile Rock
Beach*, with an arrow pointing seaward, and below that, it read
Steep Slope.

That was surely the name of the game around here.

We left the main trail, as Roger had, and started down the
stairway.

The way down was well-maintained, long dirt-packed steps
shored up by timber edges, flanked by a cable-and-post railing.
It was wide enough for two bare-chested guys to zip around us,
stair-running their way down. We descended more slowly,
down down down through woods and brush that thickly
haired this cliff face, pausing once to sample, not even drawing
a glance from the panting group passing us on their ascent.

The stairway jogged and narrowed again and was now bordered by waist-high wood retaining walls holding back the steep slope.

I smelled sea air.

More stairs, and then the slope moderated.

And finally, the woods parted and revealed the sea and the isolated beach that filled a small cove. It was a knockout of a beach, partly sandy, mostly rocky, strewn with driftwood, decorated with rock towers, dotted here and there with beachgoers, one of them constructing a new tower.

The water itself was littered with boulders and sea stacks, near and far, and I guessed that the rock supporting a lighthouse a mile or so from shore was the 'mile rock' for which this spot was named.

But none of the geology in the water or on the sand compared to the soaring promontory that flanked the beach's northern end, with its ship's-prow point. Lands End Point.

We had arrived at the final segment of the journey.

From here on, things were going to get tricky.

Some of the soils and pebbles that comprised layer one of the mud from Roger's boot soles likely came from this beach. Some likely came from the top of that massive promontory, and some from the beach on its other side. And some most definitely came from what lay beyond. All of it somewhat mixed.

If the samples we gathered indeed matched the evidence, we could confirm that Roger had come this way. That somewhere on this segment, he'd taken his final steps.

Here, possibly.

Walter took out his phone to mark the location.

I just took it all in. Envisioning Roger here. He'd had low tide, as we did. Nice wading. We knew he'd had to wade from the beach on the promontory's far side, but he might have done so here, as well, just for the fun of it, just to cool his sweaty feet.

Maybe he built one of those rock towers. Alone. Or with his killers, a group project.

Did they find an isolated spot here, around the outcrop at the beach's southern end? Was that where Roger took his final steps?

The question was tricky because we didn't know if Roger had done some back-and-forthing in this off-trail final segment of the journey.

And there was no puppy-dog ghost to ask.

I started to work, sampling my way from dry sand down to the low-tide stretch of wet sand, then continuing along the strand. Walter followed his own path, browsing for a match to his prized melange pebble.

We drew no attention. Just two more beachgoers starting a sand castle, collecting for a pebble tower.

Doing a little sand art.

When we'd finished we took a seat on a driftwood log. We spent a few moments admiring the view. Then Walter displayed a specimen dish of pebbles that promised *melange*, and I admired that.

He said, "Are you ready to walk it through?"

We'd walked it through in the lab this morning, our sketchy overview. Now in the field, we'd see what we could see.

I said, "Let's do it."

"We'll begin with the known. According to the medical examiner, Roger was killed late in the afternoon."

"No privacy right here but they might have found some beyond that little arm of cliff." I indicated the jutting outcrop that bordered the southern end of the beach.

Walter nodded. "Next, the question of the car."

Rigor and lividity suggested that Roger's body had been placed in a car trunk. On his side, jammed up. Which raised a very big question.

"Yeah," I said, "let's walk *that* through. The killers carry the body back this way, across this popular beach, in the afternoon? And then up the stairs? Having just walked down that stairway, I call it nearly impossible to carry a body back up. Two-hundred-plus very steep steps from here to the trail. And then a whole lot more steps to the parking lot. In the afternoon. In public."

Walter rubbed his calves. "Call it impossible, no qualifier. Which leaves us with the only likely alternative."

"Right. A boat."

"No objections?"

"Now that we're here?" I pointed at the boulder-littered water. "Just those."

"Indeed. The perps need a small boat. Nimble. Something like a Zodiac."

"I can do a Zodiac."

"Even so," Walter said, "they have to load the body in the boat, without being seen, even down the strand where it's *maybe* more private. So here's a more likely scenario--a 'friend' happens by with his boat and Roger willingly goes along for a ride, and they end up at the site where the car awaits."

I nodded, "Either way--whether he's killed here or at the car--we need the car. Given that he progresses to full rigor and lividity while in the trunk, let's say the killers leave him there for a long while, waiting until the middle of the night so they can arrive at the dig when it's likely deserted. And then they wrangle Roger down to his burial spot." I added, "Can two perps manage all this? One with Roger on his hike and the second, the friend bringing the Zodiac? After having parked the car, wherever. And where *is* the car parked? Got to be some isolated spot accessible by Zodiac, right?"

Walter sighed. "What we have is too many variables. Let's confine ourselves to Lands End. Somewhere in this neighborhood, the boot evidence says he took his final steps."

I glanced up at the promontory towering above us, where we'd be taking our next steps.

First, though, we energized with protein bars and hydrated with warm water from our Nalgenes.

We had a stiff hike ahead.

12

WE PACKED up and returned to the stairway.

Just above the beach we left the stairs and took an unsigned fork up a narrow dirt path. The path wound across the cliffside and spat us onto a narrower path fit for a goat that hugged a precipitous drop-off.

It was a long way down to Mile Rock Beach.

The goat path skirted a tall outcrop and then spat us onto the broad flat top of the promontory, its ships prow giving the illusion of a springboard into air, and then a long plunge down to the sea below.

We gaped.

"Well," Walter finally said, "it does not disappoint."

No. Neither the geologic map nor the satellite image could put us in the scene, like this.

We did not have it to ourselves. A couple huddled near the outcrop. A woman stood at the edge, her ponytail whipping in the wind. A man crouched nearby, looking as if he might wind-surf into the void. Out near the terminus where the prow narrowed to a point, several hikers circled and circled the giant labyrinth that claimed a quadrant of the promontory, following paths laid out by large stones. I'd seen the labyrinth in photos. I'd dismissed it, not being a fan of disturbing the geology to decorate the scenery. But now, seeing it in person, I found myself briefly mesmerized. It was haunting.

"At another time," Walter said, "on a different quest, I wouldn't mind walking that labyrinth."

I'd watch that. I said, "On this quest, let's get to work."

"Let's go out to the point, first. I want to get an overview."

We zipped our jackets against the wind and then went to take in the lay of the land.

We had to skirt the labyrinth in order to reach the point, where a narrow spit of rock jutted out. Seeing it up close now, I thought yeah, it's shaped like a ship's prow. In earlier times, a carved figurehead would keep watch on an actual ship.

Evidently, Walter was thinking the same. He said, "The *Dawn*."

I wondered if that buried ship on the other side of the city had had a figurehead. Burt Zhang would know. I thought a siren would have been appropriate, luring sailors to their graves.

"This is the way it would have come," Walter continued, "sailing across the sea, passing this point," he raised a finger, swiping from left to right, "following the strait to enter the bay, to reach the gold-rush waterfront at Yerba Buena Cove."

I followed the journey traced by my partner's finger. From open ocean to the passage between the two headlands just visible in the distance off to our right, where the orange bridge spanned. Of course, there was no bridge back then. Just the gateway, the golden gate. It would have been a treacherous journey, navigating through that strait, especially in a land notorious for its fog.

Today, now, nothing hampered our visibility.

I took in the panorama and asked my poetry-loving partner, "You know a poem suitable for this?"

He shook his head.

"Make one up."

"The end."

"That's not a poem."

"It's what I've got." He sucked in a breath. "Very well. The last frontier, before one falls off the rocky edge of the continent."

Good enough.

I gave a thought to Roger. One push off Lands End Point would have done the job. But clearly the killers didn't want him smashed on the rocks below, because there had been no push, no fall-inflicted trauma. There was throttling, asphyxia, up close and personal.

This magnificent treacherous promontory was a way-point, from one beach to the others, any of which were candidates for Roger's last steps.

Wind gusted harder. I zipped my jacket to the chin and took a step backward.

"Yes," Walter said, "let's get to it."

We found a spot and set to work. I had to resist photographing the killer view, and narrowed my focus. The soil was brownish--despite the color, this promontory was labeled greenstone on the geologic map. In its massive form, greenstone created steep green-black sea cliffs, like this one. The surficial soil, exposed up here, was weathered to a gritty brown.

When I looked up from my sampling I saw that one of the labyrinth circlers, a rangy young guy with a shaved head and Viking beard, was frowning at me. Perhaps he thought I was planning to snatch one of the stones that marked the paths.

I put up my hands. Not gonna steal from the labyrinth-- karma's a bitch.

And no need. The stones, I'd read, had been carried up from the beaches below. The promontory would have shed pebbles and cobbles and even boulders, and over time those rocks eroded into gravel, and then sand. Soon enough, Walter and I would be collecting from the beach on the eastern side of the promontory--the counterpart of Mile Rock Beach. Because from here, according to his boots, Roger Forster had hiked down to that empty beach.

And beyond.

Walter stowed his field kit. "Shall we move on?"

I stowed mine. "We shall."

We shouldered our packs and headed over to the eastern edge, and peered down. Some two hundred feet below was the rocky beach we'd studied on the satellite map. I shifted focus, hunting for the hint of the path we'd found on the map, the direct way down. I thought I saw it. Something of a scramble. The entry point was at the back of the promontory, where it was not quite so damnably steep.

As we turned to go I caught the Viking still watching, hands on his hips. I waved, my San Francisco default response to people who seem overly interested in what we are doing.

13

THE PATH down to the beach was every bit as sketchy as it had appeared on the satellite map. It began as a switchback, heading away from the sheer-sided portion of the promontory, but this was still a steep descent and we had to side-step here and there, crouching once or twice.

When we hit the sand we high-fived.

This beach was unnamed on the map so I named it--Nameless Beach.

We found a flat boulder to shelve our packs and got out the field kits and set to work. According to the map, the geology here should be much the same as at Mile Rock Beach, and when Walter found the multi-colored melange pebbles, he smiled in satisfaction.

The major difference between the two beaches was isolation--this one lacked any beach-goers. But the approach from the sea was equally bouldery, equally unwelcoming.

Walter said, "Zodiac-worthy, at best."

I studied it. "Still, doable."

We knew Roger had to have come this way, en route to what lay beyond, and the question was if he had returned here. My quick-and-dirty field assessment was that he might have spent his final minutes tramping this beach.

Or not.

Wherever he ended his day, he had first proceeded further east along this lonely stretch of coastline.

And then he'd gone wading.

We packed up and moved on, following our ghost.

The beach was more rock than sand and we had to pay considerable attention to our footing, navigating across and among the boulders.

Walter, behind me, said, "Shit."

My partner seldom swears so I turned, thinking he'd tripped, but he was upright, wearing a look of disgust.

"It's fine," he said. "My foot slipped and came down in a little pool of water."

"You okay?" I was thinking ankle.

"I simply have a slightly wet boot."

I grinned. "You just demonstrated the efficacy of seawater slopping into the tread of a boot sole, mixing up the soils near the surface." Tramp around on this beach, and that beach, step in wet sand, in wet mud, in little pools of seawater caught in depressions among the rocks, and one disrupts the chronological sequence of acquisition. And we get a top layer of stuff that resembles a smashed cake. "Nice work, partner."

"You're welcome. I still have a wet boot."

We continued, picking our way through the rocks to a stretch of pebbly sand and then into a gnarly boulder field. Nameless Beach was a long rocky strand that quickly cliffed out on our right, and quickly met the sea on our left.

At high tide, it would surely not exist.

Right now the tide was low, as we'd aimed for. The waves were laid-back and lapped at the shoreline, tumbling loose rocks. It sounded like applause.

The boulder hike brought us to a mini-cove, a sandy crescent, a prime spot to prepare.

We did as Roger no doubt did, taking a seat in the damp sand to remove our boots and socks and roll up our pant legs. No doubt we embedded a few grains in the seams of our pants. As Roger had.

We took the time to sample the tan sand and I identified the obvious--quartz, feldspar, graywacke, rock frags from the cliffs, white bits of shell and no telling what kind of animals had once called them home.

We stuffed socks in boots and tied boots to the D-rings of our packs.

And then there was nothing left but to go wading.

Walter took the lead.

I stepped into the sea and gasped. San Francisco Pacific Ocean cold. Local surfers wore wet suits. Waders needn't bother, as long as they weren't going deep. As the water rose above my ankles I wondered, how deep. The sat map image we'd studied had been taken at low tide, but I didn't know *how* low. I did know that we were going to have to skirt the big-ass wedge of cliff ahead, which jutted far into the water.

Walter called, over his shoulder, "How you doing?"

I dug my toes into the squishy sand beneath the surface. "Fine."

The sun was warm, the cliff down here at sea level blocked the wind, and I was gaining my sea legs.

We went deeper.

The water rose, wetting the rolled-up edges of my pants, and I understood how Roger got the saltwater-stained bands on his rolled-up pant legs.

We came to the big-ass wedge of cliff.

Walter disappeared around the corner.

There was a long silence, and then he shouted, "You're not going to believe this!"

I came around the wedge and saw the little cove and its slice of beach. And the stupendous cliff.

Oh yeah, I believed.

The high cliff face was eyed with windows.

We'd studied it on the satellite map. But this was different. In person, cold water up to my knees, I was a little bit reluctant to wade out of the sea and onto the sand where Walter was now dropping his pack.

A little bit reluctant to undertake the next stage of the journey.

"Cassie!"

I shifted focus to my partner, who was already untying his boots from the D-rings.

I waded to shore.

Here, up close, I tipped my head back and studied the cliff face, taking note of the darkened rock, seawater-stained, where the highest of storm-whipped waves had reached--up to window level. I wondered how much higher the highest tide now climbed on the cliff than it had back when our field-trip group studied sea-level rise. We hadn't come to this edge of the city. No reason to. One needed a solid reason to come here at any point, at any time.

I shifted my study down to the horizon where the cliff met the beach, where high tides and big waves had battered the rock, eaten away at it, undercut it here and there, leaving the beach-level cliff face looking scalloped.

I found the eroded eaten-away gouge in the cliff that Walter and I had come for. It was a tall opening, an inverted V, narrower at the top, wider at the bottom.

It was a sea cave.

It was the only way inside the cliff.

This was the way Roger entered years ago, doing research for his cousin's Sutro book. Last night after reading about this place, Walter had done some Googling and found an interview Roger gave back when the biography was published. Not only had he pitched the book, he'd also pitched his own 'exciting' research trips.

On his trip here three days ago, he'd picked up layers of mud in his boots that gave us the journey-history, the way he'd come.

Question was, did he come alone, or with company?

Walter said, "We shouldn't dawdle. We don't know how much time we're going to need. We have to mind the tide."

I stood rooted, staring up at the windows in the cliff, and I found a name for this unnamed stretch of transitory sand: Cold-feet Beach.

Walter was already putting on his boots.

I dumped my pack and took a seat and untied my boots and pulled out socks. Brushing sand off my feet, I understood how Roger had got sand in his socks. There is *always* a little sand clinging to your skin when you clean off your feet at the beach.

"Cassie." Walter stood, ready to go.

"Yeah." Clean enough. I pulled on socks and boots and laced tightly and rolled down my pant legs and then took a series of photos of the multi-eyed cliff face, just to set the scene, just to establish that this place was simply a job, and then I joined Walter in sampling the beach, and when we'd finished I saw that he was eyeing me.

"What?" I asked.

"Are you sure?"

I could ask him the same thing. Are *you* sure? Several years ago he'd suffered a couple of mini-strokes. Now, he was healthy and fit but he'd put on a few ill-advised pounds and he wasn't getting any younger. He liked to complain about his age, invoking the dinosaurs, and I liked to tell him that in a geologic time frame, he was a youngster. Still, age-wise, he was closer to the dinosaurs than I was.

On the other hand, I was the one who had a problem with tightly enclosed spaces.

For a moment we regarded one another.

And then the moment passed. The reality was that if one of us went in alone, and slipped and broke an ankle, there was no way to call for help. Up inside the cliff, no one could hear you. And there was almost certainly no cell service in there.

We exchanged nods and then stowed the field kits in the packs and exchanged our hats for headlamps and helmets, and then we approached the sea cave.

The beachy entrance was sand littered with rocks and boulders, no doubt eroded from the cliff above, in addition to those washed ashore by high tides. High tides would wash seawater right on inside this cave.

Wouldn't want to be in there with the tide coming in.

I looked up, above the cave, to study the strange column of cemented bricks that climbed from the top of the entrance up the cliff face, looking something like the exterior of a chimney. At the top of the chimney was a window into the cliff.

That's where we were headed--up to the high window.

Via the sea cave.

I switched on my headlamp and followed Walter into the mouth of the cave.

14

INSIDE THE SEA CAVE, by the light of my headlamp, I saw that the space was narrow, and very tall.

And it was nearly filled with a semi-wrecked structure made of brick. We'd seen its exterior from the beach, climbing up the cliff face like a chimney. In here, the interior portion was wedged within the cave walls, reaching almost to the top. In here, it looked less like a chimney and more like the remains of a brick tower, the lower half gutted, the edges like stanchions cemented to the cave wall, holding the tower in place. No way to tell its original purpose, or when it had broken, or why. Earthquake, maybe. Erosion. Instability. Everything--whether made by nature or human hand--was susceptible to the right triggering event.

Walter moved closer to the 'stanchion' near the cave entrance. "You see that?" He pointed to a small area of discolored brick, at about shoulder height. The surface was lightly abraded. "Possibly, someone brushed against the brick--which is crumbly, to begin with--and an edge of their pack did that. Possibly, during a struggle."

"Roger."

"It's not out of the question. And dislodged grains fell to the ground, which could account for the brick grains in the mud his boots picked up." Walter got the field kit from his pack, selected the chisel, popped off a piece of abraded brick, then stowed it in a specimen dish.

"If there was a struggle," I said, "the next question is, was it before or after he went up there?"

We both looked up, to the top of the sea cave. Short of hauling an extension ladder in here, there was no obvious way to climb up the gutted tower, to access the tunnels above, to penetrate deeper inside the cliff.

But there was a better way.

Roger's way.

In that interview, he'd given a sketchy roadmap. It led behind the brick tower. The way was via a low narrow corridor of sorts on the left-hand side, where the tower had pulled partially away from the cave wall.

Walter asked me, "Ready?"

Nothing like being in the field, experiencing it. "Yeah, ready."

We donned our helmets.

Walter took the lead, ducking into the corridor, and soon called, "Come ahead, there's room enough."

I stooped and came ahead.

It was a short unpleasant few steps that ended at the back of the brick tower. Here was another narrow corridor, between the brick and the rock wall--a slot that rose all the way to the top of the sea cave.

My headlamp washed the facing walls: red brick and rough graywacke. The place smelled sea-cave dank. There was room enough, just. A phrase came to mind: *as the walls close in*. Metaphorical. That trapped feeling. I recalled a horror flick I'd watched as a kid in which the walls of the cheesy movie set actually closed on the explorer.

All in all, this slot was a stone-cold reason why I didn't like tightly enclosed spaces.

I left it to Walter to photograph this unsettling place. I just scooped dirt.

Then Walter opened his pack and dragged out the yellow rope.

I tipped my head way back, angling my headlamp beam at the uneven top of the brick wall, some fifteen feet above us, where a chunk of bricks was missing, leaving a jutting red fist. It made a workable anchorage for a rope. Roger hadn't said how many throws he'd needed to anchor his rope around the fist. Neither had he said if the footholds in the brick wall were generous. Hard to tell, from down here.

We'd find out.

Walter tied the rope in a giant loop, and threw. It took him five tries to lasso the fist. The loop now hung down in a long pendant. It was a simple technique--upon finishing our exploration, upon descent, we'd untie the knot and the rope would hang free and we could pull it down and pack it away.

Now, preparing to ascend, Walter gave the loop a tug. Then he did it again, and again. It held, snugged around the fist. Finally, he put on his pack and cinched the hip belt.

I focused on the climb. Looked doable.

The yellow rope loop snaked down the red brick wall like a handrail alongside the footholds. Somebody had thought this through, aligning the footholds with the fist--the somebody who'd chiseled away stairstep bricks, hacking this stairway into the wall. Some zealous explorer-spelunker with tools and good balance. Roger maybe. Roger and Gregory Forster together, maybe.

"How you doing?" Walter asked.

"Fine." Rock solid.

"I'll go first.'

My partner, the quintessential gentleman. I didn't argue.

He grasped the two sections of rope loop and squeezed them together, for a better grasp. He put a boot on the first step, and then the second, hand-over-handing the rope as he ascended. He climbed slowly, smoothly. I took notice because I was lighting his way with my headlamp, assessing his stability and balance--as I sometimes did, surreptitiously, when I got the chance.

He wasn't in dinosaur territory.

My light lit the top of the cave, where it narrowed, where the brick and stone walls nearly met, where Walter was heading, where I would follow, to squeeze in between a rock and a hard place.

So many rock metaphors.

He reached the brick fist and paused to check the rope's anchorage, and then he disappeared above it.

"I'm up," he called. "Rope's all yours."

The looped rope shimmied against the brick face, then stilled.

I set my pack and tightened the hip belt. I took hold of the rope handrail and started up the steps, hand-over-handing the rope. Inevitably, my knees brushed and bumped the brick wall, and inevitably dust and grains of brick embedded in my pants, as they had to have done in Roger's pants. I appreciated the non-skid roughness of the brick footholds. All good. Climbing wasn't the problem. I moved up the steps and then as the walls started narrowing, my shoulder scraped against the rock wall behind me and I met the problem. Nose to nose with it, back to back.

Deep breath.

I focused on the number of times I've gone into caves and tunnels on the job, following the evidence--always with relief upon the exit. Always with the understanding that this came with the territory, when your territory is geology.

Not a puzzle why I ended up here. Because of Walter. I'd been hooked, as a kid, in the lab. One day he'd shown me a thin section of sandstone under the scope that revealed a world within a world. He'd explained that--wonder of wonders--the source of that rock could unravel the story of something that somebody did. A crime, a wrong, a crisis in the making. Which-- truly wonder of wonders--one could do something about. Which Walter could. Which, in time, I could as well.

I climbed.

I pictured Roger climbing, three days ago, alone or with the kind of company that pledged *we will bury you.*

Not buried here, though, much as this place resembled a tomb.

But he could have been killed in here. If so, it would have happened below on the cave floor because it was unlikely his body could have been ferried down these rough-hewn steps. If he was killed down below--that struggle we'd posited--then moved out onto Cold-feet Beach for a boat ride, his killers had to have considered the tide.

As did we.

I called up to Walter, "Doing fine."

Which was true, because the hardest part had been starting. Now that I'd squeezed past the narrowest part, now that I was coming to the fist, passing it--and hearing Walter's "over here!"--I was pretty chill. I tore my gaze from the narrowing walls to look left and saw him sitting on a rock shelf with his legs dangling over the edge, nothing but air between him and the cave floor below.

The rock shelf spanned the narrow rock wall up here.

Off to my right was a window in the cliff face, the window I'd taken note of from the beach. That narrow window let in light and framed the sea beyond.

I liked the view.

I let go of the rope loop and it slithered back down the slot and I followed the rock shelf from the top of the steps along the cave wall to join my partner.

He was smiling. He was loving this--climbing, caving, exploring.

I folded down beside him with my legs dangling over the edge. I returned his smile, liking the newfound unconfined space.

We got out water bottles and drank long, and then Walter mentioned the sandwiches. We'd bought them for lunch, not knowing precisely when that would be. My only opinion on lunch was, not *here*. Instead, we energized once again on protein bars, chewing the sticky bricks of oats and seeds and chocolate chips. Powering up for the next phase. Debating which way to go from here.

There was a tunnel to the east of us and a tunnel to the west of us. It had likely been one continuous tunnel at some point but it had clearly been eroded, breaking here at the top of the sea cave, which I assumed had once been some sort of shaft, which maybe explained the bricks, lining the shaft.

The question was, into which tunnel would Roger have gone? He hadn't specified, in that interview.

We shined our headlamps along the visible length of the eastern tunnel, which ran slightly higher and had a rough rocky floor.

And then we illuminated the visible length of the western tunnel, which as far as we could see had a smooth sandy floor, the sand presumably grains eroded from the rough rock walls.

I imagined describing it to Detective Talon: you won't believe this--there's a beach inside a tunnel high above the shoreline outside.

We decided on the western tunnel.

15

WE PACKED up and bade farewell to the narrow window and its daylight.

Yet again, Walter took the lead and I didn't argue.

We took it slowly, playing headlamp beams over the rough-hewn knobby walls. In comparison to the slot, the walls were comfortably far apart and the ceiling was high. This was a well-made tunnel. Easy walking. The beachy floor was thin sand over hard rock, too scuffed to show footprints, and our boots scattered already-scuffed sand.

We continued our slow advance, watching the walls. We did not want to miss anything telling.

The walls were the same old, same old. Graywacke. The rock was gray as its name. Graywacke got born offshore by turbidity currents--submarine avalanches--depositing mud and sand into the subduction zone, where the stuff got compressed and cemented into rock. And then, much later, it was scraped up along with other Franciscan rocks by plate tectonic movement and plastered onto the continent's edge. Graywacke wasn't pretty like, say, red-rock sandstone, but I had become stubbornly fond of it, the rock that Gregory Forster called unlovely.

The decomposed graywacke underfoot was now pebbly.

We'd left the beachy realm.

"How are you doing?" Walter asked.

I'd prefer, actually, not to keep assessing that. And I could really understand his irritation when I assessed his health and sure-footedness in the field.

All in all, though, better to have each other's back.

I said, "Doing fine, thanks."

Doing fine until the tunnel began to shrink.

The ceiling grew lower and the walls grew closer and craggier. The floor was rockier, littered with stones and cobbles and shards, debris that had clearly fallen from the ceiling, from the walls. I thought about the tunnel-builders' skill set. Most of the tunnel had withstood the years--from one century to the next, and the next--clear evidence of structural integrity. On the other side of the equation were the forces of nature: erosion, subsidences, earthquakes.

Cave-ins.

I fiddled with my helmet.

Walter said, "Here we are."

I looked where he was looking, adding my headlamp beam to his. The graywacke sandstone was now interbedded with a layer of darker fine-grained rock: shale.

We'd arrived at the neighborhood.

We continued at a snail's pace, slow as a geologic age, picking our way through the debris on the floor, scanning the rock face.

And then we found the address in the 'hood, the target we'd been hunting.

There was a small open patch of floor near the wall, a place to stand amidst the debris. In fact, it looked as though the floor space had been cleared. Rocks were piled to one side.

I bent to look. This soil was gray and grainy--decomposed shale adding its color to the mix.

Walter said, "Someone's been here."

No question. This soil was thicker than the thin beachy sand--and well churned up, the way the earth gets churned with a good deal of tramping around. I identified what appeared to be the toe of a waffle sole. It wasn't a good clean print but, nevertheless, it said *someone's been here.*

We'd chosen the correct tunnel.

We added our own prints, moving in close. We took off packs and retrieved the field kits. Took out hand lenses. Smeared the wall with our lights.

I leaned close and put the high-power lens to the rock, and there it was.

I said, "You were right."

He replied, "The book was right."

It was a thin line, the darkest gray so far. It was a lens of carbonized plant material.

Carbonized, and coaly-looking.

A coaly-looking shale.

It *was* coal, in the eyes of the nineteenth-century prospector who spotted a narrow lens of the stuff on the surface of the cliff. Money, in the eyes of the man shown a hacked-off sample, the man who owned the land--Adolph Sutro. The man who would become mayor was intrigued. He knew mining; he'd once designed a drainage tunnel for silver mines in Nevada. He knew that his adopted boomtown hometown of San Francisco, which relied on imported coal, would boom even more with an astonishing source in its own backyard.

We knew all this because Gregory Forster had written about it in his biography of Adolph Sutro.

When Walter read it last night, in the wee hours, he'd had an epiphany about the unusual shale bits in layer one of Roger Forster's boot soil.

Roger knew about it from old newspaper clippings, discovered during research for his cousin's book. And then he'd found his way to the tunnels of Sutro's mine to see for himself. What Roger found--and boasted about in that interview--was what we were now exploring. A skeleton mine, and nothing more. Tunneling was begun, and then stopped.

The great find was not useable coal.

I ran a finger along the deep gray line of carbonized shale. "First Sutro builds a railroad to bring people to the outdoor wonders of Lands End. Then he rips into its cliff, to build a coal mine by the sea. A man of contradictions."

Walter grunted. "A man of his times."

"Times damn well change."

"They rightly do."

I added, "Off and on."

"And yet here I am," he added, "happily exploring the mine's remains."

"Not *just* following Roger."

He nodded. "I am plagued by contradictions."

Who isn't?

Walter said, "I'll move uptunnel and hack a bit from the wall if you want to take on this stuff here."

I did, actually. I wanted to find bits of the coaly shale in the gray soil and match it, back at the lab, to the stuff from Roger's boot soles. I wanted to anchor him to this spot. And then I wanted to ask Gregory Forster why his cousin might have come here on the day of his death. And why Forster, during our Sea Cliff visit, had complained about Roger giving interviews at the dig and yet had not mentioned the old interview Roger gave about this place.

I knelt and scooped a generous helping and secured it in the specimen dish, then shouldered my pack and moved along to join Walter.

He was ready and waiting. "Let's continue and see if we can find anything to establish Roger's return."

"Like what? A dropped candy wrapper?"

"I was thinking more along the lines of Roger reviving the story of the lost Sutro mine, and tying that to the lost ship. Publicity. The buried past--now unburied. Maybe take a selfie looking out one of the windows. In which case, there might be a patch of floor up ahead with prints."

I nodded. Worth checking out.

Walter led the way. Uptunnel was narrower, rockier, lower, but the saving grace was the light that came in from a high window in the cliff face, up ahead. I tried to orient myself, picture the windowed cliff I'd studied from the beach, and figure how far the tunnel would go before we could go no farther.

Hard to figure.

We single-filed it, dodging debris, finding foot placements, and then we halted, in unison.

"You see that?" Walter asked.

"Yeah." The window cast a glow inside the tunnel and our headlamps lighted the floor up ahead where a patch of soil was visible in the rocky debris. Okay, then. Maybe up there we'd find some identifiable prints.

We advanced uptunnel, picking our way through the rocks, and then came parallel with the high window.

Walter said, "Oh."

I gaped at the floor. The patch of soil was muddy, no doubt from the sea mist that entered from the window. And there were indeed identifiable prints: five-digit sharp-nailed gouges in the mud, with stubby heel pads.

I burst out laughing. "Raccoons."

"In here?" Walter said. "How the devil...?" And then he

answered his own question. "The window. They're climbers. At least they are when they knock over my trash cans." He added, "The question is why?" And then he answered that one. "They're curious creatures."

Like us.

We moved on.

We didn't get far.

Up ahead was a rock pile filling the tunnel from floor to ceiling, a terminus. Our tunnel ended here, victim of a cave-in.

End of the line.

Walter painted the ceiling and the walls with his headlamp. "I see nothing in imminent danger of collapse. I'll just nip up there and have a look."

"You're not serious."

"I'll be quick."

I stared at the caved-in terminus. "You can see from here. It's all rocks. No place for footprints."

"I was thinking more along the lines of a dropped phone."

Ah. Right. Roger's missing phone. Could be. He goes crawling around up there, phone falls out of his pocket, disappears in some crevice. "How quick is quick?"

"A minute or so to look." He threw me a grin. "Plus ten seconds to take a selfie."

I rolled my eyes.

He moved into the debris field at the edge of the rock pile and began to look around. My mind jumped--Roger in here, where the tunnel had caved in, taking a selfie, great PR photo to revive interest in the Sutro book. But if the killers were with him, why? He wasn't killed here, he was taken to the dig, so why go to the trouble to come in here first? More Sutro country, sure, but this Sutro country was damned hard to access and not a little creepy to explore.

Walter returned, shaking his head. I found myself disappointed. No phone. No candy wrapper. Not even a selfie. Exploration finished.

We turned and headed downtunnel.

"I can't help thinking," Walter said, as we walked, "that the mystery is rooted here."

I agreed. "Which puts scenario two into play."

Neither of us had anything more to add so my thoughts shifted ahead, to the climb down the tricky footholds and the wading through the sea around the wedge of cliff to Nameless Beach where we could sit in the sand and keep track of the tide, where we could eat our sandwiches and enjoy the unfettered daylight.

I was, in truth, congratulating myself on finding my chill in the tunnel when I saw the headlamp beam ahead, coming our way.

16

"*STOP THERE!*"

The command echoed in the tunnel but it did not drown out the sound of my hammering heartbeat.

I could see nothing but the blinding light. It was aimed straight at us. There was no caving etiquette here. I turned my head, averting my own beam. The stranger's light still overwhelmed, a high-lumen headlamp. I squinted and put up my hands to shield my eyes and it felt like raising one's hands in surrender. Don't shoot. My gut squeezed. Roger hadn't been shot. And Roger couldn't, logistically, have been killed in this tunnel. Didn't mean this couldn't be Roger's killer, though. No logistical reason why not. I sucked in a breath. Find your chill. And keep your hands up.

Walter had his hands raised and his light beam averted.

He said, to the stranger, "Can you aim that headlamp elsewhere?"

There was no reply. But then, out of the corner of my eye, I saw a hand flick in and out of view and the beam switched from focused to flood, and then tilted up toward the ceiling.

I stopped squinting.

Okay, data point. The stranger's headlamp was multi-adjustable. So, serious gear.

I said, "We're going to tilt up our headlamps, as well. So we can face you. Okay?"

No reply.

No objection, though. We adjusted our headlamps, and dropped our hands.

The ceiling was now awash. The light shone down on us like bizarre moon-glow. I glanced at Walter. He looked spectral.

Very slowly, I turned to face the stranger.

The first thing I noticed was the long braid snaking out from beneath the white helmet, catching in the collar of the parka. The spectral tunnel glow was light enough to reveal the electric-blue color of the hair.

Before I could form a question, Walter stepped in.

"Let's proceed with introductions," he said. "I'm Walter. My partner here is Cassie."

"I know."

Whoa. You *do*? I wondered if that was good, or bad.

Walter said, "Then you have us at an advantage."

"Jane."

Jane's voice was raspy, as if mostly unused. She had a strong jawline and a long nose and pale skin. Her eyes were shadowed, deep-set. There were hollows in her cheeks but that could be a trick of the weird moon-glow lighting.

Walter said, "Why have you intercepted us here, Jane?"

I saw what he was doing. Seizing the lead, asking the kind of reasonable questions anyone would ask. Managing the situation.

She didn't reply. There was a stillness about her. Not calm. More like, assessing us.

I'd had enough. "You didn't answer, Jane. What do you want?"

Her attention shifted to me. "You're tracking my cousin."

I scrambled to catch up. "You're a *Forster*?" Of course. "So, related to Gregory as well? You his daughter?"

"Not anymore."

Whatever that was supposed to mean--estranged?--I didn't want to go there. Here, now, we had another alarming Forster.

Walter's hand was on my arm, giving it a squeeze.

He said, "Jane, we're trying to find out what happened to Roger."

"So am I."

He said carefully, "That's not a good idea."

"Why?

"Because this is a murder case."

"What's scenario two?"

Okay, I thought, second data point: acoustics in here were good enough to have carried our conversation when we left the cave-in and started down the tunnel. At least we'd stopped short of spelling out scenario two, that Roger's killers brought him from the dig to Lands End.

Walter said, "I'm afraid I can't discuss our investigation, but I can introduce you to the detective in charge of the case and you can put your questions to her."

"*No.*" Jane suddenly unzipped her parka, and I flinched, but there was nothing alarming underneath--only a sweatshirt. And I suddenly knew her identity. Not just estranged Forster daughter, but hoodie Jane. Her baggy sweatshirt was navy blue. The hood was bunched under the collar of the navy-blue parka.

I said, "Here's what *I* know. You were at the dig yesterday, watching us. You and somebody else, also wearing a hooded sweatshirt. Friend of yours?"

"Uh-huh."

"Name?"

She was silent.

"Fine," I said, "here's what else I know--last night you were at

Pier 40 on the walkway outside the warehouse where we work. So I'd say you're stalking us, and what's worse is you ambushed us in here, and that's really not cool."

She was silent.

"You knew we'd be here. You brought a helmet and head-lamp. How do you know about this place?"

She glanced at the tunnel wall.

It was the briefest of glances but her beam caught the carbonized plant material, glazing the black coaly seam. I thought she frowned. Hard to tell, in the murky light. And I wondered, were you here recently, Jane? Say, with your cousin Roger on the day of his death? That would put you in league with the killers. Or maybe you were following them. Like you've followed us. Or, more likely, you read your father's Sutro book and you already knew about this half-built coal mine.

"Jane," Walter said, "we're sorry for your loss. Beyond that, we can't help you."

"You *can*. Tell me what the archaeologist said."

Okay, I thought, we're back to the dig. And I wondered what connected the buried ship to this skeleton mine on the city's wild fringe.

Walter didn't miss a beat. "Nothing," he said. "The archaeologist told us nothing that can be of use to you, Jane."

"You're dodging."

He was. "You're asking questions I can't answer."

"*Won't* answer."

"You need to leave this to the investigators."

She stiffened.

I watched her. She'd watched us at the dig with a fierce focus. She'd seen us move from the crime scene to the ship, to talk to Burt Zhang. Easy enough to put two and two together, to figure the detective in charge of the case brought us to the archaeologist to ask why Roger's body had been dumped at the dig.

"Jane," I said, "why do you need to know what happened to Roger?"

"*I'm a Forster.*"

She'd hissed it.

I watched her. She was rigid. I thought of her father on the landing at Sea Cliff, rigid with fury because he thought I was wasting time, because the perp had threatened *we will bury you.* Future tense. And it seemed to me, now, that estranged Jane Forster had something in common with her father. Both were watching their backs.

Walter said, "Jane, you really do need to speak to the detective. We'd be happy to take you."

"I said *no.*"

"Then you need to move aside so that my partner and I can take our leave." He took a step forward.

She moved then, quickly. She whipped aside the flaps of her parka and shoved her sweatshirt up to the waist of her jeans, which were anchored by an electric-blue belt. Clipped to the belt was a black canister. The red lettering was small but I could make out the word *pepper.*

Pepper spray.

I sucked in a breath.

Walter raised a palm. "Take it easy, Jane."

"*Don't move.*"

"We *can't* move. You're blocking our exit."

Her hand went to the canister, unhooking it. With the other hand, she tilted her headlamp down, blinding us, and we ducked, and by the time my eyes stopped watering and I looked up, she was gone. Only her light remained, a firefly in the tunnel ahead.

And then the tunnel ahead went dark.

We stood rooted to the spot for longer than necessary and then we both spoke, almost in unison. "*The rope.*"

17

I ENVISIONED JANE FORSTER, in my panicked mind's eye, climbing down from the tunnel, through the slot, using the rope to steady her descent on the precarious steps of the brick wall.

And when she reaches the floor, she leaves the rope in place for us.

Or, she unties the knot and yanks the rope off its anchorage and it falls in a heap, leaving us stranded up here.

We took off down the tunnel, focused fiercely on reaching the exit. The only illumination ahead was the faint glow from the top of the sea cave where the window in the cliff leaked light inside.

We headed for the light.

Next stop, the exit.

My eyes began to water.

I squinted.

Walter let out a gasp and dragged me to a halt. I might have kept going, otherwise, charging ahead on sheer fear and fury.

But my eyes were stinging now, a searing pain that made me duck against the spray wafting uptunnel like the devil's own perfume.

I jerked my parka up over my mouth, over my nose, would've covered my eyes but Walter was dragging me again, in the opposite direction. I could barely see through my slitted eyes.

We stumbled our way uptunnel.

My throat was on fire.

Couldn't breathe.

And then I expelled a breath I didn't know I'd been holding and that was worse, shit don't do that.

When the floor began to turn rocky, we slowed so as not to trip and break an ankle.

It took an eon to travel past the interbedding of the shale, past the coaly seam, all the way to the blessed high window that let in blessed sea air.

I found that I could trust my breathing again. But my throat ached. My eyes stung. I yanked off my pack and got my water bottle, and Walter got his, and we tipped our heads and poured water in our eyes, flushing them. And then we drank, salving our raw throats. I would have drained my bottle but Walter said, "Save it."

Yes. Save the water. Who knows how long we'll be in here.

Who knows how long that spray will persist downtunnel.

I found my fury. No, didn't find it. Never lost it. Just got side-tracked trying to escape.

We kicked aside rocks and shards and cobbles, clearing a flat stretch of dirt, and then we stretched out on the floor and never mind the pebbles.

We rested for minutes. More than that.

My heartbeat steadied. My breathing slowed. I swallowed, barely flinching. My eyes still stung but no worse than after a salty swim in the sea.

Minutes passed. Hours.

We got bandanas from our packs and covered mouths and

noses and tried, again, to get out. Didn't get far. We retreated to the space beneath the high window.

Again, we flattened to the earth.

I checked my phone. Only fifteen minutes after our latest retreat. I thought it had been longer. I showed Walter the time on my screen.

He said, "We'll give it another half hour."

I wondered how he came up with that time frame. How long it takes pepper spray to dissipate, to clear a tunnel in a cliff--taking windows into consideration. That's some calculating there, partner. Or maybe he meant, he couldn't stand waiting any longer.

Yeah.

I said, "Hope the rope's there." Stating the obvious. Those steps were pretty much non-navigable without the rope but there would come a point when we'd have to try. Sure, exhausted and pepper-poisoned, we could Spiderman our way down that slot.

Time passed.

I checked my phone. Only ten minutes gone. I worked on my breathing.

Walter asked, "You okay?"

I looked up at the high window. "We could get up the wall here--it's rough enough for footholds--and then look out the window and hope for a view down at the cliff face, see if there's anything scaleable there, maybe a ledge or some crevices."

Walter said, "Are you kidding?"

"Raccoons climbed it."

He waited.

"Kidding." Crazy talk, crazy talk. Give me another half hour in here and I might just take a gander out that window.

We gave it another half hour--reconstructing the tide table we'd studied, figuring time was still on our side but why wait any longer? At some point, the tide was going to rise enough to flood the sea cave.

It was not possible to wait any longer.

We got up, wrapped the bandanas, shouldered our packs, and then started the journey downtunnel once again. We passed the coaly seam without incident. When we reached the sandy stretch of floor there was a lingering hint of pepper spray, and our eyes began to sting. We got sunglasses from parka pockets and donned them, and then we continued along the sandy floor looking like crazed chilled beach bums.

As we approached the exit, my stomach clenched because the moment of truth was at hand.

Spiderman, or rope?

The rock shelf came into view--lighted by the window--and below the shelf was the brick-fist anchorage and my heart leaped. The yellow rope was still looped there.

Walter, a couple of paces in front of me, let out a hoot.

She'd left the rope in place for us.

I wanted to hug her.

My eyes stung--not with tears of relief, but with the dregs of her pepper spray.

I didn't want to hug her.

I wanted Detective Raptor to track her down and throw her in a lightless dungeon.

18

THERE WAS a lot of noise in here.

Seventeen hours ago we'd been sunk in the hush of the tunnel, and we'd escaped it wrapped in silence. Our descent down the steps clutching the rope had been wordless--no need to nag one another about taking care. The first words we'd spoken came on the beach, taking note that the tide had turned but it hadn't yet swamped the beach and it hadn't risen so high as to keep us from wading around the wedge of cliff, although I got wet nearly to the waist. At the promontory, we passed the labyrinth circlers like ghosts. We took the goat path to the stairway and that gnarly climb up to the Coastal Trail with ragged inhales and rough exhales. The hike back proceeded in silence and the chatter of passers-by was lost to the wind. We said next to nothing on the drive back. The phone call shocking Debra Talon was brief. Dinner was the uneaten sandwiches in my pack. Work was sporadic, desultory. We made a small bit of progress. We focused on layer one of the boot mud and established one solid match. The most important match. Roger Forster had walked in the sea cave, had ascended to the tunnel to stand on the graywacke soil, acquiring his coaly flakes. We'd high-fived. But we hadn't had much to say.

In part, that was due to practicality--nagging raw throats.

In part, it was avoidance. We weren't in the frame of mind to dissect our encounter with Jane Forster.

We slept like the dead. Woke this morning groggy. Headed out for breakfast, mostly silent.

Ever since the tunnel, I'd felt like my ears were plugged, like I'd gone for a swim in the sea and dived too deep.

Now--amid the talk and the laughter and the scraping of chairs and the smoothie-making blender and the clatter of dishes--that underwater feeling dissipated, as if my ears had finally popped.

I studied the menu on the chalkboard above the curved wooden counter that ran the length of the big room.

Walter said, "The breakfast taco sounds fine."

I was leaning toward the lemon-poppyseed waffle.

My stomach growled, a familiar sound. All right, then.

We ordered, collected our coffees, then wound our way among the couches and the tables large and small, and found a two-person table by a window. Sun streamed in. We soaked up the warmth, nursing our coffees, waiting for the food. I studied the place: walls of Tuscan gold were hung with bright prints and paintings and quilts, and the bookshelves were full.

I liked it here.

I looked out the window. Across the street, the waters of the bay sparkled. A block away was Pier 40 and our lab. Down this side of the street was our rental apartment. Couldn't be more convenient.

A server who looked about fifteen brought the taco and the waffle with a friendly, "How's it going?"

"Fine, thanks," I answered, my voice working. "And you?"

"Getting better every day."

Yeah, we'd read the sign by the food counter. Crossroads Cafe was a training school for a foundation that helped people in need rebuild their lives.

Walter said, "Good place, here."

The server gave a smile and moved on.

The noise in the cafe, it seemed to me, was mellowing. No. I was mellowing.

We dug in and yeah, good place, good food. We ate in silence.

When his egg-and-jalapeno-cheese taco was nearly finished, Walter took our mugs to refill. When he returned, when he'd settled, when we'd each had time to get a start on the second coffee, he glanced at the neighboring tables and then dropped his voice and said, "What do we know?"

I glanced around, too. People were eating and chatting, showing no interest in eavesdropping. A big group at a nearby table was talking, loudly, about how to hit the bestseller list. Authors, clearly. I wondered if Gregory Forster ever came here.

So, to business. I began, speaking in a hushed mine-tunnel voice. "We know that Roger took a hike at Lands End. We know he visited a mine tunnel he had previously visited. We know he ended up, that day, across the city in a pit next to Burt Zhang's archaeological dig."

"You put Burt in your assessment."

"I did. Because Jane Forster thought Burt knew something about Roger's death."

"That's nothing to do with Burt."

I smiled. Walter was clearly a fan of the archaeologist who cast him as a gold-rush mayor.

"As to *Jane*," he said, "it's fair to say she's worried about becoming a victim of Roger's killer. Hence she wanted to know what Burt told us."

"Yeah. So we figured."

"*Hence,*" he added, "she carries the pepper spray."

"Well she used it on the wrong targets."

"She used it to keep us from following her. I suspect she's keeping her whereabouts hidden."

"You're forgiving." I sighed. "But yeah, could be."

And could be she was still following us. Last night, when we were doing our best to do good work in the lab, I'd certainly been on alert. Once, I dragged Walter outside to investigate passers-by on the walkway that flanked the warehouse. But the only passer-by we'd caught in our flashlight beams was a boat owner heading up the ramp from the marina docks.

We fell into silence again, Walter finishing his taco, me mopping syrup with my last square of waffle.

I went to fetch more coffee.

When I'd settled, I said, "Let's get back to Roger. I'm thinking of what Debra said to Forster, that Roger might have drawn the wrong kind of attention at the dig with his PR stunts for the books."

"I suspect you're about to make an onageristic estimate."

I was. An onager is a wild ass. My wild-ass guesses have sometimes paid off. Sometimes not. I said, "Try this on-- someone bears Roger a grudge and uses the PR angle to lure him to Lands End."

"You mean, posing as a reporter?"

I nodded. "The 'reporter' asks for an interview about the Sutro book. Suggests doing it in Sutro country."

Walter rubbed his chin. "That's a valid scenario. But why Lands End? The grudge, presumably, is connected to the discovery of the ship, since Roger's body was placed at the dig. So why not kill him there? Why take Roger to the other side of the city?" Walter added, his voice gone raw again, "To that damnable mine."

The thrill of tunnel exploration had evaporated, for my partner. Couldn't agree more.

Walter's phone rang. He answered, listened, mouthed *Debra*, then put the phone on speaker and set it on the table between us. He leaned in. "You're on speaker."

"Great. Hello to the both of you." Her speaker-voice came loud as a raptor's cry.

"We're at breakfast," Walter said, "in a public place."

I glanced again at the nearby tables. Nobody was taking notice.

"I'm guessing Crossroads," she said, lowering her voice, and when Walter confirmed, she continued, "great place, I should have told you about it but doesn't matter, you found it on your own, and I hope you're nearly finished because I need you on the road in fifteen minutes, tops. If you're not done eating, get one of those to-go clamshells. I'll text you directions. I assume you didn't bring your gear to breakfast, so you'll need to grab that before you come."

"First," Walter said, "we're going to need to know what you're talking about."

"We've got a line on her."

There could be only one *her*. I said, "Jane Forster?"

"You got it." Detective Talon added, "You're not going to believe this."

19

IT WAS JARRING.

Yesterday, we hiked the Coastal Trail. Today, we stood above it.

The knoll upon which we stood rested atop the rugged cliffs that buttressed Lands End. But the topography was steep enough that we couldn't see the wild land down below, from up here.

Up here, on the knoll, it was tidied, not wild. The terrain was haired with oaks and graceful cypress and pines and groomed in rangy green grass and marked, here and there, with colored flags. We couldn't see all the flagged holes--they'd be scattered among the trees. We could see, in the distance, the expanse of blue sea and the strait that ran through the headlands--through the golden gate--and the bridge itself, flame orange in the morning sun.

The golf course draped the knoll like it had been laid out for the views.

I wondered how often tourists trespassed onto the course while gawking at the panorama.

At the moment, the only 'trespassers' in sight were two

uniformed police officers, their long shadows trailing like dogs, part of the force that had scattered in search of Jane Forster.

The last person in the world, at the moment, I cared to find.

My throat ached.

Debra had no doubt pulled rank and shooed away any golfers. Debra, herself, was not in sight. She'd replied to Walter's text when we arrived: *gimme ten.* And so we'd wandered off to take in the lay of the land.

Now, we headed back toward the clubhouse and spotted the detective, true to her word, striding toward us. She wore a variation on her dig clothes--gray slacks and blazer, white T-shirt, black sneakers. Aviator shades.

"Bathroom break," she said, drawing up, "sorry I missed you, let's go."

She turned and led the way to the low-slung clubhouse.

Gregory Forster stood waiting on a small patio. He looked gutted. Not the jaunty Forster of Sea Cliff. He wore baggy black sweats. The sweatshirt was hooded; like daughter, like father. He wore his scuffed deck shoes, no socks. His white hair was mussed. I thought, he'd risen, found out, phoned Detective Talon, and done nothing more than throw on what was quick. Didn't take the time to don his casual chic, or even comb his hair. An ungroomed Forster.

We exchanged greetings.

We took seats around a small picnic table. The white paint was chipped. The modest clubhouse itself looked in need of a paint job. And more.

"All right," Debra said, "let's get into it. Cassie, Walter, I filled in Forster about your encounter with his daughter in the mine. Anything you need filled in?"

I asked, "You still thinking the note could be from Jane?"

"Could be. It was email, and my IT wizards are trying to trace the sender. Seems to be one of those bounce-around-the-internet back channels. The wording itself? A variation on the note pinned to Roger Forster's shirt. *We will bury you* on one line, and then *Jane Forster* on the next. You could read it that the name is a signature, Jane being the sender. Or, the *you* in juxtaposition to *Jane Forster* makes her the intended victim."

Forster made a pained sound.

"Sorry Forster, I'm not good with the niceties."

"If Jane's the sender," I asked, "how would she know the wording of the original bury-you note? To repeat it."

"Dig gossip? Burt and his team found Roger's body. Saw the note, of course. No doubt the Fencies hear all the gossip."

That widened the field.

"Whether she's the sender or intended vic, Jane seems to have poofed. Forster has a phone number for her but he regretfully admits he gave up trying after she kept hanging up on him. That was years ago. So far, no luck finding a new listing for Jane Forster. New name, new account..." Debra shrugged. "The only other thing in the email were the GPS coordinates that brought us here, meaning our working assumption is that whoever sent it knows about Forster's connection to the golf course."

"What connection?"

"He heads the management team for the Lincoln Park Golf Association. He's their big name. He's the man."

The man himself listened, dazed, to our back and forth.

"And the *bury you*?" Walter asked. "Any signs of burying on or around a golf course would be apparent."

"My people are looking."

It took Forster a moment to register that. He stared at our packs, at us. His eyes were reddened.

"Forster," Walter said, "once again, we're sorry to meet under difficult circumstances."

He said, strained, "Was she all right? In the mine?"

I said, "*She* was." My eyes had been reddened this morning, a holdover from his daughter's pepper spray. "You want to tell us why your daughter chose *that* place to confront us?"

"I don't know."

"She have a connection? Other than it's featured in your Sutro book?"

He appeared taken aback. He shouldn't have been. He'd loaned Walter the book.

"No? Yes? She knew enough to follow us there."

"I said I don't know."

"Really? A place that all you Forsters have in common."

He said, pained, "She cut me out of her life."

"Because...?"

"It's not your business."

"It is now. We're here because of you, and your daughter."

"Surly teenager," he snapped, "overprotective father. And that's the end of it."

"All right," Debra said, "let's talk about the note. Forster, it seems your daughter might bear you a grudge. Fair or unfair-- par for the course with family, right? But it's possible that's what's going on here. Roger's murder shocks her, ignites the old family dysfunction, and now she strikes out at you. She sends the note."

"No," he said, curtly, "she wouldn't."

Oh yes, I thought, tunnel-Jane would.

Walter said, "Somebody's coming."

We all turned.

The man was burly, jowly, gray-haired, tanned to earth brown. He wore olive-green shirt and pants and as he neared, the logo on his shirt was readable: a white-on-red sketch of the Golden Gate Bridge, framed by the words *Lincoln Park Golf Course.*

Forster quickly stood. "Ned..."

"I know, Greg, cops told me. Crap, I'm sorry."

"Appreciate it, man." Forster gathered himself. Turned to us. "Ned Cunningham here is the course greenskeeper. He keeps this place going."

Debra introduced us, by name and by title.

The greenskeeper swung on the detective. "Any reason your cops can't search without tearing up my course? Divots all over the place."

She stood. "I'll have a word."

"Didn't just come for that. Came to tell you about something you wanna check out."

"What?"

"A grave."

Forster seemed to reel and Ned grabbed his arm. "Oh *crap*, Greg, sorry, it's not her."

20

We trooped behind the greenskeeper.

The Lincoln Park Golf Course was laid out in two sections: upper and lower. The upper section had its flat greens, its dips and curves, but it followed the gentle rise of the knoll.

To our right was a view of the sea pouring into the bay beneath the bridge.

Up ahead, crowning the knoll like a citadel, was a massive creamy-gold building, all columns and ramparts and statues.

"Museum," Debra said, at my side.

The golf course flowed around it.

We skirted the museum and then the lower course came into view, meandering downhill. It was a sweeping vista of rolling green edged with thick woods.

Down there, presumably, was a grave.

A breeze brought the scent of new-mown grass.

Ned charged down a paved path that wound through sections of green, leading us to the very edge of the course where the grass met the woods, on the brink of a steep cliff.

Despite the expanse of green, it felt isolated. No searchers in sight.

I took a step and felt the ground squish and looked to see water oozing up through the grass. Forster, behind me, said, "Drainage problems, watch your step." An echo, Forster at his cliff-hugging stairway: *watch your step.*

Ned wound into a thicket of trees and bushes.

We crowded behind him. The undergrowth was spongy with leaf litter and unidentifiable decomposed organic material.

"Show you this first," he said, "you geologists." He knelt and plunged his hands into the detritus, clearing the stuff away, revealing naked soil. A dank odor rose. Rotting vegetation. Something moved down in the soil, some burrowing wormy creature that had been disturbed.

Ned stood and moved aside, leaving us a clear view.

A wound appeared, several feet long, a gouge in the earth.

Walter crouched for a closer look. "When did you find this, Ned?"

"Week ago? Was covered with leaves and sticks. Only found it looking for lost balls in the underbrush--flyers. People lose 'em, I get to collect 'em."

Walter straightened. "Well, it's definite ground cracking."

"Earthquake?"

"Possibly. That could cause fissuring. A year ago, so I understand, there was a moderate quake that caused damage here and there. But I wouldn't worry about this, Ned."

"Not *worried.* Would take the Big One to take down my course. Just thought this'd maybe explain the grave."

"Then let's see it," Debra said.

The greenskeeper led us a few yards deeper into the woods, then stopped and pointed.

It was deeply shaded here and the ground was the color of the shade. It took a few moments for my eyes to adjust. There was another gouge in the earth, or perhaps it was an offshoot of the first. Dirt and leaf litter were piled to one side. A shard of age-blackened wood nosed out of the dirt pile, looking ready to decay into dust. The rectangular hole was edged by shards of that decaying wood, clearly the remains of a coffin.

Forster made a sound. Sounded like relief. Confirmation that It was a skeleton down there, nothing more.

Most of the skeleton was still buried but a truncated midsection was laid bare. What stood out were the buttons. There were four, in a line that ran down the spinal column. Earth-stained ribs curved out from the vertebrae. They looked delicate. One rib was detached, as though cast aside.

"Found this same time found that ground crack," Ned said. "Was looking around, saw that piece of wood poking up, dug down to find out what it was. Got to the coffin, stopped. Covered it again. Keep it safe." He toed the edge of the litter pile. "*Today*, was hunting around the woods, trying to help. Looking, you know for..." He gave Forster a little nod. "And found the grave all uncovered, like this."

Debra frowned. "You're saying someone cleared it off. *Today*?"

"Sometime since I found it."

"Let's back up, to *when* you found it. Didn't you tell anyone?"

"Sure. Called that archaeology man, been in the news."

The four of us--Debra and Forster, Walter and I--exchanged glances.

Debra asked, "What did he say?"

"Didn't talk to him. Was his office number. Left a message."

"You didn't try again?"

"Nah, man's busy. Grave isn't going anywhere, been here since 1880, thereabout."

"How do you know?"

"They're all old."

"All?"

"All the graves. Lincoln Park was a graveyard back then. Now, you golf with ghosts."

21

DEBRA SAID, "I don't believe in coincidences."

"Me neither," Ned said. "Greg's daughter missing, grave gets cleared off. Why I showed you."

"Hang on," I said, "same perp, maybe. But how did they know about the grave?"

The greenskeeper scowled. "*I* didn't tell anybody."

"You left a message on an office phone."

"All right," Debra said, "let's clear it up. I've got Burt's personal number. I'll ask if he got Ned's message, and if he didn't, who in his office picked it up." She got her phone, dialed. Waited. Left a voicemail. "Hey Burt, it's Debra Talon. Got a newly-found ancient grave here at the golf course you might be interested in. I'll text you the deets."

She ended the call and flashed us a smile. "That'll get to him. Ancient grave. Archaeologist. Catnip."

Forster snapped, "We're wasting time on old graves."

"Maybe." The detective regarded him. "But this does fall into the realm of how-about-that. The note says *we will bury you*. Threatening to bury a Forster--no way to dance around that.

GPS leads to the golf course, and now we find this." She gave a short laugh. "You learn something new every day. At least, I do. Good thing I'm not a golfer, walking on the dead--I get enough of the dead in my nightmares. Anyway Forster, I assume you already knew your course was built on an old cemetery." She cocked her head.

"Yes."

"You might have mentioned that. We've been talking *bury* all morning."

"Well I goddamn didn't know about *this* grave."

"Somebody did," Walter put in. "The question then becomes, not only *how* they knew, but how they were certain *we'd* find it?"

"If Ned hadn't gone looking?" Debra folded her arms. "My search team, who haven't yet had the chance to search everywhere, would have found it. I guarantee you, we don't fuck around."

We started up the hill, heading for the clubhouse to wait for Debra's team to expand their search.

Along the way, the archaeologist returned Debra's call. The talk was brief.

"He'll be here pronto," she told us, ending the call. "Catnip."

We reversed course, heading back to the edge of the woods to wait for Burt Zhang.

Ned found us a dry patch of grass to sit and wait, apologizing, red-faced, for the irrigation drainage problems. He waited with us--proprietary about the course. He told stories about helping Forster improve his golf swing, trying to lighten the mood. Forster smiled grimly.

It felt like a strange campout, sitting on the green, listening to golf stories.

That new-cut grass smell was up my nose. I stifled a sneeze.

Grass releases volatile chemicals when cut, I'd read somewhere, the plant's way of signaling distress.

22

THE ARCHAEOLOGIST MADE it in twenty-three minutes.

He phoned Debra from the parking lot and she directed him to this slice of golf course hugging the cliff edge.

He approached our little 'campsite' in a hurry, responding brusquely as Debra greeted him, as she reminded him who Walter and I were, as she introduced the greenskeeper and Forster.

Burt Zhang was antsy. His hair was in ropy strands, helmet hair. His T-shirt was dirt-gray with white lettering--*Dig It*--beneath a sketch of a trowel speared into a mound of dirt. He said, in that deep-canyon voice, "Where's the grave?"

Yup, catnip.

"This way Burt," Debra said, "and then we have a few questions." She led him into the woods.

Ned followed. His find, after all.

We three waited, Forster ever more jittery.

We heard them. Burt's exclamation, "*When* was this discovered?" Ned recounting the find. Burt talking arrangements for temporary protection. Debra interrupting, "After we've finished chatting."

They emerged from the woods and joined us.

The six of us stood in a circle, like a deployment.

"What I'm wondering," Debra said, "is who picked up the message Ned sent you last week."

"I wouldn't know," Burt said. "The dig gets so much publicity our office is swamped with messages."

"Then it's fortunate I have your personal number." She gave him a smile. "Now, let me explain why we're all here."

The archaeologist listened carefully. When she'd finished, he said, "I'm unfamiliar with the missing woman."

"I'm told she was a regular at the dig."

"Many people are regulars."

Walter cleared his throat. "Evidently, she saw us talking with you at the dig, Burt. She thought you might have told us something relevant."

"About?"

"Her cousin--Roger Forster. You'll recall we discussed him."

"Yes, I recall. You'll recall I wanted nothing to do with the man. He was using my dig as a PR stunt to sell books."

Forster spoke up. "*That* bothers you?"

The archaeologist shifted his gaze to Forster. "Yes."

"How about *this*? My cousin was murdered and dumped at your dig."

"I'm aware. A calamity. My sympathy."

"Save it. My focus now is my daughter."

"My sympathy, again."

"Save it. *Again*."

"Take it easy, Forster," Debra cut in, "this isn't a pissing match. We're all trying to find your daughter. Burt, to that end, you're the archaeologist, so help me out. The perp uncovered this old grave, presumably for our benefit. But I'm at a loss as to why. Do you know of *anything* in connection with this place that can help us find Jane Forster?"

"Possibly."

That took her aback. "And you're just getting to it now?"

"I'm here because you phoned me about the old grave."

"I phoned you about *that* because it appears to be some kind of sick message from the perp. And now you appear to know something relevant which you've been hoarding ever since you got here. For whatever reason."

"There's a reason. I had no wish to get dragged into the Forster family drama."

Forster stiffened. "How do you know jack shit about my family?"

Burt fixed Forster with a speculative stare. "I received an anonymous email this morning, on the subject. It linked to a nineteenth-century newspaper article--ugly stuff. Your ancestors left quite a trail."

That took all of us aback.

Forster managed, "That's bullshit."

"Is it?" Debra asked Burt.

"You wanted to know why you're here. Follow the trail."

"To?"

"To begin, grave robbing."

23

MY HEAD SPUN.

This was some place, this Lincoln Park Golf Course, previously a cemetery, in some way associated with Gregory Forster's ancestors.

The man certainly looked as though he'd been time-shifted. Adrift.

"Forster," Debra said, "you're building up quite the track record of withholding information."

He sucked in a breath. "I have no idea about any grave robbing."

"No? Let's hope not. Because, yanno, *we will bury you*."

He just shook his head.

She turned to Burt. "So, about that newspaper article."

The archaeologist waved a hand, encompassing the stretch of green. "First, you need to fathom the past. What do you know about the old cemetery here?"

"Only that Ned told us it *existed*. What should we know?"

"In the nineteenth century, this area was known as 'outside lands' due to its remoteness--which is why the cemetery was located *here*, to segregate the indigent and immigrant dead."

She gave a soundless whistle. "Forster, I assume you know *that* much. Being on the golf board."

He shrugged. Nodded.

She held up a palm to Burt. "Go on."

"According to the article, the Forster ancestors worked as cemetery caretakers. They employed a Chinese immigrant by the name of Li to do the grunt work, fix rotting fences, repair rutted paths. It was Mr. Li who witnessed the grave robbing--in the indigent burial sector. The newspaper didn't mention what was stolen, just what happened next. The Forsters fired Mr. Li. He had no recourse, his word against white men's word."

Forster opened his mouth to speak. Closed it.

"Mr. Li," Burt continued, "could not find other employment. He became destitute. He fled down to the sea and took shelter in a cave. Set up a rudimentary home there. Learned to fish. Occasionally, curious beach-combers dropped by and he would tell his tale about injustice. Word got back to the Forsters, who complained to the police. Mr. Li was arrested, under the city's anti-vagrancy law. He sickened in jail. He died there."

I caught Walter's eye. Holy hell.

"*That*," Debra said, "is a tragic tale. And I'm having trouble, Forster, understanding how you didn't know it. No family stories?"

"*Damnation*," he exploded, "I am not my ancestors. My daughter isn't our ancestors. Neither was Roger. Here's what I know about the ancestors. They got tired of Barbary Coast crime and moved here looking for a new start. This was decades before they moved on to Sea Cliff. Here, they found a patch of empty land, built a place, found work on a nearby potato farm. When the opportunity arose, they accepted the job of cemetery caretakers. If one of them was involved with that Mr. Li, it's news to me."

Debra regarded him. "I'd say it's a cautionary tale for all of us--look into the ancestors and we might not like what we see. But yes Forster, I think we can all agree that your daughter is not responsible for what happened here in the past." She turned to the archaeologist. "And you certainly have no relation to any of this, so I'm wondering why the message was sent to *you*."

"Presumably," he said, voice hard, "because I'd be familiar with the cemetery's segregation."

"So is Forster, as I've just learned. Point is, it seems the message-sender wanted you, Burt, to come here and reveal this unknown part of Forster's past. Again, I'm wondering why you?"

"So am I," Burt snapped.

"The ship?" Walter put in. "If we're looking for a connection, we have Jane and Roger Forster at your dig. We might consider the morning's other message, the bury-you email sent to Forster--which is an echo of the note pinned to Roger's body at the dig." Walter regarded Forster. "You told us your family has no connection to the ship."

"We don't."

"Well. That would have tied things together. Someone carrying a grudge against your family, the past unburied, an echo across the ages."

Forster said, icily, "That's almost operatic, Walter. And my daughter is still missing."

I considered what my partner had said. I could believe that Forster lied about his family having no connection to the ship-- but I wondered why. Still. I hated to credit Gregory Forster with any valid point, but he is not his ancestor. Nor were Roger and Jane their ancestors. And then I thought about Jane's estrangement from her father, and the idea we'd been kicking around that she was the one who'd sent him the bury-you note. In which case, perhaps she was also the one who'd sent the newspaper link to Burt. Tying things together.

I asked him, "Does your daughter know the family history?"

He turned a venomous look on me. "My daughter is the victim here."

"Burt," Debra said, "where was that cave?"

24

BURT TOOK THE LEAD.

He knew where that cave was. He'd recognized the location described in the newspaper article--'a deep cleft in the cliff that extends like a fist into the cove'. And he was thoroughly familiar with Lands End. He'd surveyed indigenous shell mounds where Sutro Baths was later built, and sites of hunting camps along the cliffs where the Coastal Trail now ran, their names for this land erased by history.

Ned walked alongside Burt. It was his neck of the woods, as he put it, proprietary not just about the golf course but also the land below the cliffs. The rest of us trailed. Walter and I had exchanged a glance when Burt quoted the article--we knew where we were headed. *Fist. Cove.*

We followed the paved path that skirted the woods, which led us out of the golf course and onto a short steep rutted dirt path.

The sea came into view, far below.

The path quickly intersected the Coastal Trail, and I got my bearings. Yesterday, on this trail, Walter and I had seen nothing above us but thick woods. The only reason we'd known there was a golf course somewhere up above was because we'd studied our maps. Otherwise, we'd not given it a second thought.

Now, I thought of Mr. Li heading down these cliffs in search of shelter.

A track-suited runner passed us, and then a young couple in jeans and T-shirts and lime-green running shoes.

All of us tramping in ancient footsteps.

Before I could time-shift further, we came to the sign for Mile Rock Beach and turned onto the steep stairway.

Ned called, over his shoulder, "Long way down."

I didn't need reminding.

I did think about synchronicity. Two days, two descents, tracking Roger Forster's journey yesterday, and now hunting for Jane Forster. I fixed on her father, two long stair-steps below me, descending stiffly, like a man who did not want to reach the bottom.

Hikers on the ascent passed us in ones and twos and threes, panting, not panting, running, not running.

We descended, and the stairway narrowed, and then it jogged, and steepened, and we met the retaining walls.

I smelled sea air.

Finally, the woods parted to reveal the wedge of beach edging the rocky cove, and the promontory looming above. The fist.

We tramped onto the beach.

Forster took a seat on a driftwood log and poured sand out of his deck shoes. Ned stood above him. Burt stared out to sea, hands jammed in his pockets. Debra toed a tower of flat rocks stacked like pancakes, as if testing the structural integrity.

We joined them.

Debra abandoned the tower and scanned the cliff face. "The cave, Burt?"

He said, "Tide's too high. We'll have to wade."

Walter shot me a glance.

Yeah. Synchronicity.

We all joined Forster on his log to remove footwear and roll up pant legs.

Burt led the way into the icy water. At lower tide, we could have walked along the beach. At highest tide, we'd have to swim. It was a roundabout route but we didn't have to wade far. Burt herded us toward a line of sand at the base of the promontory. Much of the rock was in shadow, down where it met the beach, and so I did not see our destination.

And then I sloshed closer to shore and saw the deep cleft in the rock face. It was a dank-looking inhospitable place.

We waded into the shallows and stepped onto the sand. There wasn't much of it. Wave action pulsed water right up to the cave entrance, and inside.

Debra said, "Cave gets wet."

I assumed Mr. Li would have built some sort of barricade, to keep the cave dry. He certainly benefitted from lower sea level.

Debra moved closer and called into the cave. "Helloooo."

There was no answer. She tried again. There was no answer.

Forster moved.

She laid a land on his arm. "Why don't you wait out here?"

Ned said, "I'll wait with you."

Burt said, "I explored this cave years ago. I've no need, now."

"So it's just us," Debra said, to Walter and me. "Either of you got a flashlight in your pack?"

I retrieved mine. And by dint of that, I took the lead.

Daylight illuminated the front of the cave, which was just that, a sea cave, walled with the greenstone rock of the cliff, floored with sand and pebbles and crushed seashells and bits of rotting kelp, which raised a stink. It was an unremarkable-looking place. It must have made a very humble abode. I assumed Mr. Li had acquired the rudimentary necessities. A bedroll. A pot to cook in. A circle of rocks to set driftwood afire. There was no sign of that now, of course. No artifacts.

Walter and Debra crowded in behind me.

The back of the cave was murky.

I switched on my light and swept the area, realizing I was holding my breath. I felt Debra's breath on the back of my neck. I felt Walter's shoulder as he squeezed in beside me.

And then we all breathed easier. There was nothing in the back of the cave.

To be thorough I expanded my field of search, playing the beam along the walls, up to the low ceiling.

Walter flinched.

I saw what he saw, thinking *snake*, Walter's phobia, largely conquered but the body remembers.

Yeah, there was sure something snaky on a rock shelf partway up the wall at the back of the cave. But there were no sea snakes in San Francisco waters and a land snake wasn't going to shelter in a sea cave.

Debra said, "What *is* that?"

I switched my beam to spotlight. And I knew what it was. Snaky looking, twisty sure, but the color alone gave it away. That electric-blue hue was unmistakable.

Jane Forster's severed braid draped across the rock shelf.

25

DEBRA JOINED the others outside the cave while Walter and I prepared to sample inside.

I heard Burt say, "My sympathy."

I didn't catch Forster's response.

Walter and I focused on the job.

I took a panorama photo of the cave, lit up in the phone's flash.

Walter lensed the sandy floor. "No footprints, other than ours."

No surprise, I thought. The perp would surely have known the tides. The previous low tide, I calculated, had been around dawn. Unlikely to have been nosy beach-goers then. The perp could have easily accessed the cave, unnoticed. And then throughout the morning the tide rises and washes inside, erasing any footprints. Similar scenario if the braid had been deposited last night.

Perp was smart.

Nevertheless, Walter knelt to collect samples of the sandy cave floor, on the chance the perp had deposited some foreign bits, which survived the tide, which could be traced.

The perp being a kidnapper, or a killer, or Jane herself--hacking off her own braid, leaving it here, a message to her father. I hoped it was that.

I crossed the cave floor to the rock shelf. I opened my field kit and got a plastic garbage bag, folded the top down, and placed it on the floor. Then stood, facing the shelf. It was at my shoulder height--high enough to keep the braid well above the incoming tide, low enough that it would be found. The braid was secured by elastic bands, top and bottom. That double-banding made my job easier. I pulled on latex gloves. Carefully--so as not to dislodge grains from the weave of the hair--I moved the bright blue braid from the shelf into the bag. I felt a twinge. Round about this time yesterday, the woman whose hair I was bagging had ambushed Walter and me in the mine tunnel. Now, she was in need of finding.

I got a specimen dish and collected sand and pebbles from the rock shelf.

When we finished, and exited, Forster asked for a look inside the plastic bag.

I showed him.

He whispered, "Her hair was brown last time I saw her."

We retraced our route back to the beach, Debra delaying Walter and me as we waded ashore. "Maybe it goes without saying, but I'll say it anyway. Technically, the Jane Forster case--it's now, officially, a case--is not the job you were hired for. But you're on it, now. Whether Jane is victim or perpetrator, I intend to find out. I just want to make sure we're on the same page, case-wise."

Walter said, "The two cases would appear to intersect. No need to adjust our fee."

She laughed. "I hadn't even considered that. My point is, in terms of priority, Jane comes before Roger. There is, I hope, a life to save."

"We're on the same page," Walter said.

We returned to the log and put on our footwear.

The others had moved on, beginning the climb up the steep stairway, Burt on the way to investigate the past, Ned returning to his greenskeeping duties, Forster heading for Sea Cliff in the hollow hope his daughter would turn up there.

Tramping across the sand, following in their wake, scuffing footprints, considering timing scenarios, I thought, if the perp came this morning then his prints could still be here because today's incoming tide would not yet have reached this high. No way to ID them, though.

A lot of footsteps on this beach.

All of them history by tomorrow.

26

I REGARDED the long braid on my work table.

Under the operating-room lights of our trailer-lab, every blue strand was illuminated. Against the stark white plastic of the modular table, the tiniest mineral grain that fell out would be visible.

But something else held my attention.

I asked my partner, "You ever cut your own hair?"

He looked up from his microscope. He ran a hand across his scalp, worrying the thinning gray strands. "I haven't enough left to risk it."

Indeed, he was wearing it longer these days, making up for the lost square footage.

I said, "I tried cutting mine once, back when I wore it long. Made a mess of it."

He indicated the braid. "You think she cut it herself?"

The top of the braid, the thickest part, was held in place by an elastic band and above that the cut end was noticeably uneven.

I said, "I could make a case for, and against. The cut end is almost angled, as if she'd brought the braid around to easily access. If someone else did it, still be hard to cut cleanly through that thick stalk of hair."

"Either way, a ragged cut."

"Either way," I agreed.

Walter rose and collected the clamshells that sat on one of the modular tables. "I'm going to step out and put these in the compost bin."

"Thanks." The lingering odor of lemon chicken was distracting.

The clamshells contained the dregs of our lunch. Not many dregs. We'd been ravenous. Despite our big breakfast at the cafe, the morning's events--at the golf course, at the beach, in the cave--had drained us. So we'd grabbed take-out on the way back from Lands End and as soon as we'd settled into the lab, we'd eaten.

Damn, it had been a long day and it was only mid-afternoon.

Walter stepped back inside and returned to his work.

We were interrupting the completion of the Roger Forster journey-history to concentrate on the Jane Forster case, as Debra had requested. Walter was analyzing the cave soils and so far he'd found the expected: grains of beach sand, shards of seashell, bits of kelp. What he'd not yet found was any foreign soil tracked in from someplace else. But there was always the chance the next specimen dish would contain a prize.

I returned to the braid.

Before removing the bands, I was doing a minute inspection of the plaits, searching for bits of mineral. I expected to find material from the cave, given that the braid lay on that sandy pebbly shelf. Like Walter, I hoped to find something foreign that could lead to the place where the braid was cut. Assuming it wasn't cut in the cave.

Walter abruptly looked up.

"What?"

"I believed I saw someone pass by." He grimaced. "Evidently, I can't just let the world go by outside the window."

"We'll buy curtains."

He grunted and bent to his work.

I returned to mine, plucking out mineral grains from the weave of the braid. The hair felt slightly sticky, perhaps from salty sea air. As expected, the braid had acquired and held onto the sticky cave soil.

My scalp began to itch, as if grains from the mine tunnel were still lodged in my hair, although I'd thoroughly washed it last night after returning from the lab to our apartment.

Jane, too, might have had the chance to shower and shampoo after leaving us in the mine, might have re-braided her clean hair, before it was cut off and deposited in the cave.

I removed the bottom hair band, fanned out the blue plaits, and found more salts of the sea.

Bottom line: she didn't shampoo.

In fact, one might think she'd gone for a swim before the braid was cut off.

───────────

I'd taken a break, sitting back from my table, rolling my neck to work out the kinks, when I caught the flicker of a shadow outside.

I looked.

There was a hoodie on the walkway.

I turned to tell Walter and by the time I turned back, she was at the window. She lifted a finger and circled it. Message clear. She was coming around to the end of the walkway, to the warehouse entrance.

WE OPENED the door of our trailer-lab, and waited.

It didn't take her long. She strode down the wide cement corridor that ran through the warehouse, past the porta-potties, past the maritime businesses. I recognized the jeans and the purple hooded sweatshirt. She drew up to our trailer, halting at the steps. She pushed the hood back. Her hair was electric blue--and very short.

For a moment I thought, she *did* cut off her braid. And swapped sweatshirts with her friend. The moment passed. This wasn't Jane. A vivid image of Jane was lodged in my mind: pale face, long nose, hollow cheeks. This hoodie had an upturned nose, large green eyes, and a tanned round face that made her look very young--but for the deep squint lines around the eyes.

She climbed the two wooden steps with a smile. "Hi, I'm Maxie Swift."

It was head-snapping. I'd been dwelling on the hoodies since the dig. First we meet wild Jane Forster. Now smiling Maxie Swift, casually dropping by as if we'd been expecting her.

We introduced ourselves.

"I know who you are," she said, "from the dig."

I vividly recalled.

"But it's nice to meet officially." She peeked into the lab. "Smells good in there."

"Lunch."

"Yum."

"I'm afraid it's all gone."

"That's cool. I'm not here for lunch."

I said, cautiously, "Why are you here?"

"About my friend Jane Forster."

There was no universe in which that should surprise me. But it did.

Walter recovered his manners and invited her into the lab.

Inside, she took in our workspace. When she spotted the unbound braid fanned on my table, she said, "Wow."

I tried to parse that. "Wow, what?"

"I mean, she mentioned that, but *seeing* it..."

Walter and I exchanged a glance, surprise doubled. There were a dozen questions to ask but I began with the one that mattered most. "You talked to her?"

"That's why I'm here!"

Walter said, "Does she realize the police are searching for her? Do *you*?" He nodded at the fanned-out braid. "What do you think we're doing here?"

"I guess that's what she wants? To have you all, like, watching out for her?"

"Well, she got that."

"Okay. But now she wants to talk to you."

"Fine," Walter said, "have her give us a call."

"Um, she's keeping her phone off so nobody can track her. We just text now. I'll show you." Maxie got her phone, tapped the screen, and held it out.

I took it and read the message out loud: *Cut off braid, faked kidnap. Need help. Bring geologists to island.* The sender's name was Jane. I thought, sounds like brusque tunnel-Jane.

I returned the phone. "What island?"

"A place we like. It's called Red Rock. I drive a sightseeing boat, *Best Bay Tours*." Maxie removed a laminated card from her wallet and passed it to me.

Walter drew close and we examined the card. It was a U.S. Coast Guard Six-Pack Captain's License, allowing Maxie Swift to pilot a craft carrying up to six paying passengers. Her smiling photo was in one corner.

"Yeah," she said, "I was doing a tour when I got her text. Just got back to the marina, so good thing you're here!"

I returned the license. "You want us to get on a boat with you--who we've just met--and go to this island?"

"We're not really strangers, Cassie." She winked. "We waved at the dig."

"I recall. Why the hoodies?"

"To cover this." She touched her hair. "We dyed it to match for fun but after what happened to Roger, we're keeping a low profile."

"As in, spying on us here?"

"That was Jane."

Good to have it confirmed. "Why?"

"She wanted to see what you do. And where you'd go. She was kind of keeping watch."

"She saw where we went, yesterday. Here's the problem, Maxie. Your friend sandbagged us in a mine at Lands End, to ask about Roger. She used pepper spray on her way out."

"She *did*? Wow. Yeah, she can work herself up. She carries the spray just in case. But you guys are okay, right?"

Define *okay*. I said, "Unharmed."

"Whew, good. And she'll be cool with you this time."

"Maxie," Walter said, "you're getting ahead of yourself. To be clear, we'd go nowhere without consulting the detective in charge of the case."

"Okay."

He added, "Due diligence."

"I get it. Okay. So I'll leave you to talk it over. I'll be at the boat." She pointed out the window, to the marina. "You go down the ramp, go all the way to the far end of the dock. Boat's there. If you're coming, bring parkas. And I guess you might as well bring your tools."

I glanced at the braid on my worktable, which had so far yielded no mineral clues to follow. But now, presumably, Jane herself was going to show up at that island--which would solve our case.

I stopped Maxie as she headed to the door. "Not so fast."

She turned.

"What are the logistics? How would you time this meetup?"

"Jane knows my schedule's flexible--the owner's pretty cool." She grinned. "That would be me."

"How would Jane get to the island?"

"Drive to this harbor nearby and rent a kayak. Or catch a lift with a boater."

"Why not come on your boat?"

"She does if we've arranged it. Since we didn't, for today we'll just do the alternate, meet up at the island. We've done that before."

"Maxie," Walter said, "we'll consider. Should we decide in favor, we'll phone the detective and discuss the proposal."

"So if it's cool, you'll come?"

"We'll let you know."

"Ten minutes?" She added, "And you'd better tell the detective nobody should follow us. Jane would freak. That means, I see a police boat anywhere near us, I give you a tour of the bay and that's all."

Walter and I talked about Jane Forster's method of requesting help.

We talked about her state of mind.

We checked our map and found the island.

And then we phoned Detective Talon.

28

WE LOCKED the lab and exited the warehouse and found the ramp that led down to the dock and walked to the very end where, as promised, a small white motorboat was tied up. The *Best Bay Tours* logo was painted in purple. There was a seating area in the bow, and another in the stern, and in between was the elevated cockpit. Maxie sat up high in the captain's seat. She'd donned wraparound sunglasses and a white bucket hat with BBT stitched in purple across the front.

She swept a hand. "Welcome almost aboard."

Walter said, "Just so we're clear, everything we learn we'll report to the detective on the case."

"I figured."

We stepped into the bow of the boat. Padded bench seats with padded backrests lined the interior. It was a cushy setup. I wondered how much sightseers paid.

We took seats on opposite sides and put on parkas and hats.

"Okay," Maxie said, "I just texted her we're on the way!"

On the way, I hoped, to closing the Jane Forster case. "She respond?"

"Doesn't need to. When she turns her phone on, she'll be happy to see we're coming."

I hoped so.

The engine roared to life. We motored out of the little harbor, into the bay, and promptly turned left on a northerly heading. The skyline ahead was bisected by the Bay Bridge, its steel polished in the afternoon sun.

A big yacht tacked beneath the bridge, sails billowing.

The wind whipped us and the water was choppy but Maxie found her speed and smoothed out the ride.

"Bay Bridge coming up," she called over the clamor of the wind, "links San Francisco to Oakland."

Part of the sightseeing spiel, I assumed, calling out landmarks. Habit.

"And on the starboard side--that's to your right--is Yerba Buena Island."

As we approached the bridge, the island it was tethered to rose into closer view, rugged and mountainous--where I'd camped on that field trip eleven years ago. Now, as we moved beneath the steel span of the bridge, I twisted on my bench to scan the shoreline but the closeup view told the same story as the binocs scan two days ago. A sliver of the past fully submerged.

Maxie called out, in her tour-guide voice, "And next to it, Treasure Island."

The two islands were connected by a causeway. This one wasn't much of a treasure--it was a flat manufactured island built of quarried rock and dredged mud for a long-ago world's fair. Our team had measured subsidence there. Now, it bristled with buildings, sinking land evidently not a worry.

I turned my back on the islands and faced the San Francisco waterfront, spotting the long pier that fingered into the bay, where Walter and I had eaten lunch two days ago.

"On the port side," Maxie said, "to your left, is Yerba Buena Cove."

There was no cove in sight, of course, but I figured she was landmarking the past. We all had that in common, 'meeting' at the dig where the ship had been abandoned nearly two hundred years ago, then buried as the cove was filled in. The now-nonexistent cove would not be a tour landmark. This was for us. I took note.

We motored on.

The bay waters were busy with boats--sailboats and cabin cruisers and fishing boats big and small, windsurfers darting in between. I looked for a boat with SFPD lettering, and didn't find one. Good. Otherwise, we'd get a tour of the bay, and nothing else.

Maxie called out, "Alcatraz coming up port-side."

I saw the high-bluffed prison island topped by the mammoth fortification--now a tourist attraction--and thought, Alcatraz wouldn't make much of a hideaway these days.

"To the west of Alcatraz...you gotta know that orange bridge!"

Indeed. The boat gave a good angle on the bridge spanning the golden gate entrance to the bay, connecting San Francisco to the headlands north. As always, it held the eye.

We motored on in silence for a couple of minutes.

The bridge and the prison island were now in the rearview.

A much bigger island was dead ahead.

Maxie called out, "That bad boy coming up is Angel Island. Immigration detention back in the old days."

Walter called back, "Primarily, Chinese immigrants."

"You know it?"

"I'm a history buff."

I imagined another history buff--Burt Zhang--would have a story or two about it. And I wondered what Jane Forster thought the archaeologist knew about the murder victim dumped beside his dig.

Perhaps we'd find out, up ahead.

We were moving into northern bay waters, new territory for me. My grad-student field trip had been restricted to the two small islands and the San Francisco mainland, and I'd seen little of the bay itself. I'd learned about it--formed, like everything else around here, by movement of the earth's tectonic plates, which created a massive fault system, whose own activity down-warped the land, resulting in a bay that extended some sixty miles, much of it to the south of us, enough of it to the north, up ahead.

I noticed Walter looking beyond me, at the land mass east of us, where his alma mater UC Berkeley sat upon a hill. I asked him, "You do any boating on the bay, back then?"

"The occasional excursion."

"You mean a party boat?"

"That's what I mean."

I smiled, then swiveled to face into the wind.

The *Best Bay Tours* plowed onward through the wide channel between land masses east and west. I tracked the western shore-line, and then the eastern shoreline, correlating the landscape with the map we'd examined in our lab, calculating that our destination was coming up. In the distance, a utilitarian bridge spanned the expanse of the bay, one more link between eastern and western shores. A landmark of sorts, although Maxie did not call it out.

Instead, she said, "To starboard, that harbor with the long wharf, city of Richmond, that's where Jane drives to and rents a kayak. Or gets a lift. Time to start keeping an eye out."

We looked.

I saw a big cargo ship at the wharf, and a number of small craft in the nearby waters.

Walter said, "Tricky place to kayak."

"That's where she learned! Richmond was a transit hub to ship coal from other states overseas, but the community got sick of coal dust everywhere and got it stopped. Kayaktivists joined the protest--Jane was one!"

It took me a moment. Kayak. Activist. Nice. Walter gave a thumbs-up. I added mine. Times do change. And coal pops up again. Yesterday Jane ambushes us in Adolph Sutro's half-built coal mine on the cliffs of Lands End. Today, we learn she protested modern-day coal, here. I took note.

And I kept an eye out.

And then Maxie called, "Up ahead."

I snapped my attention from the harbor, to look ahead. There it was, almost within spitting distance of the utilitarian bridge.

We'd seen it in the lab, a speck on the map.

In the field, it was a peculiar sight, a knobby cone of red rock rising out of the water. Actually, I thought, that tiny island was a good hideaway. Hidden in plain sight. Compared to the port and the boats and the bridge, the island appeared inconsequential.

Maxie swung the *Best Bay* eastward, heading directly for a long reddish beach backed by a high rough cliff face. The dark mouth of a tunnel opened above the southern end of the beach.

The boat idled to a stop.

"Close as I'm gonna get," Maxie said. "Then we do a little wading."

I sighed. What's new?

29

"SHE'LL BE HERE," Maxie said.

There was no sign of her yet. As we'd motored in, we'd seen that the entirety of the island's western shoreline was empty. Adjacent to the long red beach where we now stood--where the shore turned rocky--a little hill led up to the dark mouth of the tunnel I'd spotted from the boat. Nobody in sight there. Or on the clifftop high above. The other side of the island was beyond our field of view.

Walter asked, "She knows to come to *this* beach, specifically?"

Maxie nodded. "Could take her awhile--I mean, traffic gets gnarly, and then she has to catch a ride or rent a kayak--but she'll get dropped off here, or paddle to this side of the island. She knows I anchor here."

"How often do you come here?"

"On and off. Ever since we met."

"When was that?"

"Couple months ago, when the dig started. We met at the fence and, um, hit it off."

"And you became regulars?"

"Yeah."

"And what is it that brings you two *here*, on and off?"

"Um, Jane's part of the story too, when she comes we'll..."

He stopped her with a lifted palm. "Maxie, this won't fly. We came along with you because your friend is, officially, missing and that's our case. I understand the logistics--the drive, and then the boating. But here we wait. You need to be more forthcoming. Why did you two form a connection at the dig? Why is this island your getaway? There are other islands, other getaways. Why here, Maxie? Why us? While we await your friend, you need to explain."

She held his look. "Okay." She added, "But only what's mine to tell."

He folded his arms and cocked his head.

"First," she said, "you've gotta know about Red Rock. There's maybe fifteen islands in the bay, but almost nobody learns about this one. Or even comes here. But back in the old days it was used for mining manganese." She pointed in the direction of the tunnel. "You guys would know about manganese, right?"

"We would," he said. "It's a metallic element that occurs in several forms--like manganese ore. It's an ingredient in metal alloys, among other uses. By the way, mining it produces hazardous dust, so you'd want to stay out of that tunnel." He took a moment to scan the cliff face, nearest the tunnel entrance. "That's it there, that narrow black band."

I looked at the reddish cliff with its kinked vertical layers, tentatively identifying the alternating layers as shale and chert, part of the ubiquitous Franciscan Complex. The interstratified layer of black manganese was a bold contrast to the adjoining reddish rocks.

"As for red rock..." Walter poked around the sand and found a red pebble and passed it to Maxie. "That's chert. The red coloration comes from oxidized iron, which has also reddened the gray shale on the cliff. Thus you end up with an island that earns its name." He regarded her. "But you didn't invite us for a geology lesson."

"*Jane* invited you, but... I mean, we both watched you at the dig and talked about this stuff so I guess it's okay if I ask you now." Maxie returned the pebble to Walter. "Can you find out if somebody walked on something like this?"

"Somebody?"

"From that ship. The *Dawn*."

It took us a moment--Walter turning to me just as I turned to him--the two of us catching on. Maxie Swift was saying the *Dawn* had come *here*, to this little island. The ship that Burt Zhang was currently unearthing in San Francisco.

Which meant there was no way, I thought, that Maxie and Jane came here, on and off, simply because they were looking for a getaway. They came because they thought the old ship had come here--bizarrely--and because they thought somebody from that ship had picked up a pebble like the one Walter still held. I pictured the dig--Burt showing off the boot found in the husk of the ship, explaining the bullet holes, and then Walter extracting the pebbles. All the while, up top, the hooded students watched, and figured out who was who.

There was only one logical reason Maxie would connect that boot and that ship to this island. "Maxie," I asked, "were your ancestors on the *Dawn*?"

She said, "Yes."

I caught Walter's nod of concurrence. He'd put two and two together.

I pressed Maxie, "And Jane's family? Also connected to the ship? Is that what brought you two together?"

"I said I'm only telling you my part."

"Okay." For starters.

"Okay, all I know is stories I heard as a kid, from old letters-- patchy stuff. We used to come here, me and my family, for fun, and also because our ancestors came here. But back when the ship came here, it wasn't for fun, it was for work."

"Work?" Walter's bushy eyebrows rose above the rims of his shades. "Giving tours of San Francisco Bay?"

"You're joking, right?"

"I'm compensating. Your story is scrambling my grasp of the ship's history."

She laughed.

I saw what he was doing. We'd been a bit tough on Maxie-- now we were a friendly audience. And I liked her for the laugh.

"Okay," she said, "so the Swifts were from Oregon and they made their living shipping goods up and down the coast. When the gold rush came they moved to San Francisco because business was really good there. So, their new business became-- they'd sail the *Dawn* out through the golden gate and up the coast to Oregon, buy vegetables and stuff from farmers they knew, and bring that back to sell in SF."

I asked, "Where does this island come into it?"

"They'd found it exploring the bay, and it had this abandoned mine tunnel. So they saw a way to have a paying load on the trip *to* Oregon. They built a dock here, and they'd stop to pick up rocks for ballast, and when they got to Oregon they'd sell the ones with manganese for paint pigment. Bunch of people there had a pottery business." She added, as if it were simply an aside, "Then on one trip they met a family that wanted to go hunt gold, so the Swifts decided to try hauling prospectors instead of vegetables. On the way here they got friendly with them, a family called Packington, and decided to join up to look for gold too."

"Packington?"

"Yeah."

"Not Forster?"

"I said I'm not telling you Jane's part." She paused, then

shrugged. "Okay, I guess you just guessed that part. So, the Packingtons changed their name to Forster later."

I said, "Jane's father claims that the Forster ancestors came overland from Los Angeles to San Francisco. He claims they had no connection to the *Dawn*. He claims they weren't gold hunters."

"He lies."

I almost laughed. She'd said it off-handedly--of course he lies, he's Forster.

She added, "But that gets into the rest of Jane's story."

Good start though, I thought.

"Maxie," Walter said, "I'm afraid I'm lost. When did the *Dawn* bring the Packingtons here? According to the dig archaeologist, gold-rush ships would anchor at Yerba Buena Cove, and from there the gold hunters would have to catch a smaller ship..."

"The *Dawn* was a smaller ship, with a shallow draft. Once she sailed through the golden gate, she could just go directly north up the bay, past this island, all the way up to the inlet with the Sacramento River, and then they take the river up to Sacramento. From there, they go overland to the gold fields. Oh, and they leave the ship anchored at Sacramento. Just to keep it straight for you."

Walter nodded his appreciation.

"And they do find gold--I mean, like a lot. All of them. When they return to Sacramento they board the ship because the Swifts have a contract to ferry the Packingtons back home. They stop off here, as usual, to load up on the rocks because they want to keep the regular business going. And that's how they all end up here. My family's first and last trip hauling gold hunters. Here's where it happened." Her voice had tightened on the *here*.

Walter asked, "What, precisely, happened?"

"A fight."

"Over gold?"

"What do you think?"

"I think it's not out of the question."

"That's a squirrelly answer."

He said, "I'm endeavoring to fill in the blanks."

"I don't like telling this part, okay?"

"You're the only one here who can."

"Yeah. But *you* have the evidence."

He waited.

"At the dig, that archaeologist showed you the boot. I could see bullet holes. I could see you dig out pebbles from the sole."

"You think the boot belonged to a Swift?"

"No shit."

"You want to know if he got shot here."

"No shit, Sherlock."

"*Why* do you think the victim was a Swift? Rather than a Packington?"

"The guy who got shot maybe lost a leg, right?"

I put in, "If he survived."

Her attention swung to me. "You know if he did? Lose the leg?"

"Just supposition." Same thing I knew when I spun my scenario at the ship, when Burt cast me as the victim, assuring me I could have survived but lost my leg in the process. Nothing more than supposition.

She blew out a long breath. "Okay, there was this one-legged man--Pegleg, in the family stories. Rude, but that's how they talked back then. If he was in that fight, and got shot here, you can find out, right?"

Walter shook his head. "Even if we could determine that the pebbles came from here, that doesn't tell you the *shooting* occurred here. The ship was found at Yerba Buena Cove. The boot was found on the ship."

"Don't forget the bullets in the hull. Like, maybe the Packingtons tried to execute the Swifts."

I thought, she and Jane *did* get a good look. Still, fifty-one bullets, missing their targets. Weird attempt at execution.

"There is still the question," Walter said, "of the ship ending up in San Francisco. Who sailed it there?"

"I don't know."

"How did Pegleg survive?"

"I don't *know*."

"Maxie," Walter said, "there are gaps--understandably. And you're jumping to conclusions."

I thought, be fair Walter. We jump to conclusions and call it spinning scenarios. Walter had spun one at the dig: the gouges on the boot suggested there was a fight on land, and then likely boot-guy fled back to the ship and got shot there, since the boot was found aboard. He removes his boot to tend his wound, and somehow escapes. And lives on in the Swift family memory and myth, as Pegleg. What we couldn't say was *where* the shooting took place. Here at Red Rock Island. Or at Yerba Buena Cove, the ship's final resting place. We certainly couldn't say who shot who. Or what the hell happened to the hull. I took in Maxie's pained expression, her round friendly face transformed. I kept my *couldn't-says* to myself.

"Maxie," Walter said, gently, "why does it matter? Where Pegleg was shot, and how?"

"Because the boot might be proof of what happened back then, and that might explain why somebody killed Jane's cousin. And maybe my cousin."

"Hang on," I said. "*Your* cousin?"

She lifted her chin. "Louis Swift, coolest guy ever, a history professor up in Sacramento. When the ship was discovered he came to town to see the dig. And then he went off exploring, and he, uh, fell off a cliff. And that killed him."

My head spun. "Holy shit."

"Yeah. It was shitty. And I had to call his brother and tell him. I'd met him once. He lives in Nevada, along with some Swifts who gave my folks trouble back before they died, long time ago but I want nothing to do with the shitty Nevada Swifts."

"Why do you say someone killed Louis?"

"He was too good a hiker to fall off a cliff."

"What cliff?"

"At Lands End, it sticks way out, place with the labyrinth." She added, "Near that mine."

I thought, small world. I said, "When was this?"

"About three weeks ago."

I caught Walter's eye, and he nodded.

She watched us. "You know something?"

We knew where Roger Forster took his final journey, crossing the promontory on the way to Sutro's mine. Three weeks after Louis Swift fell off that promontory. That was some major synchronicity.

Walter said, "Maxie, I'm deeply sorry for your loss, but I'm afraid we can't share details of our investigation."

"Well shit," she said. "So, at least you could find out if Pegleg walked here?"

"Well." He rubbed his chin, as he does when he's weighing pros and cons. "Technically, your Pegleg is not part of our case. So I suppose we can give it a try."

"Yeah? You *rock*."

My partner grew a small smile.

30

As Walter and I gathered grains and pebbles from the red beach, I visualized boot-guy here, heading for that mine tunnel to gather chunks of manganese-bearing rock. Maybe the whole gang came ashore. Then, the argument--which gets settled back aboard with a Colt. Then more shooting. Then the *Dawn* sails on to Yerba Buena Cove.

For whatever reason.

I watched Walter sampling and thought, he's not just doing this for Maxie. Eh, neither was I. Burt Zhang and his artifact had put us both in the story.

When we'd finished and packed up our field kits, Maxie said, simply, "Thank you."

Walter nodded. "To be clear, this will take a place in line behind our active cases." He gave her a long look. "Jane is the current priority."

I added, "And we can wait here only so long."

Maxie got her phone, texted, watched the screen for a full minute, shook her head, and pocketed the phone. "Yeah, like I said, she's keeping her phone off--but she'll be checking when she can. You know, she *could* have meant for us to meet up top.

We do that sometimes. If she got here early, she could be waiting and just didn't see the *Best Bay* coming in. Like, maybe she took a pee break or something. And, I mean, she wouldn't hear us talking down here--the wind really howls up top. So I think we should go up and check."

I tipped my head and gazed up the sheer cliff face. From here, the summit of the island was not visible but I calculated it was at least a couple hundred feet above this beach.

"Not *here*, we climb from the other side of the island." She added, "Or I could just go alone, no problemo."

Walter and I consulted. It was decided we'd all go up top.

Walter phoned Debra and updated her.

And then we set off for the other side. Maxie led the way up the long red beach to the island's northern end, disturbing a gaggle of seagulls, which noisily took wing. From here, the view of the bridge was unobstructed. And the view *from* the bridge of us tramping along the tiny northern beach would be unobstructed, should Jane still be on the way, taking that route.

We rounded a sharp bend and then came to the island's eastern shore. I was struck by three things. One, the slope above the beach was gentler here--still steep enough, but not a forbidding cliff face. Two, dense brush mantled the slope. Three, there was no kayak on the beach.

Across the water was the Richmond harbor.

Maxie said, "She could have hitched a ride and gotten dropped off here--to go up top."

Walter stared up the brushy slope.

"Not that way, it's really thick and you get all scratched. There's a couple other ways, and I'm taking you to the one we use."

We continued along the deserted beach and then arrived at Maxie's choice. The slope here was exposed rock again, although much gentler than the steep cliff face on the western side.

A yellow rope snaked down the slope from above.

This was surely a day for echoes. The echo in this case being the sea cave that led up to the tunnels of Adolph Sutro's mine-- and the rope that we'd deployed, the rope that Jane had thankfully left in place.

Maxie gave this rope a tug. "There's a secure tie-off up top. You two okay with this?"

Walter cast me a look: don't even go there.

I didn't intend to. I said, "We're good."

She tightened the chin strap of her hat. "Windy up there." She scrambled with agility up the slope, with an assist from the rope. She reached a place that was lightly haired in brush, and then disappeared. Her shout came, "Next!"

The rope flapped against the rock, then stilled.

We set our hats.

Walter said, "After you."

I began my ascent, hand-over-handing the rope, finding my way up. It was a substantial climb and in several places I was glad for the rope's support. Soon enough I reached the brushy area, breathing hard now, inhaling the scent of sage and other unidentifiable vegetation. And then I came to the top--a narrow ridge--where Maxie was waiting.

"Easy-peasy," she said.

Mostly. I released the rope and called down to Walter. "All yours!"

He ascended in silence. I heard the cries of gulls and the wind hissing over our ridgetop, but from Walter, silence. He's climbed worse. When he finally appeared, he threw me a weary smile.

Easy-peasy.

We let our heart rates settle, giving it a few moments, taking in the view.

The view was stupendous. The sky blazed blue here but in the distance, to the west, the hills were hatted in a fog bank rolling in from the Pacific Ocean. I turned to the eastern shore-line, with its busy harbor, boats darting out into the bay. Defining the skyline was the no-nonsense bridge that linked east to west. Two boats passed underneath, one a sailboat and one a ferry bristling with passengers.

Up here, the closeup view was limited by thick brush and tall chaparral.

"If you're ready," Maxie said, "we'll go look."

There was only one route to take, a path of sorts along the narrow ridge that comprised the top of the island. We were somewhere in the middle, I calculated. Maxie turned us left-ward, toward the ridge's southern end. The ridgetop was scrubby with sage and the path was hemmed with the half-dead chaparral, which grazed my shoulders as I passed. We single-filed, giving each other room, watching our footing on the uneven beaten earth. We didn't get far because the ridge began to angle downward and, from what I recalled of the topography I'd glimpsed on the boat ride here, this southern end of the ridge terminated in a steep cliff. Indeed, Maxie stopped us.

There was nothing in sight but wind-whipped vegetation.

I scanned the waters between the eastern harbor and the island and saw no kayak heading our way, no motorboat with a hitchhiking Jane.

"So we'll try the summit," Maxie said.

We reversed course and navigated our way back to the yellow rope tie-off, and then as we continued I noticed that the path had begun to steepen. Otherwise, it was scrub and chap-arral, the path snaking here and there to avoid boulders. And then like a surprise, the way opened up as the ridge rose to a hump where a fat pine tree held its own, dug into the thin soil, its needles shivering in the wind. The little summit sloped down to a shoulder thick with brambles and brush, and a couple more pine trees. This was the top of the cliff we'd seen from the beach, the way not to climb because we'd get all scratched.

There was no sign of Jane on or around the summit.

Maxie had her phone out, texting. "Telling her we're up here but we're gonna come back down and meet by my boat."

Walter put up a hand. "A moment's rest first."

I refrained from asking how he was doing. "Works for me."

Indeed, the air had gone out of all three of us. We folded ourselves down to the reddish earth beneath the fat pine. If this day hadn't already been so long, if I hadn't felt so weary, so suddenly drained, I would have suggested a time frame for our rest. A short while, I decided.

Maxie braced her arms behind her and stretched her legs in front.

Walter and I used our packs as backrests.

I took in the view, not just because it was a stunning panorama but because I was taking note of line of sight. There was no question of Jane having taken a pee and missing our incoming boat--Jane wasn't up here. If we'd missed her approach while we were up here, if she'd just reached the beach--any of this island's beaches--we couldn't tell, because we had limited line of sight down from this ridgetop. If she was down there, she would have seen the *Best Bay*, and turned on her phone, and answered Maxie's text. But no problemo, I thought, channeling Maxie, Jane could still be on the way. Bay Area traffic was nothing if not gnarly.

Walter stirred. "Maxie," he said, "I have a question."

She turned to him.

"Down on the beach you said the shooting of your ancestor Pegleg might explain what happened to Jane's cousin Roger, and to your cousin Louis. Nearly two hundred years after the fact. How?"

"Um, that gets into Jane's story."

"We either get into it, or it's time to take us back to the marina."

Maxie drew up her knees and hugged them. "Okay, what if we make an agreement? I'll tell you what I know, and you promise to do the pebbles *today* when I take you back?"

Walter straightened. "Deal."

She appeared surprised. I wasn't. Walter our finance man knew how to negotiate, and he could easily deliver on this deal. It would not take him long to put pebbles from the boot and pebbles from the long red beach under the comparison scope and see if he had a match. If need be, he'd use the X-ray fluorescence analyzer to build an elemental profile on both. Meanwhile, I'd finish the analysis of the grains from Jane's braid. We could juggle both jobs, and be in compliance with Debra's request--the Jane Forster case took priority.

Walter said, "Go ahead, Maxie."

"Okay. Okay here's what I know. When Jane was growing up her family had stories, too, about the ship and the island. Her dad and Roger even took her here, like an adventure, and they played at searching for gold."

"They find anything?"

"Nah. Neither did my family when we went." She shrugged. "I don't know what Jane's dad thought, but he told her the *Dawn* thing was just a little argument over lost gold, no big deal."

"He spun the story."

"He wanted her to think Forsters were good guys."

"Did she?"

"For a while."

"What changed?"

"What she found out. When she was seventeen, Mr. Forster

wrote a book about this old-time San Francisco mayor and it talked about that mine he was building."

"We're familiar with both."

"Right. Anyway, Jane went once with Roger when he was researching and she found out there could have been a *coal* mine at Lands End. That got her into protesting."

"Is that what led to the trouble with her father?"

"No, he didn't care about coal. He cared about gold."

"Playing at it?"

"He got serious. After the book was published, Roger did more research, for publicity, and he found employment records for the mine. One of the workers was a mining engineer named Larry Forster."

I thought, holy moly.

Walter said, neutrally, "That would have made quite a hook."

"Yeah, no, Roger and Mr. Forster didn't *use* it. They started talking again about gold from the old stories, like maybe their ancestors really *did* steal it, and the engineer hid it in the mine. And Jane overheard. All of a sudden she sees that her dad and her cousin are cool with their ancestors being thieves and murderers. So she decides to do her own research into the family past, and finds some online archives, only there's nothing about the *Dawn*. Instead, she finds an awful story about the Forsters when they were cemetery caretakers at Lands End. She asked her dad if *that* was true and he said, all holy, we are not our ancestors. But he was sure interested in that mining engineer. So she said the hell with him."

I had no trouble believing it.

Walter asked, in his studied neutral tone, "And did she say the hell with Roger, too?"

"Yeah, she was real hard-line. I mean, she left home and didn't see either one for years. Until the dig. Roger was around, he was just this super-eager guy glad to see her. She couldn't

avoid him. So they ended up talking, and then she had to introduce me, and then Louis when he came to see the dig. We all
ended up talking about stuff."

"Jane and Roger were reconciled?"

"Maybe a little?"

"I understand Roger was pitching his cousin's books at the
dig. Did you all talk about the Sutro book? About the mine?"

She eyed him. "You mean, about the gold?"

Walter waited.

"I know what you mean," she said. "You think that's why
Louis was hiking at Lands End. You think he was on the way to
the mine."

"Do you think that? Does Jane?"

She said, strained, "We talked about it. Like, maybe somebody pushed Louis. And then maybe somebody wanted revenge
for that and killed Roger."

"You realize *who* you're talking about?"

"Yeah. A Forster killed Louis. And then a Swift killed Roger."

I thought, Maxie Swift puts two and two together just fine.

Walter asked, "Does Jane believe her family is complicit?"

"She won't say it. Not after Roger was killed. That really tore
her up."

I recalled fierce Jane Forster confronting us in the mine
wanting to know what we'd learned about her cousin and I
wished I'd given her a better answer.

"So," Maxie said, to Walter, "that's what I know. And you'll
keep your end of the deal?"

"Certainly."

She lifted her little finger. "Pinky swear?"

Without a pause he raised a hand and hooked pinkies
with her.

She turned to me. "I didn't think he'd do it."

Neither did I.

"Okay, so like I said, let's go down to the beach and we'll give Jane a little bit longer and then if she doesn't come, and her phone's still off, I'll take you back to the marina and you can get going on the pebbles. And when Jane answers my text I'll tell her what you're doing, and if she still needs to talk to you then she needs to get a better way to meet up."

Walter said, "Excellent plan."

Maxie rose with the nimbleness of a twenty-something. Walter and I got to our feet. We shouldered our packs and set off, following Maxie. When the broad summit started narrowing into the brushy path down the ridge, we single-filed, Maxie in the lead, then Walter, then me. I grinned at my partner's back--pinky swear!--and knew I'd file that in the don't-ever-mention department.

The path snaked and he disappeared, and as I rounded the little bend I heard a shout up ahead, Maxie's voice floating my way. *"Jane!"*

Really? Finally?

I picked up my pace to close the distance between me and Walter, who was picking up his own pace, stumbling once on the uneven ground, slowing again, and I came up behind him, angling for a look beyond him, and I caught a glimpse of Maxie's white hat up ahead as she plunged through the narrow channel in the chaparral.

There was a sound, whipped on the wind, like a wave crashing against rocks.

And then Walter halted and I nearly slammed into him.

He turned and grabbed me around the waist and pulled me down to the hard earth, knocking the wind out of me. He hit the ground beside me, half into the chaparral. When I recovered my breath I lifted my head to look down the path and I saw Maxie on the ground. On her back. Her head tipped back, her hat jammed forward, her arms flung out to the sides like she had tried to take wing. I stared, uncomprehending, until I spotted the wet stain growing on the chest of her purple sweatshirt.

Walter crawled forward and took hold of her wrist.

And then he inched his way back to me.

We lay flattened, hidden, silent.

After an eternity, he mouthed *we need to move.*

There was no question of crawling, we rose to a low crouch and without another glance back started up the ridge, the two of us crowded on the narrow path, arms scraped by chaparral, stumbling until we reached the open ground of the summit, and then we straightened and ran. We topped the summit, passing the fat pine, then scrambled down the little slope to the thick brush. When we couldn't scramble any farther we dropped to our knees and then our bellies and wormed into the brambles. My mind skittered, landing on logistics. The slope was too steep and the brush too thick to worm all the way down to the beach, and there was no way in hell we were going back down the ridge path to the yellow rope.

When my pounding heartbeat eased, I listened for footsteps.

After an eternity, I heard Walter say, "There's been a tragedy."

I looked at him, huddled beside me. He was whispering into his phone.

Oh.

Good.

He'd called Debra.

My mind just skittered.

And then it settled with pain on Maxie.

31

DETECTIVE TALON CAME BY HELICOPTER.

In our brushy nest below the summit we heard the clatter of the approaching chopper. The helicopter was coming in to land on the long stretch of sand where Maxie and Walter and I had waded ashore.

We stayed put, because Debra had said stay put until she gave us the all-clear. But I didn't think the shooter was still on the island. Could have shot us. Didn't. During our eternal wait for Debra my mind had skittered from suspect to suspect. First choice was Gregory Forster, because I'd seen enough of him to place him first. Second was his daughter, who was supposed to meet us here, but didn't. The Forsters and the Swifts, locked into a deadly feud. Third were the shitty Nevada Swifts, who didn't like Maxie. Fourth was the archaeologist, who Jane suspected of knowing something crucial.

The incoming clatter grew louder and I saw the SFPD helicopter lowering down out of the sky. And then it sank out of view. And then the clatter ceased.

I felt relief.

And then another feeling reared, swift as a sneaker wave.

Fury. My face must have shown it because Walter put a hand on my arm.

"I truly liked her," he said.

So did I.

We heard Debra before we saw her. She bellowed, "Next on the rope come on up!"

And then she shouted to us, "Stay put until you hear otherwise!"

We were too stiff to argue.

It took her a while. I figured she'd found Maxie. She cursed once, and then motormouth Detective Talon went silent.

I looked down at Maxie. The stain on her chest had stopped spreading. There was a small hole in the middle of her sweatshirt, dark like the pupil of an eye, fringed by filaments of severed fabric. The white bucket hat still covered half her face. The fall, the impact of her head against the ground, had knocked it awry.

I fixed hard on the purple BBT lettering.

When my eyes had stopped tearing, I looked at Debra.

She stood several feet back, arms folded, scanning the ridgetop, what could be seen of it beyond the hedgy chaparral. She wore what she'd worn last time I'd seen her--midday at the golf course, heading for our cars after the long climb up from Mile Rock Beach. Gray slacks and white T-shirt and black sneakers, everything dirt-streaked from the climb up here. She'd swapped her blazer for a black parka, and a black ballcap, both with gold SFPD logos. The lenses of her aviator shades were dusty.

It felt wrong being at a crime scene with nothing to do. Normally, we'd be collecting earth evidence. But there was no need. There was no question about the shooting that geology could answer, in this case, at this point, right here.

One of her team had already come up the rope and been dispatched down the ridge to search for spent shell casings. It had been preliminarily established that the shooter had fired from the path near the rope tie-off. Crouched in chaparral, firing slightly upward at the approaching Maxie, judging by the entry angle of the bullet.

"All right," Debra said, "as soon as Danny comes up the rope, you two can go down. Somebody'll show you what to do."

"Anything," I said.

She waved me off.

Okay. This was how she worked a scene, with the victim present. I'd only seen her work a cold scene. Now, with the vic here--and I was already calling Maxie the vic--Debra was taciturn.

Walter and I were escorted around the northern end of the island--back the way we'd come--to the western side.

We came to the long red beach, where the SFPD helicopter was parked, and beyond the chopper, Maxie's boat had been brought to shoreline, its bow nosing the sand.

We skirted the *Best Bay Tours* and clambered over the boulders below the tunnel opening and continued to the southern end of the western side of the island. There was a slight cove there. A decent beach. According to our escort, the team had ascertained that the cliff here was climbable, with a slight saddle that led up bare rock to a low point below the ridge. According to our escort, there were no prints on the rock route up from this beach.

I turned to the water. A boat could come in and anchor in this little cove, possibly right up to the shore. From up top, we wouldn't have seen it. Farther out in the bay it would have been just one more watercraft.

We did our job. Photos, measurements, sampling. It was the familiar red sandy shore. The sand was soft and pebbly enough that our boots left little more than gouges, rather than identifiable footprints. Squat yellow marker cones marked a corridor where Debra's team had come and gone, leaving their own gouges. Possibly, there had been prints in the wet sand at water's edge. If so, the water had pulsed enough to erase them.

Still, we combed the area at the base of the cliff.

We combed the beach.

Our escort left us to it.

When we'd collected all that could reasonably be collected, we returned to the long beach. And there we took a seat on the sun-warmed sand and waited for Detective Talon.

Debra appeared half an hour later.

She looked done in.

Long ugly day, for all three of us. Started early at the golf course. It was early evening, here at Red Rock Island.

I was empty to the core.

She sat facing us. "What can you tell me?"

She listened while we summed up what we'd learned from Maxie. About Louis Swift, and the shitty Nevada Swifts. About the ancestral Swift family business. About the *Dawn*. About the Packingtons, AKA Forsters. About Jane Forster's learning curve.

When we'd finished, she rose and motioned us to follow her to the waterline, to Maxie's boat. "My techs have done their thing and there's no indication the perp boarded this craft. So we're going to take her back to the marina."

She climbed over the bow.

We followed.

The detective headed for the cockpit and took the captain's seat.

I must have flinched, because Debra said, "Yes, I can drive a little boat like this, I grew up in the city by the bay and I spent many a day out on the water. My buddies and a cooler of beer and sandwiches and off we'd go, find ourselves a beach or an island, but yanno we never did make it to *this* one. Guess I can check this one off my list." She took off her sunglasses and cleaned the lenses with the hem of her T-shirt. Staring down at us from the raised seat. "I'm going to get this perp."

There was cold fury in her pale green eyes.

32

We took our old seats, Walter on the port side and me on starboard.

Two cops shed their footwear and pushed the boat away from the shore.

Debra started the motor and hightailed us away from the island, expertly navigating the *Best Bay Tours* to skirt a large ferryboat and larger yacht, while giving a clutch of kite-surfers a generous patch of space.

I didn't see any kayaks.

We motored down the channel between the western and eastern shorelines and then passed Angel Island and then Alcatraz and the golden-gate entrance from the sea to the bay.

I saw flat Treasure Island and its mountainous neighbor Yerba Buena coming up. Fifteen islands in the bay, Maxie had said. I'd now visited three.

Debra, up in the cockpit, was immobile, a ship's figurehead. No tour-guide spiel from her.

Walter was swiveled on his bench seat, staring straight ahead. He'd taken off his hat. He needed a haircut. The gray strands blew in the wind, like smoke.

As we neared the San Francisco waterfront, I twisted to look. I thought I could pick out the tower that neighbored the dig, the tall parking garage where Roger Forster had left his car.

And then we passed beneath the Bay Bridge and in short order came to the marina bordering the pier with the massive warehouse.

Debra drove the boat to the long dock where Walter and I had boarded a number of very long hours ago. She shut off the engine and came out of the cockpit to face us. "I don't know where the slip is for this boat. I'll find out. And I'll contact the marina manager and explain the situation." She jerked a thumb over her shoulder, toward the warehouse, toward our trailer-lab. "You two able to work at this point? Any fuel left in your tank? I'd like to have those samples you took ready for a match. Ready as you can get."

Walter cleared his throat. "Ready, how soon?"

"Soon as I check something out."

"You have a suspect in mind." He stated it, rather than asked it.

"Don't you?"

33

I REFILLED our water bottles and raided the snack box for energy bars, to get us through the next hour.

Walter set the specimen dish of pebbles from the long red beach on the lab's modular shelf, next to the specimen dish of boot-guy's pebbles--at the end of the line, behind our current cases.

And then we set to work on the newest case, laying out the samples we'd collected at the southern end of the island where Debra's people had decided the suspect most likely parked the boat, tromped ashore, came and went.

The evening light dulled.

I glanced out the window once, at the marina.

A man in a parka strolled by on the walkway.

He was nobody.

Debra knocked once and opened the door. She held a Trader Joe's shopping bag. She said, "I need you now."

Walter said, "We're not quite finished."

I looked up, rubbing my eyes. Had been staring at blood-red sand under the high-power lens of my scope.

We hesitated a moment too long, and Detective Talon barked, "*Now*."

I asked, "How did you know it was here?"

We were deep into the marina, halfway down a long dock, with a multitude of watercraft big and small between us and the warehouse.

"There are only a few marinas in the city," Debra said, "so I phoned around and talked to the managers and played my detective card and asked if a certain boat owner parked at their marina and when they made noises about client privacy I said this is a murder case, and you won't be surprised to hear how the word *murder* gets attention. I learned the boat in question is parked in *this* marina, and got the slip number."

The name painted on the white hull was *Maverick*.

"Gregory Forster's," Walter said.

"Well yes and no. The slip is still registered to Roger Forster. But--as *Gregory* told us two days ago, and my *god* was it only two days ago?--the boat is his now."

I remembered the photo on the table in the Sea Cliff living room with puppy-dog Roger and sleek tan Gregory standing on the boat deck, arms around each other's necks.

The *Maverick* was small and sleek and fit neatly into its U-shaped berth, enclosed by concrete arms that branched off the long concrete dock that stuck out into the bay. It was a cabin cruiser, and I thought *smart*, Forster, you were hidden inside the cabin when you approached Red Rock Island. Unseen and unseeable should anyone up top look down at the water and take note of the approaching boat. Unseen and unseeable after you'd finished your business and motored away.

I said, "Convenient that Forster's boat and Maxie's boat and our lab are clustered here."

"You noticed." Debra nodded. "As to your lab, space for visiting consultants costs an arm and a leg in this city, and the department gets a good deal on the trailer. As to the boat slips, this is a popular marina."

I nodded.

"Here's the deal with Forster's boat. I'd love to get into that cabin and check out the GPS and the logbook and the Garmin and whatever fancy-schmancy electronics he has, but the cabin's an interior compartment and I haven't yet got a warrant so that's out-of-bounds for now." She paused. "The deck, though..."

Walter said, "In plain view."

"Right with you, Walter. Deck's in plain view and we're lawfully present--so you get the deck. Probably no joy, though." She pointed to the teak floor near the bow. "A little water pooling. It's been hosed down. Responsible boaters rinse off their craft after use. Especially if they tracked something aboard they don't want examined by people like you with hand lenses and microscopes, on the off-chance that people like me follow up on that."

I took note of the stanchion on one concrete arm of the berth, where a hose was coiled on a bib beside a spigot. The concrete beneath the hose was damp.

Smart, Forster.

"Still," Debra said, "worth checking out." She withdrew a box from the shopping bag. "I keep protective gear in the trunk."

Walter and I covered our island-contaminated shoes with booties and climbed aboard the *Maverick*.

The deck proved to be squeaky clean.

"All right," the detective said, "no joy, no surprise. Once I get that warrant maybe we'll get lucky and find a gun and a pair of dirty boots stashed in the cabin but truth be told I suspect they're at the bottom of the bay. So let's move on. I've got another long shot in mind. You two ready to rock and roll?"

34

WE TOOK Debra's car across the city, talking long shots.

We'd all gotten a second wind--a full-steam-ahead tailwind--and we talked and we talked and we threw around what-ifs and we spun out the scenarios.

As Debra dodged and weaved and climbed and descended the berzerk streets of San Francisco, the lowering sun threw long stripey shadows, pointing toward the end of the day.

The day had begun so long ago with long stripey shadows across the green of the golf course.

Fatigue fuzzed my mind.

And then we were going over scenarios again, repeating ourselves.

By the time Debra slammed to a halt at the curb in front of Gregory Forster's estate--all rich warm terracotta Mediterranean knock-off display--we were juiced.

We piled out of the car and Debra led the way across the slate-tiled driveway, past the white-paneled garage, past the slate walkway that led to the grand entrance to Forster's spread. And then we came to the tall hedge ramparts that separated Forster's estate from the estate next door. A path arrowed between the hedges, a nearly hidden walkway that Forster had described to Debra when she phoned to say we were on the way.

We plunged ahead.

When we reached the back patio, there was that show-stopping view--glorious sky, wild seascape, and in the distance the lowering sun turning the orange bridge red. Gave it all a glance as we descended to the lower patio, then passed the statue of the metal-limbed miner hatted with the orange traffic cone.

The gate in the wall bordering the patio was open.

I took the lead down the zigzag stairway, recalling how Forster had put me off my stride, last time. Not this time, no. I warned Debra and Walter about the cracked paver. We descended without trouble to the little landing quarried out of the cliff face.

As promised, Gregory Forster waited for us there, slouched in his cousin's lawn chair. He lifted a hand in greeting.

Debra crossed in front of Forster and leaned against the far cliff face. Walter and I took side-by-side seats on the bottom step. The paver still held its sun warmth.

Debra began. "Thanks for seeing us, Forster. We'll be out of your hair in time for you to soak up the sunset in peace." She nodded at the paintbox sky.

He said, "I'm not here for the sunset."

He looked wrecked. Worse than he'd looked this morning at the golf course, at Mile Rock Beach, at the cave. His white hair was spiked, plowed. The sinking sun bronzed his tan face with a patina of gold but he was a rough replica of jaunty Forster, like a metal gold miner pitted by sea air. He wore baggy black sweats, the top hooded. This morning's sweats, maybe. Or fresh ones. Maybe he kept a whole closet-full.

I took note of his feet. Tanned, clean-looking. He wore black flip-flops. Footwear to hose off the deck of a boat? Maybe he kept a pair aboard. Or maybe these were kept by the sliding glass door to the patios, footwear to slip into in a hurry.

Debra said, "Then what brings you down here, Forster?"

"Roger."

She made a sympathetic face. "I know how a loss hits people. Day by day, you pull yourself together but then it pops up without warning and you fall apart. That what's going on?"

He shot her a look. He wasn't buying the sympathy. "That's right. I lose my cousin, who I grew up with. And then my daughter disappears, and the fact that she'd left my life years ago makes no difference. She's all I have left. So I'm sitting here in Roger's chair feeling sorry for myself. Despairing. Thanks for understanding."

"We all understand, Forster."

"Then are you here with news?"

"In regard to your cousin?"

"My *cousin*. My *daughter*. What other news does it look like I'm in need of?"

Debra nodded to Walter, and Walter took over. "Cassie and I are close to learning what happened to your cousin. Have faith. This is what we do. Evidence is taking us on the same journey Roger took and we're almost to the end. When we arrive, we'll bring it to Detective Talon and she will do what she does."

"And are you close to finding out where my daughter is?"

"I'm afraid we haven't yet traced the braid beyond the cave where it was found."

"It's *evidence*. It's what you *do*."

"Not all evidence yields helpful results."

Forster slammed the arms of the rickety lawn chair.

Walter slammed a hand on the paver.

Forster flinched.

Walter sat forward, hands braced on the step. "Forster, I'm going to tell you about emotion." Walter's voice was deadly calm.

"I've been at this job for decades and I've seen a lot of death. After the fact. Today, I saw someone killed--right in front of my eyes, as the saying goes. I didn't see the killer. I saw the victim. I'm telling you this now to explain that I understand how emotion drives us. I feel a rage, at today's killer. Vengeful. As you must feel, at the person who murdered your cousin."

Forster sat utterly still.

"Don't you?"

He didn't answer. He was getting it. Wary now.

I watched him figuring what to say. Should he disavow the legitimacy of vengeful feelings? Should he ask Walter, whose murder did you witness today? It's the obvious question. But Forster wouldn't want to go down that road, because that road led nowhere good. He had no idea what we knew, or suspected. Safer to sit in silence, exhibiting respect for Walter's shock.

Debra watched him with a raptor's keen focus.

He caught her look. He caught his mistake; he should have asked whose murder. There was no pivoting from this. He said, thickly, "What... I mean, *today*, who...?"

Walter cut in, "A young woman named Maxie Swift was shot to death."

I felt, again, today's anguish. The evening air seemed to thin. I sucked in a long breath, and Debra followed suit, the two of us seemingly in need of extra oxygen.

Forster said, "That's terrible."

Walter waited.

Forster had no choice. "Who was she?"

"A friend of your daughter's."

Forster cast about. "I don't..."

It was almost too easy, throwing him further off his stride.

"Don't you?" Walter asked mildly. "Presumably, your cousin saw Jane and her friend at the dig. Not a leap to think he reported that information back to you."

"It *is* a leap. Jane and I were estranged. Roger knew not to broach the subject."

"But now we find ourselves enmeshed in the subject of your daughter. You asked when we would find her. For a while, today, Cassie and I thought we had."

He straightened. "What do you mean?"

"Maxie Swift came to our lab and told us your daughter wanted to meet up."

"*What*? Did you, did she...?"

"She never showed up."

Forster seemed to deflate. I thought, he probably does care, in his way. But he didn't ask where Walter and I were supposed to have met up with his daughter. Where Maxie had taken us.

I figured he saw it coming.

Debra took over. "That brings us, Forster, to an ugly lump of rock in the northern bay called Red Rock Island. Do you know it?"

He faced her. "Heard of it."

"Ever been there?"

"No."

"How about your cousin?"

"No."

He's Forster, I thought, he lies.

"I ask," Debra said, "because of Roger's gung-ho interest in the dig, in the unearthed ship."

"Him, along with a thousand other people."

"A thousand other people didn't piss off the archaeologist, barging into the dig, pitching your books."

"That's Roger. Enthusiastic. So?"

"So I'm thinking your gung-ho research assistant might have dug up interesting tidbits about that old ship and its history."

"Where is this going, Detective?"

"To Red Rock Island."

He spread his hands. "Then I don't follow."

"Then my geologists will lead you." She leaned back against the cliff face and nodded to us.

Walter took it. "The history of the *Dawn* is rooted on that island. Maxie Swift told us the story, just hours ago. Her ancestors operated the ship, with stops at the island to collect manganese rocks to sell for paint pigment in Oregon. On one return trip they ferried gold seekers--by the name of Packington--to Sacramento, to try their luck in the gold fields. The Swifts joined them. They made some finds, and on the return they stopped again at the island. There, gold was stolen, and at least one Swift came to grief." Walter paused. "You need a moment to take all this in?"

"I have no interest in taking this in," Forster said.

"Have patience. There's more. Ms. Swift told us a number of things, including the sad fact that, about three weeks ago, her cousin fell from that promontory at Lands End, to his death."

Forster didn't even flinch. "A shame."

"His name was Louis Swift. Ring a bell?"

"Should it?"

"At the least, it's coincidental. Don't you think? Maxie's cousin dies three weeks ago. Your cousin dies five days ago."

Forster lifted his palms, at the irrelevance of the information.

"*Forster.*" Debra pushed off the rock face. "The problem with your professed ignorance about all things Swift is that you were caught out in a lie today. At Red Rock Island. Which makes it difficult to believe your protestations now."

He didn't respond.

"The lie I'm speaking of is the one you told us last time we gathered here. You said your ancestors came to San Francisco from Los Angeles, overland. You said they never boarded a ship."

"Yes. So?"

"According to Maxie Swift, your ancestors were on that ship.

I think that's why your cousin was so interested in its discovery. I think you've been equally interested."

"Think what you like." Forster started to rise.

"Stay put. We're not done here."

He settled back in the chair, stretching his legs, crossing his ankles. The flip-flops dangled.

Debra turned to me. All yours.

I gathered my thoughts. I felt a deep fatigue, like I was sinking, like the dying day's sun. I tried to recapture the buzz that had propelled us across the city, that fed my fevered march down the zigzag staircase, that singed my nerves.

Forster caught my hesitation. His mouth curled, edging on a smile.

I rallied. "Forster, let's go back to the issue of your daughter."

"Who remains missing."

"Who liked to hang out at the dig."

"I wouldn't know. I stayed away."

"You were at the golf course this morning when we talked about Jane sandbagging us in the mine, about her insistence that the archaeologist knew something in regard to Roger's death. That was, what, ten or so hours ago?"

"You asking if I can keep track of my day? Yes, I recall this morning."

"Good. Fast-forward to a few minutes ago when we mentioned that your daughter and Maxie Swift were friends. That began at the dig. And today at the island Maxie told Walter and me something she'd learned from Jane--about that half-built coal mine at Lands End, the one you wrote about in your Sutro book."

Forster's face was stone.

"According to Maxie, after the book was published Roger did some research to prep publicity. In the process, he learned about an engineer named *Larry Forster* who worked on the mine." I waited for a reaction. Got none. I continued, "Evidently, Jane overheard you and Roger talking about the *Dawn*, about stolen gold, about the possibility that your ancestor Larry hid it in the mine. And she confronted you about your ancestors being thieves and murderers. You recall that?"

"You expect me to comment on something my daughter supposedly told this Maxie?"

"As in, you are not your ancestors?" I let a smile flicker. "I've been learning about your ancestors. Let's see if I can put it together. After Red Rock Island, your ancestors--and the *Dawn*-- somehow end up in San Francisco. They flee the lawless Barbary Coast for the undeveloped western part of the city, where they change their name from Packington to Forster, and become potato farmers. And, who knows, stash their gold in the root cellar. Their gold, plus the gold stolen from the Swifts--the whole jackpot. Eventually, they become cemetery caretakers and get accused of grave-robbing--were they, perhaps, not robbing but *burying* their remaining gold in an empty grave? In time, an even better option becomes available. One of them becomes an engineer on Adolph Sutro's mine, and voila--creates a nifty hidey-hole. How much gold was left at that point? Who knows? But you and Roger thought it was worth a look?"

Forster said, brusquely, "You're mixing fact and fiction. Potato farmers, cemetery caretakers--I've acknowledged that. Everything else is bullshit."

"I think there's some truth to *everything else*."

He lifted his hands, his go-to dismissal.

"Why did Roger gift you the gold miner statue?"

"Because he worked on my book about the Barbary Coast, which was born in the *gold rush*. And he got interested. He would have loved having ancestors who struck it rich. We didn't. He settled for the miner statue. I added the traffic cone. It became a running joke."

"Not so funny now, though. Three people dead."

He seemed to be counting.

"Louis Swift. Roger Forster. Maxie Swift. You notice the pattern?" I focused, fiercely, on his stony face. "I think, today, someone shot Maxie Swift in revenge."

He shot me a dagger of a look. "I think we're done here."

"*Forster*," Debra cut back in, "you want to explain where you went boating this afternoon?"

His attention snapped to her.

"I ask," she said, "because your boat the *Maverick* is parked in the marina next to the warehouse where my geologists have their lab. Looked like it'd been washed down, after use."

"Not by me." He added, easily, "People borrow hoses. People get things wet."

"I'm not talking *people*. I'm talking *you*. Let's take a boat tour to Red Rock Island."

"No thank you."

"No choice," she said. "At first, I was puzzled that you didn't rent a boat under a fake name. Instead, you took *your* boat to Red Rock Island. Risky. If my geologists had seen it they would have recognized the name, from that photo of you and Roger aboard. Would have then placed you at the island, around the time of Maxie Swift's murder." She wagged a finger. "But lucky for you they didn't see the boat. No view from up top."

"This is fantasy."

"Let me ground it for you. Let's start with the discovery of the *Dawn*, two months ago. That kicked things off. The dig, Roger and Jane and Maxie. Roger reporting back to you. The past is rearing up. Here's a Swift, claiming her ancestors owned that ship. And on top of that, she has a cousin in Sacramento, who has a brother, and on top of *that* there are Swifts in Nevada. All of them descendants of the *Dawn* Swifts. And you, understand-ably, start to worry. The last thing you want is Swifts looking for their stolen inheritance. Maybe even looking for revenge. Turns out your worry is justified, because Louis Swift shows up. You worry that Jane--who is not your biggest fan--told Maxie about the mining engineer, and Maxie told Louis. You worry that'll send Louis poking around the mine. I assume you and Roger hadn't yet found gold there. But you held out hope, didn't you? Don't you, still? You're smart, determined. Walter tells me there are modern techniques, like ground-penetrating radar, to find lost artifacts. Hidden things."

"I wouldn't know."

"You weren't worried about Louis Swift showing up?"

"As I said, never heard of him."

"How about his death?"

"No idea."

"A death at *Lands End*? Your neighborhood."

"I don't patrol it."

"Neither did I. My division only responds if homicide is suspected. The death was termed accidental. Could have been. Certainly, the name didn't raise a flag at the time. Now it does."

"The name doesn't raise a flag with *me*. Then or now."

They were batting it back and forth, question and answer. She was trying to trip him up. He was dodging with ease.

She saw that. She pressed on. "*Forster*. Were you there, on that cliff? Giving Louis Swift a helping hand over the side. Or was it Roger? I can believe that, impulsive Roger. Gets carried away. Whichever, bottom line, now you have a new worry. It's spelled revenge. And damned if that doesn't turn out to be justified. Your cousin is murdered. Dumped at the dig, a note pinned to his shirt! *We will bury you*. 'We' being you-don't-know-how-many Swifts. 'You' being you. You're spooked. You hope to hell that the killer gets found. In the meantime, you keep track of the closest Swift, Maxie. And you arm yourself."

The waves boomed in the cove below.

Forster settled more comfortably in the lawn chair.

"And then," Debra continued, "we learn your daughter has been kidnapped. *Another* bury-you note. That's enough to freak out anybody. And you *were* freaked, Forster, this morning at the golf course. To start with, Burt Zhang rips you a new one. And then we find your daughter's braid in the sea cave. Forster, I saw you. You were beyond freaked at that point. You were overwhelmed. Pushed to the brink."

"That's the only part of this fantasy you have right, Detective. I'm overwhelmed."

"Then hang on for the ride because I'm not done yet. You'll recall earlier in our conversation when Walter talked about vengeful feelings. So we have you overwhelmed this afternoon-- after we all went our separate ways. And let's add vengeance to the mix. You don't know where Louis's brother, or the Nevada Swifts, are to be found. But you do know where Maxie works. You've researched her. So you drive on over to the marina. Planning, let's say, to find out what she knows. About your missing daughter. About your cousin's last day. And, given your state of mind, it's not surprising if you're thinking something more than talk."

"That's enough," Forster said.

"You asking me to stop the story?"

"Yes."

"That sounds like guilt."

"You're talking slander."

"On the contrary," she said, "I'm not publicly accusing you of anything. Your reputation is intact. This isn't an interrogation. I'm just spitballing here. So hear me out. When I finish, you can call bullshit if you like." She cocked her head. "That work for you, Forster?"

He said, "I call bullshit now." But he didn't tell her to stop.

I thought, he wants to know what we've got, what we haven't got. What we suspect. What he needs to watch out for.

"All right, then," the detective said. "So we have you waiting for Maxie to finish her last tour--and *then* Cassie and Walter join her for a boat ride! What the hell, right? What are you gonna do? Follow. Oh, and here's where I answered my own question, why you didn't rent a boat. You didn't have time. So you follow the *Best Bay Tours*--easy to stay back, stay unnoticed. Then they reach their destination--Red Rock Island! Well...*wow*, right? Of course, you know about the Swifts and the ship and the island. That's *your* ancestors' history, where it all intersects. So I imagine you just motor around the vicinity, wondering what Maxie is telling the geologists, wondering what to do. And then you see them climbing up to the island's summit. On that damnable rope, jeez what a climb. Of course, you didn't go up that way. You had to park your boat where it was least likely to be seen, from the summit, and then scramble your way up. You knew the island. You and Roger took Jane there gold hunting when she was a kid. You go again, after the *Dawn* was found, the past rearing up? Take another look? Jane and Maxie sure went, poking around in the ancestry. Bottom line, Red Rock Island got a lot of action."

He looked cornered. The sun had lowered and no longer bronzed his face. Then he flicked a look at Walter and me, with a little head shake, as if to say, did you two come up with this bullshit?

Debra continued, resolute. "So Forster, we have you angry and armed and when you reach the summit, you find your target. What I wonder is, why didn't you kill my geologists too? My god, I'm glad you didn't. But what happened? You were angry and a little crazed and you took your shot and then in the aftermath, you were in shock? You aren't a stone-cold killer? After shooting Maxie...the finality of it. And, you'd gotten your revenge. Not only that, you sure as hell sent a warning to other Swifts: we're all locked in a blood feud that's echoed across the centuries. Do they want to continue?"

He shifted in the lawn chair. Stretching his back. "Are you finished now, Detective?"

"Not quite." She stepped away from the cliff face, curling her back, stretching, mirroring him. "Let's move upstairs, into the house. You won't mind if we take a look in your closet. Shoe rack. Dirty clothes bin."

"I do mind."

This, I thought, was why he met us down here, rather than in the house. Why he rushed into the flip-flops.

"And we'll appreciate access to your garage. To your car."

"This is harassment."

She sighed. "Then I'll be getting a warrant."

"Whatever." He smiled. He'd fended off everything we threw at him.

Almost. He'd tripped on Red Rock Island: never went there. Roger never went there. He'd lied.

But we needed proof.

He said, "Sunset's taking too damn long." He rose. When Detective Talon didn't tell him to sit back down, he folded Roger's lawn chair and leaned it against the graywacke cliff. He addressed Walter and me. "You're blocking the stairs. I'd appreciate it if you'd get out of my way."

We rose and stood aside.

He started up the staircase, flip-flops slapping the slate pavers.

Debra crossed the little landing to join us, and we followed him, at a distance of three pavers.

At the summit, he went through the gate, onto the lower patio, ignoring the cone-hatted miner statue, ascending the next two patios, heading for the hedges, calling over his shoulder, "I'll see you out."

Worked just fine for me.

We followed him through the hedge tunnel, toward the driveway. At the slate walkway that led to the grand entrance of the Forster estate, we stopped following.

He took another couple of steps, realized, turned. "Something *more*?"

"Yeah," I said. "Your doormats."

35

WALTER STATED IT. "IN PLAIN VIEW."

Forster pretended to be puzzled. Perhaps he was.

So Debra explained: Everything from the driveway to the front door along the arrow-straight walkway was in plain view. We were lawfully present. The potentially incriminating character of the object was immediately apparent.

We bagged the F-monogrammed mat at the front door.

Debra had to help, holding the black trash bag wide open while Walter and I inserted the doormat, trying not to dislodge anything.

If we did, no biggie.

We were just being thorough, taking this one.

We hadn't bothered to suggest a stop to collect the doormat on the back patio. We weren't interested in anything any Forster tracked up from the cove or the landing.

The doormat we wanted was flanking the side door into the garage.

I took another trash bag from the field kit.

Debra, expert now, knelt to open it.

I held up a hand, *wait*.

I turned to Forster. I didn't need to say anything. He made no effort to stop us. He just stood watching, shoulders hunched. But I couldn't resist. I wanted to slam him with it. See him squirm. Smell the sweat on him.

So I said, "I like the way you designed this, with the decorative brick edging the doormat, sequestering it from the walkway. Dresses it up. Sets it off. And very handy, snuggled right against the door to the garage here. So, you drive home from wherever and park in the garage and if you've got mud or sand or dirt on your shoes, you don't want to track it across the garage floor. I'd expect your garage is floored in something nice. Better to come out here first, wipe your shoes, and then, if need be, shake out the mat in the flower bedding. Keep this area neat and clean. Then you go back through the garage and use the interior access. Walk through the laundry room or kitchen or whatever without tracking in dirt."

His breathing was heavy, like the long day had just caught up with him.

I waited for something from him. A protest. An explanation that did not involve the opportunity to clean one's footwear when one returned from the marina after trips to Red Rock Island.

He wouldn't be worrying about today's trip, because today's footwear likely rested at the bottom of the bay, as Debra had suggested.

But earlier trips?

After they put on flip-flops and hose off the boat, after they put their shoes back on and walk to the car, they scrape the soles on the curb, or whatever is handy. Keep the car clean.

I've done it.

But it's nearly impossible to dislodge everything.

And then, back at the Sea Cliff garage, maybe, just maybe, they take the extra measure of stepping out the side door to wipe their shoes on the mat--Forster being obsessively neat, Forster having 'civilized' his cousin, training him to wipe his feet.

But it's nearly impossible to dislodge *everything*.

I said, "Did I get it right, Forster? Why you have a doormat *here*?"

He rallied. He flicked me a scornful smile. "Same reason anybody would."

I nodded my understanding. He knew it was a long shot. He knew it was unlikely we'd find mineral grains from that damnable island enmeshed in the mat.

It was.

But we were going to rock this long shot.

36

WALTER SAID, "WATCH YOUR STEP."

I hadn't stumbled but clearly Walter, above and behind me on the stairway, thought I was in stumbling territory.

Focus.

My thoughts had been elsewhere. Several elsewheres. Flicking from Red Rock Island to Sea Cliff to the lab, which we'd left in a hurry an hour ago. We'd gotten an early start this morning after a largely-useless session last night upon returning from Gregory Forster's estate, both of us wrecked. On autopilot and heading for a wall. When our eyes blurred, we called it a night.

I said, over my shoulder, to my partner, "This feel like deja-vu to you?"

"It feels steeper this time."

And emptier. No gung-ho beachgoers passing us on the way down. No mellowed beachies on the ascent. Just us, beachgoers of a downbeat sort.

We descended, step by deja-vu step, down down and down.

By the time the stairway narrowed and I tasted salty air, I'd stopped mind-tripping.

By the time we hit the sand, I was fully focused on the here and now.

Detective Talon saw us and gave a come-here flick of the wrist.

She wore her responding-to-emergency uniform, same as she'd worn on Red Rock Island: T-shirt, slacks, sneakers, black parka and ballcap with the gold SFPD logo. Her shades reflected the low afternoon sun. She stood beside the remains of a rock tower, with two pancaked rocks left standing. I wondered if she'd tried to kick it over.

Beyond her, two cops were scouting the scene.

It wasn't, technically, a scene but it was clearly headed that way.

I looked at the rocky bouldery water of the cove and the green-blue sea beyond, just turning gray at the far horizon where the fog had at last made an appearance. I looked up at the promontory. There was nobody at the edge gazing down at Mile Rock Beach.

We headed for Debra.

She said, as we drew up, "Still no luck."

When she'd phoned us an hour ago, she was brief: another message, Forster missing, get to Mile Rock Beach ASAP.

Walter said, evenly, "From the beginning, please."

"Beginning was the email, that back-channel anonymous shit, same method as the one sent to Forster yesterday that brought us all to the golf course, his daughter missing, yada yada. Only this time the GPS coordinates lead here. And this time *I'm* the lucky recipient. And this time the threat isn't directed at Jane Forster. This time it's, we will bury *him*. I wasted fifteen seconds considering who the 'him' is. You need time to figure it?"

Walter shook his head.

I said, "No."

"Good. First thing, I phoned him. Rang once then went to disconnect. I assumed he wasn't the one who shut off his phone so I scrambled a team. We get there, we knock, no answer, we make a forced entry--exigent circumstances, assume he's in danger. Search the whole place and that took some searching, place could be a hotel. No Forster. No note. No nothing. Maybe *he* got a message from the perps, same as me, get yourself to Mile Rock Beach. Maybe not. Whatever, we can hope that he left home of his own volition."

A cop passed, on the way to somewhere, shooting Debra a questioning look.

"Keep searching," she snapped.

I thought, she's expecting the worst.

She refocused on us. "So now my team's hunting here, and every damned route between Sea Cliff and here."

"If he comes here of his own volition," Walter said, "why? Given that the perps appear to be targeting *here*."

"Assuming he doesn't have a death wish, he wouldn't. Of his own volition. So maybe the perps showed up at Chez Forster, issued the invitation in person. In which case, if he's on the way here, he comes with the perps. On foot, gun to his back. In a car, tied up. In the trunk, expired."

I said, "If they're aiming for the beach, a boat's easier."

"Yes, right, Roger Forster and your Zodiac theory."

I glanced at the cove, with its lowering tide.

"We also should consider," Walter said, "that it's a hoax."

"Yes yes, thought of that. Like we considered with Jane-- who may or may not be missing of her own volition. We'll hope for a hoax, now. The Forster family, hoaxers par excellence."

I said, "Roger wasn't a hoax."

She blew out a breath. "No. Roger was verifiably not a hoax."

Whatever this turned out to be, Detective Talon was grimly

getting ready for it. The beach was cleared. Just cops. And us. And a lot of empty sand.

"Before you ask, I'm also considering that he *did* get messaged. And ran." She added, "That cover it for you?"

"Almost," I said. "Except for the fact that the email was sent to *you*."

"Yes, that. Perps had to figure we'd scramble to Sea Cliff, and then with Forster gone, that we'd follow the GPS here."

"But why would they want you here?"

"Not just me. They'd know I'd bring a team. You better believe I thought hard about that. My best guess? They want witnesses. They want us, me--and now they get you too, a bonus--to witness something."

"How would they know?"

"That I'd follow their instructions? Come here, like a good girl? Thought about that one too. Another guess but that's all I've got--they're keeping watch, hiding in the woods up there, eyeballs on us right now. Or, in a car somewhere, Forster in the trunk, watching us on their phone." She added, "Remote surveillance camera, couldn't be easier. That's how I'd do it."

We looked up, scanning the steep cliff above, the heavily vegetated slope, a gift of concealment--a vast green cloak where one could hide and watch. Binoculars, if need be. Or, Debra's remote camera perched on an outcrop or in a tree or some such, too small to be spotted, camouflaged, but with a line of sight to the beach.

"I agree," Walter said, "doable."

I said, "So they've got their witnesses. Now the question becomes, witness to what?"

"Burial." The detective shrugged. "As the email threatens. That's why I called you--you've explored the territory more thoroughly than I have. Any thoughts? Where is Gregory Forster going to be buried? Or..." she grimaced, "is he already here?"

Walter spoke first. "There is the obvious. The cave."

"Been checked. Clean and tidy. As much as a sea cave can be."

"Then I'd suggest checking the woodsy areas around the beach. A lot of places to hide in there."

"And to bury, yes. My team's on it."

We looked. I saw a uniform disappearing into the thick brush at the base of the cliff, down the beach. I glanced back at the stairway we'd descended. I knew it well, by now. Used it yesterday, with Burt Zhang leading the way. Used it day before, tracking Roger's journey, then sat here on the beach with Walter talking scenarios. I had no scenario now, for this. All I had was the worry that Mile Rock Beach was a crime scene waiting to happen.

"What else?" Debra asked.

Walter pointed to the bouldery cove.

"My rescue swimmer checked it all, when she checked the cave."

I said, "The sand. Dig a burying-deep hole."

She sighed. "Yes. Checking."

Walter said, "Then I'm afraid we've covered the territory. Perhaps we should consider a different angle--why *here*?"

"Yes, good, I've been all over that but let's do it again. The GPS, why bring us here? To be specific, the coordinates pinpointed there," she jerked a thumb, indicating the top of the promontory, "and we checked but there's nothing up there. So I'm assuming the perps were sloppy with their GPS. Because *here*, this beach, is the obvious, if Forster is the target. This is ground zero for that sordid Forster ancestor history-- which we learned about courtesy of another anonymous email."

I nodded. The old newspaper article--Mr. Li, cemetery worker who accused a Forster of grave-robbing, who fled down here to the cave, got arrested thanks to the Forsters, and died in jail. "Courtesy of Burt Zhang."

"Yes. My people should be at the dig right about now, discussing this with our archaeologist friend."

Walter said, "Let's not overlook our greenskeeper friend Ned Cunningham. He found the old grave that set things in motion. Of course, there is the question of motive."

"Golf buddy of Gregory Forster?" Debra laughed, harshly. "Motive enough."

I added, "And Jane Forster comes to mind." Missing, not missing? Definitely estranged.

"Yes, she does. I don't suppose there's anything new on the braid?"

I shook my head.

"All right. I do have something new for you two. You told me Maxie Swift said her Sacramento cousin fell to his death from the top of the promontory. I checked the department report on that. No witnesses. Judging from the scene, Louis Swift fell from the western edge, into the cove. Hit his head on a submerged rock, just about in line with that big boulder cluster. Hopefully, that knocked him out before he drowned."

I looked. Cringed.

"Burial," Walter said, "at sea."

"Yes," Debra said, "you're with me. Is this why Forster's a target, why we're here talking bury? Louis Swift died here, possibly with a push from a Forster."

"It certainly is coincidental, otherwise."

"More coincidence--Roger Forster dies here. Can you nail that?"

"More likely, he takes his last steps on the eastern beach, on the other side of the promontory. Or, possibly, at the beach outside the mine."

"When can you pinpoint it?"

"When we get more time in the lab."

"I keep interrupting you, don't I? For now, let's look at this beach as a place to exact revenge, not just for ancestral crimes but also for the modern--the death of Louis Swift. I'm looking at his brother, and the so-called Nevada Swifts. Literally. They are being looked for." She added, "Which brings me to Maxie Swift."

My gut clenched.

Walter said, "Not now."

"Don't worry, I don't believe in ghosts, especially vengeful ghosts. But Maxie is on my radar for the murder of Roger Forster." She watched us. "You don't like it. I don't like it either. But you have to see Maxie as a suspect."

"We do," my partner said.

We had. I hated it. We'd spoken it, in the lab. Motive, means, opportunity. Maxie's cousin Louis had been, perhaps, pushed off the cliff, perhaps by a Forster. Maxie drove a motorboat. There was no reason she couldn't drive a Zodiac. She'd need help--our scenarios, the car, moving the body. So, Maxie and Louis's brother. Maxie and the shitty Nevada Swifts.

But as far as being today's suspects, the Swifts were one person short.

"Speaking of Swifts," I said, "speaking of Red Rock Island, speaking of Forster, I've got a prelim on the doormat outside his garage. I found grains of manganese and did a chem analysis to characterize them. Red Rock Island is the only local source."

"No place else in the area?"

"Manganese, yes. *This* manganese, with specific percentages of the oxides of barium and silica and potassium and..."

She put up a hand. "I take your word."

I found a strained smile. "No need. The geology does the talking. Only thing I'll add is that the grains were deeply embedded in the weave of the mat. No telling when they were deposited. Or which Forster wiped his feet." I added, "Or hers."

After a very long moment, Debra said, "I can work with that. For a warrant. Later." She added, "Now, we've got a hunt on our hands."

Walter rubbed his chin. "Perhaps the perps *weren't* sloppy with their GPS. Perhaps they meant to pinpoint the promontory. You said you already had a look but why don't we take another? Get the lay of the land, all around here."

Debra nodded. "Go ahead. And, FYI, there'll be a chopper doing a sweep soon. Meanwhile, I'll redeploy my people up to the trail, expand the search area. And I'll do some scouting farther down the beach."

All righty, I thought, we have something of a plan.

37

IT WAS WINDY UP HERE.

We zipped our parkas and set our hats and discussed our strategy--in essence, take in the lay of the land.

We stepped onto the broad flat top of the promontory, which, like the beach below, had been cleared of visitors.

We decided to split the landscape, take two different paths.

Walter began counterclockwise, heading for the eastern edge.

I went clockwise, beginning where the goat path fed onto the western edge, at a cautious distance from the drop-off.

The ship's-prow shape of the promontory meant that I was soon heading for the pointed end of Lands End Point. First though, just ahead, the labyrinth sprawled. It looked purposeless without its circlers, without Viking-beard guy patrolling.

I halted near the edge of the stone spiral, wondering if Louis Swift, on his visit here three weeks ago, had done the labyrinth, and then headed over to the edge to take in the view--and leaned too far, taking that long plunge down to the sea below. Or, was he helped with a push? No witnesses, Debra had said. I could, actually, believe that there had been people up here, paying no attention, because one could lose oneself taking in the view in just about any direction. Probably could lose oneself circling the labyrinth, eyes on the ground in order to keep inside the stone pathway that led to the center, where all things converged. Taking no notice whatsoever of a guy at the edge, or even two guys at the edge.

I beelined to the spot where I judged that Louis had stood, in order to have fallen to the rocky cove below. According to Debra, he hit the water in line with that boulder cluster. I peeked down at the site of his watery landing. There was nothing below but the expected, greenish water lapping against rock, making white foam.

I shifted position to look at the beach, a wedge, with its pointy end terminating at the stairway that climbed up the cliff, up to the Coastal Trail.

I stared for a full minute. Anyone coming down the stairway would be visible once they reached the final twenty or so steps to the sand. Should the perps be bringing Forster, on foot, against his will, or under some pretext, they'd still have to get to the stairway undetected--but the trail and the cliff were currently subject to a full-on search. Should Forster, alone, be swaggering down the stairway to hoax us, same issue. Neither scenario was in the least likely.

There was nobody on the lower stairway approaching the sand.

The only person in sight was Debra, farther down the beach, now poking into the brush at the base of the slope.

Should the perps be hiding somewhere in the green expanse of the slope--watching us--they were not in my line of sight.

Nobody. Nothing.

Just us here.

I didn't like it.

I was ready to move on, to complete my circuit and meet up

with Walter, but something made me pause. There was something down there that required attention.

What?

I stared. Saw nothing new. Certainly no eye-catching shiny thing.

Then *what*?

I scanned the stairway yet again, what I could see of it before it disappeared into the woods and brush as it climbed up, and if anything was moving higher up, that thing was well hidden.

I tipped my head and looked all the way up toward the Coastal Trail, not visible from here but I knew where it would be, I'd become a frequenter of this corner of Lands End, three visits in as many days, each burned into memory. Not a question of deja vu. I just knew where things were.

Something tickled my brain.

That not-shiny thing, which had nevertheless insinuated itself. Here and gone again. Elusive notion.

All right, the thing to do when a notion is just beyond reach is to free the mind and look elsewhere.

I turned and looked for Walter and found him on his counter-clockwise stroll nearing the ship's prow. I set off, completing my own section, then meeting up with my partner at the point.

He was staring out to sea.

I asked, "A boat?"

"Sailboat. And what appear to be two fishing boats."

I glanced out to sea, where the fog still hovered. "You think someone could be monitoring the beach, from the boats?"

Walter got his binoculars and scanned. He shook his head and passed the binocs to me. I scanned. Nobody on the boats was looking shoreward. At the moment.

I returned the binocs. "You spot anything interesting on the eastern beach, during your patrol?"

"A grand and definitive nothing. You?"

"Nothing." Maybe if I walked the labyrinth, circled to the center, I'd free my mind and find the elusive *thing*.

"Then let's trade. You take my route. I'll take yours."

"Okay."

We went our separate ways.

There came the whine of a helicopter--Debra's promised chopper doing a search for the missing Forster. I watched it pass over Mile Rock Beach and then it rose and headed past us, for Nameless Beach and beyond.

I resumed my patrol, setting off along the eastern edge, traveling Walter's route, thinking about targets. Possibly, it was irrelevant that Louis Swift had fallen to his death in Mile Rock Cove; in the fevered perp mind, isolated Nameless Beach on the eastern side might well be the preferable target. Alternatively, to be thorough, since the GPS pinpointed the promontory, we had to consider that *this* was the target; perhaps the perp intended to get Gregory Forster up here and throw him over the edge.

In any case, from up here we had a birds-eye view.

I continued on Walter's route, doing what he had done. Look down and think burying.

To start, where the cliff dropped down to Nameless Cove, burying would be a watery affair. Bouldery. Lethal.

I moved another couple of yards, to the back section of the promontory. Here's where Walter and I had stood on our field trip, checking out the sketchy path that led down to Nameless Beach. Now, I looked down and checked out the beach itself.

Rockier than its cousin on the other side.

Not as pretty.

Otherwise, not much different.

To be thorough, I scanned the shore as far as I could see, the long stretch to where the beach cliffed out, beyond which was the little cove where Walter and I had removed our footwear in order to go wading, beyond which was the big-ass outcropping we'd waded around in order to reach the next beach where the tall cliff rose with its windowed eyes.

If the perps were hiding there, they'd have no view of the promontory.

Still, I looked, in case they were on the way here.

Cove, beach, cliff.

Water, sand, bare rock face.

Far above that, woods, and then the invisible Coastal Trail.

I glanced over my shoulder and saw Walter at the western edge near the labyrinth, looking, I assumed, down at Louis Swift's watery grave.

I snapped my focus back to the task at hand.

Cove, beach, cliff.

My stomach growled. I wouldn't mind a sandwich right about now--one of those San Francisco goat cheese and arugula concoctions. It was well past lunchtime and we'd had only a snack of trail mix and apples, not wanting to interrupt our lab work to go foraging. And then Debra had phoned and we'd rushed off, me leaving a dish of soil under the scope and the geo map laid out on the white table.

I was doing another sweep--cove beach cliff, thinking *buried*, thinking Forster, thinking perps with fevered brain--when my own brain suddenly ignited. I could *see* that map, in my mind's eye.

Holy shit.

I turned and dashed across the promontory's broad middle to its western edge and halted a cautious distance from the dropoff and looked at the wedge of Mile Rock Beach. The thick vegetation hid much but not all. It did not hide my shiny thing. I recognized it, now. Hell, I knew it by heart. The stairway--shiny thing hidden in plain sight.

The elusive notion bloomed in my fevered mind and turned me cold as ice.

But...how?

I was frozen in place but my thoughts didn't stand still, they roved that mind's-eye map--up and down the Lands End coast--and then, suddenly, jumped across the city, and the years, to my field-trip work on that narrow beach on Yerba Buena Island. And then ricocheted back here.

Holy holy shit.

I took out my phone and jumped online and started Googling and damn it did not take me long to start finding what I was looking for.

"Cassie?"

Walter was suddenly beside me.

"*Cassie?*"

I pointed, and blurted, "The alignment."

Now *he* looked, gazing down at Mile Rock Beach. He slowly took in the expanse, from cove to beach to stairway, past the goat-path turnoff we'd just taken, disappearing up into the wooded area, continuing on its path up to the Coastal Trail.

I explained.

He said, "It's a reach."

Yeah, literally.

"Still." He took another minute to look. And then he said, "We should get Debra up here."

Debra was returning from her scouting trip, weaving among the little rock towers, and I thought surely now she'd kick one over.

As if that mattered.

Walter cupped his mouth and bellowed, "*Debra!*"

38

"EVERYONE, EVERYWHERE IN THE ZONE." Detective Debra Talon paced across the broad top of the promontory, Walter and me in her wake. "I don't *know*. It's an informed guess but we have to assume the worst so forget the search, focus on evac, all resources, and set up the command center behind the museum."

I pictured the museum at the top of the hill, wedged between the upper and lower golf courses.

We came to the eastern edge of the promontory and paused there, Debra staring up at the cliffs, looking no doubt for a perp's vantage point.

"*Yes*," she snapped, into the phone, and then she spun and charged off in the other direction, Walter and me flanking her now, as if we might need to stop her from charging right over the edge. "Yes, the *lower* golf course, get them the hell out of there."

I recalled tramping down the lower course and got a memory-smell of newly mown grass, those volatile chemicals screaming distress.

We reached the western edge and did the sweep--cove beach cliff, and then the stairway, twenty-five-step climb before it disappeared from our view into the woods. It did some zigging and zagging up there, but all in all it took a straight line from Mile Rock Beach to the Coastal Trail.

I knew it by heart.

Debra hung up and turned to Walter. "You get hold of your guy?"

"He's on a conference call."

"Interrupt him."

"Not doable. I left a message."

She shook her head; *she'd* find a way to interrupt. Instead, she dialed her phone again. Waited. Cursed.

I had to confirm. "Forster?"

"Yes. No. Ring to disconnect. Phone still off."

Reflexively, I looked down at the beach, scanning.

"Don't bother. He's the least of my worries now."

Walter said, "Unless he's the initiator."

"Unless." She took off again, heading for the point of the ship's-prow.

We followed.

I felt useless, traipsing after her. There was more Googling I could do, a real deep dive into the literature, see if that would give me more confidence in the runaway train I'd set off. And if it didn't, what would that change? Nothing. Things were in motion. Things needed to be in motion. Anyway, my battery was low; conserve, just in case. I desperately wanted to run through it again with Walter, but we'd already done a hurried consulta- tion before Debra came charging up to join us. And he'd concurred. And he'd started Googling specialists. I picked up my pace to be within grabbing distance of Debra as she charged toward the nubbin of Lands End Point, because I didn't want to be here without her--without her and her invisible team who were scrambling, *doing something.*

Walter blocked her at the point.

She was on the phone again. "*Yes*, they say this is the best place we can be, something about the rock, same hard rock that anchors one of the bridge towers and *that* keeps standing, but we're gonna want a chopper ride as soon as you can get it here." She listened. Snapped, "I know, *I'm* the one who sent it to goddamn find him so have them finish the grid search until they're sure they can't goddamn find him."

She hung up. Swung on us. "No place else you want to wait?"

Nope. The rock here was massive greenstone, highly resistant to the forces of nature, and this mammoth fist of a promontory was testament to that geology.

I looked at Walter, who was looking out to sea.

I thought of the poem I'd asked him to concoct: *The last frontier, before one falls off the edge of the continent.* Not a poem, but suitable nevertheless.

"*Cassie*," Debra snapped, "you sure how this plays out?"

"There is no *sure*," I snapped in reply.

"How close to sure?"

"You want a percentage? Ninety percent sure?"

"That's what I want."

"I can't give it to you."

"Then guess."

I just waved a hand. Ninety percent. Ten percent. Fifty. Who knew? We needed more information.

"Debra," Walter said, turning his attention from the view to the detective, "there's no point in quantifying. What if we're only five percent sure?"

"That's a damn long shot."

I wanted to suggest she take a spin in the labyrinth, circle herself into some Zen-chill state. I wanted to take a spin, myself.

Instead, I said, "The perps *showed us* yesterday. GPS brings us to the golf course. Perps uncover the old grave, which alerts Ned the greenskeeper, who shows us the grave *and* the ground cracking from the old quake. Perps send Burt an email with a

link to that old newspaper article, which leads us down to Mile
Rock Beach and Mr. Li's cave. And the perps tell us again today--
the GPS brings us back, this time to the promontory. They
weren't being sloppy with their coordinates. They wanted us up
here. The perps *showed us the way*."

The detective just listened.

"You said it yourself, the reason they summoned *you*. To
witness. Damn fine place to bear witness, up here."

She folded her arms, fingers splayed, gripping the material
of her parka.

I fixed on her black-tipped French manicure. The nail gloss
gleamed in the sun. Utterly irrelevant. But that manicure
reminded me that this detective dives into a case like a bird of
prey and doesn't stop until she's got her talons into the perps.
Something I'd like to see, right about now.

I said, "I hope I'm wrong."

She laughed. "This is batshit crazy. And I seem to be buying
it. Because, *we will bury him*."

Yeah. Perps told us.

"What was that word you used earlier?" she asked.

"Alignment."

"No, the other word."

"Topography," I said. "The topography is a bury-him waiting
to happen."

39

DEBRA TAPPED WALTER'S ARM. "Call him back."

"I left a detailed message--another one."

"Try again."

"In five minutes," Walter said, testily.

"Why wait?"

"Because I need his expertise and five minutes is polite."

She laughed, strained. "Fine, the geology's yours. The search is mine. We're going to search. While we wait for my helicopter, we're going to use the time."

I thought that was a splendid idea. I was glad to have her refocus. We conferred, and then we all set out in search.

We paced the promontory, taking different paths, crisscrossing, scanning the coves and the beaches and the cliffs, searching as Walter and I had searched half an hour ago only then we were searching for some indication of what the perps had in mind, what sort of burial was intended for Gregory Forster. And then finally I'd taken notice of the alignment, the topography, and then time-shifted to that narrow beach on Yerba Buena Island. And made the leap.

Now there were three of us and we searched anew.

For Gregory Forster. Hoaxer, or victim.

For the perps. Bringing Forster. Hiding, watching us.

Walter phoned his guy again; left another message. Debra phoned her team again; relayed the status to us. The chopper crew was covering the grid, the roads and the paths, the cross-country route, angling for visibility through the trees. There was no sign of Forster, en route, or here.

There was nobody on either beach, nobody coming down the stairway. No sighting of watchers in the woods or an obvious surveillance camera perched on an outcrop.

We also searched the alignment, the topography. We had an unparalleled view from up here, and the time to look for small things.

Disturbed patches of vegetation.

Anything non-natural. The wrong color.

Sunlight glinting off some sort of container.

Nothing. Yet.

There was no way for Debra's people to do a ground search for explosives without putting themselves in danger. There was no way for us to do a ground search, same reason.

I checked my phone. Only seventeen minutes since we'd summoned Debra up to the promontory. It felt longer.

We continued our circumnavigation.

I neared Debra and she shot me a look. She didn't ask. Didn't have to. I shrugged; still couldn't give her the odds. She scowled and said, "If it was me I'd just lure him to the beach and hide in the bushes with a gun." I shrugged; perp might be planning that. Or the other thing, which sent a shiver creeping down my spine.

We moved along.

Walter was just ahead, near the labyrinth, and I saw him take out his phone, put it to his ear, and give us a thumbs-up. *Finally*--he got through. I hurried toward him, getting close enough to hear him ask, "Then this is a credible scenario?"

I halted beside my partner, hoping for a smile, hoping that the guy on the other end was saying that this was *not* a credible scenario.

But Walter's face was grim.

Debra drew up and joined me in the listening.

"Melange, yes we're aware," Walter said. "Clay matrix. Sheared rocks. Thank you, we've done some reading. Some fieldwork."

I thought, Walter's guy is complimenting our research. Walter's San Francisco geologist whose field of specialization is highly relevant thinks we know what's what.

Shit.

A sudden gust of wind shifted the bill of my ballcap.

Walter turned his back to the wind and ducked to protect the phone. So I missed some of his side of the conversation. Next thing I heard, Walter was talking golf course and ground cracking from the old quake, talking drainage problems on the lower green. And then he went silent. Listening.

Debra watched me, face tight.

My face, no doubt, mirrored hers.

"Yes, thank you so much," Walter finally said. "We wish you were in town, as well. I do need to conserve my battery, so I'll get back to you if we have more questions." He ended the call and pocketed the phone and stared out to sea.

I looked, as well, focusing on the creeping fog, which was still well offshore, but should it live up to its San Francisco reputation and roll in, we'd lose our visibility.

Then Walter began. "My colleague," he said, turning to us, "says that Mile Rock Beach is a highly plausible target for a landslide."

40

"Highly plausible," Debra repeated, voice tight. "Because of Cassie's scenario? The perps showed the way?"

"We didn't talk perps," Walter said. "We talked history."

"You gotta be shitting me."

History? I tensed.

"Not shitting you, detective," Walter said, with an edge. "My colleague explained that Lands End geology is notoriously unstable, especially where the rocks are a weak type known as melange. I was aware--old landslide deposits are shown on the geologic map--but I didn't give that much thought, previously. I do, now. *And*, we talked the history. *Precedent.* When Adolph Sutro built his railroad back in the 1880s, it ran along the Lands End cliffs and was plagued by slides. I read about the railroad in Forster's Sutro biography but didn't give it much thought, because it wasn't relevant to our investigation. It's relevant, now."

"All right," she said. "All right, but why don't I know this? I grew up in San Francisco. Never mind, I'm not a history buff. But sure, you hear about slides at Lands End now and then after big storms. Small slides. Not a big one, like we're talking."

"We're now talking the *likelihood* of a big one."

"All right, talk to me."

"According to my colleague," Walter said, "there is a more disturbing precedent."

"What do you mean?"

"A number of decades ago there was a landslide that reached from the cliff adjacent to the lower golf course, all the way down to the sea--in the neighborhood of Mile Rock Beach."

I tensed. I hadn't come across *that*, in my rushed not-deep-enough Google dive.

Debra stared. "All right but...*decades* ago. Nothing since?"

"The area was stabilized, to an extent, when they built the Coastal Trail. Channeling storm runoff, building retaining walls. That sort of thing."

"But?"

"But the old slide plane remains. The only thing keeping that stable is the integrity of the cliff. Destabilize that--take out that buttressing--and we could get a new slide within the old slide scar."

"Destabilize with explosives? What we talked?"

Walter threw me a nod, acknowledging my leap across the years, from Yerba Buena Island to Mile Rock Beach, from that little quake-initiated pebble slide to a big blast-initiated slide here. I didn't want acknowledgment. I wanted to be wrong.

"Yes," Walter told Debra. "Blasting could take out the buttressing."

"Where?"

"At the toe."

"Toe?"

I said, "Bottom."

She swung on me. "I get that, Cassie." She swung back to Walter. "Start a slide from the *bottom*?"

"Yes, at the toe of the old failure slope. And then that propagates up the grade, creating the momentum to pull down the rest of the slide plane with it."

"And did the old slide start with a blast?"

"The old slide," Walter said, "was likely primed by heavy wave action undercutting the cliff, at the toe. Then activated by heavy rains, which wetted the slippery clay in the melange rock."

"This is summer. Hasn't rained for months."

"There are other water sources. You'll recall the ground cracking at the edge of the golf course. If last year's quake caused that, and perhaps others, winter rainwater could have channeled deep into the slope."

"Could have."

"And you'll recall the greenskeeper said the course has had ongoing drainage problems. That could have created a pathway, funneling water down into the slide plane."

"Again, could."

"*And* with sea-level rise, conditions will have worsened, which could have further undermined the cliff."

"*Could could could.*"

"*Debra*, these are unknowns."

She took ten long seconds, then said, "So give me a known. Your blast starting this big slide. Likely, unlikely, somewhat..."

"Ninety percent."

She flinched. "*Now*, you'll quantify it."

"Now we're talking a pre-existing condition."

41

THE DETECTIVE WAS on her phone again. Pacing.

Walter and I were at the promontory's western edge, looking for any sign of the old landslide scar but the lush vegetation carpeted and smoothed the topography.

Debra passed by, shouting into her phone, "*Refueling*? Can they get here first? Enough fuel to..." And then she passed beyond my earshot, heading toward the eastern edge, and then she turned to face us across the expanse of the promontory and gave a thumbs-up, and I got it. The helicopter had enough fuel to get here, before going wherever to fill up the tank. We started for Debra. And in confirmation I heard the distant engine whine, the sound carried on the wind, and Walter threw me a grin. And then Debra, who was still on the phone, gestured at us and then the ground, and we got it, we were standing on the landing spot, so we got a move on, dashing back to the western edge, making way for our ride.

Debra followed us. Her head was bent. She was studying her phone.

The whine of the approaching helicopter grew louder.

Debra turned to look to the east.

We looked, as well.

We saw it, then, coming our way.

Walter and I exchanged another grin.

I was readying a quip about the labyrinth--glad we didn't need to clear *that* for a landing because Viking-beard guy would unleash a major frown--when Debra shouted, "*Go back!*"

At first, I thought she meant us. But that made no sense. She was shouting into her phone.

And then the helicopter that had been coming our way made a turn, a full one-eighty, and headed back the way it had come.

What? Refueling, after all?

Debra joined us. Her mouth was set. I couldn't read her eyes, shaded by her ballcap, hidden behind those aviator shades. But I could read her rigid body language. I thought, not refueling.

She spoke before we could ask. "A text message. From Forster's phone."

I said, "Is the helicopter..."

"*Gone*," she cut me off, "as in, not coming back."

I gaped.

Walter said, "What?"

She held up the phone. "Text says *stay put*. That part's for us, here. It also says, *no helicopter*. That part's for me, and I just had to make the goddamn call to send the chopper back because if I let it land and things go sideways--and don't ask how, I don't fucking know *how*--if the perps who goddamn sent the message, using Forster's phone, which is now dead again, if the perps have the means to shoot it down, to send a drone after it, who the hell knows, then I can't take the risk. Maybe it's a bluff. Probably is a bluff. But this is entirely my call and you get no say. These are my people." She hissed out a long breath. "Any comments?"

If I saw an option, I'd speak. I didn't.

Walter shook his head.

"Good," she said. "Now, *I* have questions. Two of them. First, your landslide. How the hell could the perps plan it? Know about the old slide? Know you could start a new one by blasting the toe of the...what's it called, failure slope? Who even knows those terms? Aside from you two, and Walter's specialist. How could our un-specialist perps *know* this shit?"

I found my voice and said, strained, "Google."

"You're shitting me."

"I'm not. It took me maybe half an hour to get an education. I never got to Walter's precedent slide but I did find a slide in Norway started accidentally by a blast at the toe." I added, "Admittedly, I Googled with a blast-initiated landslide in mind."

"*Exactly,*" the detective said. "You started with the idea. We don't know that the perps have that idea."

"We kind of do," I said. "They showed us the way, yesterday. Today, they messaged you to come *here*, pinpointed by GPS. And *we* came up here, because of those coordinates. They want witnesses. Like you said."

She shook her head. "What if we *hadn't* come up?"

"I don't know, they'd send you another message? The key is they waited until we were up here, when it matters. When the chopper's on the way. *Then* we're told to stay put. Bird's-eye view, great place to bear witness." As long as the damn fog stayed offshore. "I hope I'm wrong but shit, Debra, seems to me a landslide is not out of the question."

She spun on Walter. "Our un-specialist perps?"

He said, "Conceivably, they could get an education."

She stared into that distance where the fog grayed the sea and the boats still hung about.

"And your second question?" Walter asked.

She snapped her attention back. "Are we nuts to stay put?"

"We'd be nuts to do anything else."

42

IT NOSED out of the fog.

I almost missed it because the nose was gray, fog-colored, a rounded rubbery leading edge, and then the rest of the body emerged, rubbery gray sides, a small cabin taking up most of the interior, the cabin a blue plastic-looking shell with a windscreen, open at the back, and at the rear of the boat there was an outboard motor.

I said, "Zodiac."

"No," Debra said, "SFPD uses a Zodiac. That's not one."

Didn't matter. This was some make of motorized inflatable that fitted the scenario Walter and I had conjured two days ago to account for transporting Roger Forster's body, and an hour ago to speculate how the perps might transport Gregory Forster to Mile Rock Beach, and I'd been using *Zodiac* generically because that's the only make of inflatable I was familiar with, and the make didn't matter because this one was heading straight for shore.

Free of the fog now, speeding up, nose rising, throwing a foamy rooster tail in its wake.

We were moving as well, the three of us in sync, heading for the ship's-prow point, me tramping right through the outer edge of the labyrinth because it was in the way, and I kicked a stone and then another, hoping karma was off-duty.

We reached Lands End Point and halted just shy of the edge.

We lined up, shoulder to shoulder, staring out to sea.

Walter said, "One person visible in the cabin."

I squinted. Hard to see through the salt-encrusted windscreen.

Debra said, "Pass me the binocs, Walter."

I didn't need binocs to see that the sailboat and one fishing boat were gone. The remaining fishing boat was chugging southward. The inflatable was the only boat currently in play.

Debra glassed it. "The vessel ID plates are gone. Cabin left."

The boat was close enough, now, that I could see the rectangular slice of dark blue where an ID plate must have been affixed. Like a darker spot on a wall where a picture was removed. Boat had been hiding in the fog, I thought, perp likely monitoring the cell-phone camera feed or chatting with an onshore collaborator. I swiveled to scan the beaches, Mile Rock and then Nameless, and their coves, and cliffs, and if anybody had a vantage point, they were well hidden.

I turned back to watch the approaching boat. The wind brought sea spray to mist my sunglasses. The wind was so strong I felt I could lean right over and not fall off the edge.

All three of us were holding onto our hats.

The boat was nearing the cove now. It slowed, nose dropping. Even this close, the cabin's dirty windscreen impaired visibility. Still, I thought I could see that the person at the helm wore a balaclava, the eye-holes and mouth-hole dark as night.

Debra was on the phone, telling her team to stay away.

The boat idled down and the rooster tail died. It hovered at the edge of the cove, where that invisible line of demarcation separated cove from open sea.

We moved, too. In sync again, abandoning the point for the promontory's western edge, with a straight-down view of the boat. From this angle, all we could see of the cabin was its top. Perp inside was fully concealed. Behind the cabin, the back of the boat was empty.

Walter said, "Forster must be in the cabin."

Debra shouted. "*Identify yourselves!*"

There was no reply.

Debra shouted, "*Call me*. You've got my number."

She held her phone at the ready, like a test.

Waiting.

She shouted again, voice raw, "You want revenge? I'm about to get a search warrant with Gregory Forster's name on it. Hop skip and a jump to an arrest."

Nothing from the boat.

We were in another realm from search warrants and arrests.

Suddenly the boat revved up and sped deeper into the cove, swerving around the big boulder cluster that marked the watery grave of Louis Swift, and then it did a showy half-turn and stopped dead in the water.

We got a new angle of view. The cabin's open back was visible. There was a shape inside, big parka, balaclava. And then a second shape edged around balaclava-guy and came out of the cabin. Stumbling. Falling. Then catching itself with one hand braced on the tubular side. Barefoot. It wore black shorts and a long-sleeve gold T-shirt. Bare-headed, quartz-white hair.

It was Gregory Forster.

Circling his left wrist was a black zip-tie, with a cut end dangling.

He looked back into the cabin. Something spooked him, or convinced him, and he levered himself over the rubbery side and fell like dead weight into the water, rolling onto his belly.

Walter expelled a long breath.

I held mine.

Debra shouted, "*Forster!*"

He rolled his head, face coming out of the water. He was in the shallows--the water foamy and silted--and so I couldn't see beneath the surface but I could see his shoulders moving, his upper arms working, and I imagined his hands were clawing the bottom, trying free himself from the sucking sand. Finally, he lifted his torso. Then pushed himself onto hands and knees.

"*Forster!*" Debra shouted again, "*get out!*"

He looked around. Then lost his balance and pitched forward. Then righted himself. And looked around.

"He's drugged," Debra said.

Yeah.

The boat revved.

We switched attention from Forster to the boat.

It sped away to that cove-sea demarcation then made another showy turn and halted, facing shore again.

"He wants to watch," Walter said.

We turned our focus back to Forster.

He was crawling through the water to shore and when he achieved the sand, he collapsed.

Debra shouted, "*Get up!*"

It took him a full struggling minute to push up onto his knees. And then to his feet. He stood, shakily, another full minute. Testing his balance. Then he moved, small steps, turning himself to face back out to sea.

Worrying that the boat was going to return? That it wasn't?

Debra shouted, "*Forster, up here!*"

He turned himself to face the promontory and slowly tipped his head to look up at us.

And then he collapsed to the sand.

I said, "Maybe it's safe to..."

"It isn't," Walter cut me off. "You know it isn't."

"What's the timing?" Debra asked.

I knew the timing she was asking about, the time it would take the perp in the boat, or a perp ashore with a vantage point, to remotely detonate the explosives at the toe of the slope in order to destabilize the cliff, to start a process that would propagate up the grade, to pull down the works. The time it would take a landslide to reach Mile Rock Beach. The time it would take one of us to dash down there and drag a drugged Forster up twenty-ish stairs to the goat path that led to the promontory. Any way you sliced and diced it, time wasn't in our favor.

"No," Walter told Debra.

She took a step closer to the edge and cupped her hands around her mouth and bellowed, "*Landslide!*"

Forster, in a heap down below, looked up.

He was sitting squarely in the travel path--the route a slide would take, given the topography--straight down the stairway.

Debra shouted, "*Run!*" and I wondered where she'd have him run to.

She pointed, showing him the way. Run down the beach. Run southward.

It wouldn't work, would it? Even if he could coordinate enough to run, he'd have to cover too much distance to get out of the way. We knew the likely travel path that Walter's guy had spelled out but we didn't know all the runout-zone probabilities, how far it would spread once it reached the lower failure slope.

Still, there was no other way.

"*Damn it, Forster,*" she shouted, "*landslide.*"

He looked up again, craning to get a good angle on us. Shading his eyes with his uncuffed hand. Recovered enough to act like he heard, understood. And when Walter and I took up the shout, he finally showed something like alarm. Looking around. No idea why we were shouting *landslide* because there wasn't one. And now we all shouted *run down the beach* because there was no other way.

I wondered if the perp in the boat had told him anything more than, jump overboard. Did he say what awaited? Savor the shocked expression? And if so did Forster weigh the options-- jump, or get pushed. Or shot. Did he at that point understand what was going on?

Did he now?

Maybe, because he was now getting to his feet.

He looked up at us, and yelled something. It was lost on the wind. We yelled back, *run run run.* Run for all you're worth Forster, not a whole lot but it's your only option. He didn't move. He just flung out his arms and lifted his palms. Like, what the hell? Like, get down here and help me. The zip-tie cuff dangled like a bracelet. There he stood in his shorts and that shabby-chic torn T-shirt he'd worn at his estate, just as expectant now as then. And when we didn't move from our perches on the clifftop, he shook his head. I read, anger. I thought, good. He's coming to. Coming back to his arrogant self.

I screamed, "*Landslide!*"

He lowered his head, turned from the promontory, and started to walk.

"*No,*" Debra screamed.

He was heading in the wrong direction, back the way he'd come. He moved more confidently now, that arrogant Forster move. He moved right into the shallows at the mouth of the cove and when the water reached his knees and the wading became sluggish, he angled toward the promontory.

And I got it.

So did Walter. "He's going for the cave."

I yelled, "*No!*"

Debra grabbed my arm. "Why not?"

I took a step closer to the edge and leaned as far as I could safely lean and caught a glimpse of his gold shirt and then he disappeared from my line of sight. I couldn't spot the cave from up here but I could visualize it--waded into it just yesterday looking for Jane Forster. "Too shallow," I told Debra, "won't get him out of the way."

We waited for him to reverse course and return to the beach and take the only route available.

I glanced out to sea, at the inflatable boat emplaced like a brute.

Walter said, "I can't see if..." He did not complete the sentence.

We froze.

It started with a *whump*, sound like a gunshot, carried on the wind, and at the same moment a dark cloud lifted at the toe of the slope, where the woods ended on top of the small rock outcrop at the south end of the beach. And then there came a clattering sound, like waves tumbling stones, and I spotted the stones emerging from the woods, tumbling down the outcrop's rock face. Then more. Stones rained down onto the already stony beach below.

Debra gasped.

Walter gripped my hand. I gripped back.

I turned to look at the cove and I couldn't spot Forster and I pictured him crabbing to the back of the cave, and then I heard another gunshot-whump, and I spun to look back at the cliff above Mile Rock Beach and saw another dark cloud, this one closer to the stairway, where the woodsy slope gradually shallowed to the beach. Stones began to roll out from the vegetation onto the sand, slowly, like someone was gently tossing them.

Then everything stopped.

I knew I should turn and watch for Forster on the chance he'd returned to the beach but I couldn't look away from the cliff above the sand.

There were no more blasts, but the sound of rolling rock continued, expanded, rocks raining down from the cliff, and then, again, everything stopped. Everything went quiet. Eerie.

Debra whispered, "Is that it?"

We didn't answer.

We didn't know.

I took that stretch of eerie silence, that interim, to shift my viewpoint back to the cove. Empty and silent.

And then there came a terrific roar that made me jump, made Walter grip my hand so hard it hurt, made Debra shoulder up against me, nearly shoving me off my feet.

When I turned back to the cliff I saw the middle of the slope deflate, a stretch of brush and trees that simply sank. And then that section detached, leaving the cliff face bare, and the newly bared rock face started to decompose, spitting out pebbles and stones and then boulders, the lot of it charging downhill.

It ran over the beach all the way to the wet sand. Losing momentum there.

I didn't give a thought to Forster, he was on his own, if he wasn't already swamped in the cave, he was going to be buried very soon.

Another slice of the woods detached and the newly bared ground rippled like the sea, rippling upward, vibrations propagating up the grade, and the noise grew and grew, roaring and tearing, and the entire slope began to undulate, and the cliff shook, and then there was movement everywhere, the woods that had carpeted the slope were coming down, onto the beach, and the cliff itself was cracking and splintering and spitting out rock.

I fixed on a single tree, a giant, not far from the stairway, which was still untouched. The tree slowly tipped. Like a drunkard. As it fell forward, downward, its roots and the earth that still clung tipped upward. The tree, upended. Wrong way up. And then fully free of the ground it tumbled down the slope, its giant branches snapping off, and then the trunk itself splintered. I lost sight of it before it hit the beach because it was overwhelmed by a mass of rock and trees and brush and dirt and wood planks all racing downhill, and even that mass didn't race fast enough because yet another piece of the buttressing cliff failed and overtook the failing piece below it.

The dying cliff roared and the slide engendered its own weather and the wind blew our hats off.

I saw my copper-colored ballcap disappear into the gray storm.

We backpedaled, the three of us cemented shoulder-to-shoulder, backing away from the blitz down below.

We still had a line of sight to the stairway.

It was covered in stones and rocks.

It was fogged by clouds of dirt.

But still I could make out the steps. I could use it as a marker to keep track of the alignment.

The stairway was the final travel path of the landslide.

Up above, way up, somewhere around the Coastal Trail, the cliff shuddered and then shook off its woodsy cover, and that slice of Lands End came roaring down the slope, down down down the steep stairway, the same route Walter and I had traveled three days in a row.

And then there was no more demarcation between slope and cliff and woods and bare rock, there was just an uproar bearing down on Mile Rock Beach.

My mind skittered.

I wondered if the lower golf course had gone, too. And with it, the old grave.

I wondered if everyone way up on the top of the bluff--up at the museum, up there where Debra's command center was set up--if they could see the ground down below disappear.

And then my focus snapped back to the beach below, littered with rocks and trees and planks and pipes and a brown metal shard with a white painted arrow that had once been a sign we had no doubt followed. And then it was all gone--the beach and its debris--as the landslide charged out from the remains of the cliff, roaring across the beach, a runaway train that ran headlong into the only obstacle left.

The cove.

The water boiled up into a mini-tsunami that rushed the beach, that battered the foot of the promontory. Somewhere in that maelstrom was Gregory Forster. A small ugly part of me thought, he ends in Mr. Li's cave, or washed out into Louis Swift's watery grave.

Walter said, "Can't see the boat."

I looked. Couldn't find it. The mammoth dirt cloud sailing out to sea and the mist thrown up by the boiling water obscured the boat. The onslaught from the land had met the fog bank at sea and built an impenetrable wall of nothingness.

43

WE WERE STATUES.

Cemented in place, draped in dust.

Realizing it was over.

My legs went soft and I wanted to drop to the ground, cement myself there. Just sit until I could breathe freely. I wore my bandana. Walter wore his. Debra had pulled up her parka. The air was thick with dust. With particulates. With the pulverized aerosolized remains of what had existed half an hour ago.

Debra coughed.

Reflexively, I coughed.

Walter cleared his throat. Spoke. "Call your chopper, Debra." His words were muffled by his bandana.

But she caught them. Coughed. "Not till I know where that damn boat is."

From our position at the promontory's western edge, the view out to sea was murky. There was fog, sea mist, suspended dust. The damn boat could be heading for the cove right now and we wouldn't see it.

The cove was a slurry.

I tried to think of Forster down there. Washed out of the cave by the surge, buried in the congealed cove.

I couldn't focus on him.

I shifted my focus to the near view, to the labyrinth, which I could identify by the faint outline of stones beneath the thick dust. Majorly bad karma.

Reluctantly, I turned to look down at Mile Rock Beach. It was a field of debris topped by floating gray clouds of dust. The cliff that backed the remains of the beach was hollowed out, a gaping gray wound. There was no indication of a stairway.

Walter said, "Let's move to the eastern side. Maybe it'll be cleaner."

I fell in behind Debra, who flanked Walter, and we tramped across the broad top of the promontory. Stirring up dust with every step, making footprints in the moonscape.

When we reached the eastern side I saw, in relief, that Walter was right. The dust was marginally thinner. Visibility was marginally better.

Farther away--to the east, where the sea narrowed into the strait that ran under the Golden Gate Bridge--it appeared that the sea was mantled by good clean fog. The boat was possibly hidden in that gray cloak. Possibly--work done--it had hightailed off to wherever it came from.

I looked down at Nameless Cove, Nameless Beach.

It was another country down there. Intact.

The three of us sank to the ground.

And then Debra got her phone and called someone and reported that we were safe, and asked if everyone else was safe, and--pausing to cough---said, "We'll be wanting the chopper."

When she hung up, she told us they'd prefer to wait until the air cleared.

I used my parka sleeve to wipe dust from my sunglasses and

then stared into the distance, resting my eyes on the thick green vegetated unmolested clifftop to the east.

My breathing steadied. I lowered my bandana, sampled the air, then raised my bandana. Nothing to do but wait. One could lie back in the dust and go to sleep. Instead, I closed my eyes. Maybe slept, sitting up.

"*Shit*," Debra said.

My eyes snapped open. She was on her feet. Walter was saying "*What*?" and levering himself up from the ground. I followed suit, dizzy, adrenaline spiking.

She was staring down at Nameless Beach.

She said, "It's Forster."

44

GREGORY FORSTER WAS DRAPED on the rocky sand of Nameless Beach. On his back, arms flung out, legs splayed. Eyes open or closed, I couldn't tell from the angle of his head, but he wasn't moving. Battered. Bruised. Blood matted his white hair. Blood covered his right ankle. A big cut there. I could see that, from up here. Up close, it would be worse.

"How..." Walter began.

I found my voice. "He swam it."

Debra looked at me as if I'd said he'd flown.

"He told me he's a swimmer. A fit rough-water swimmer." I tried to work out angles, the distance from Mile Rock Cove to Nameless Cove--shorter if you hug the promontory but then you have to keep the waves from battering you into the base of the cliff you're trying to swim around. I tried to work out a recovering Forster's top swimming speed, the possibilities. No style, just brute force.

Debra was shouting again.

We'd been shouting at him...how long ago? Half an hour? I wasn't sure. I'd lost time. He'd been drugged, then. Confused. And then slowly recovered his senses. Hell, he'd roused to become his arrogant self. And that's how he'd found the where-withal to get going, get a head start, get around the point. Dodge the cataclysm. With arrogance. With skills from his daily swims. We hadn't seen him because we weren't looking. Even if we'd thought of it, we'd have needed to stand at the very edge and look straight down to see his swim path. But we weren't looking because we were watching the onslaught.

"*Forster!*" Debra shouted.

His left arm twitched.

All right then, not dead. Sure, I could believe that Forster survived. In fact, it was now hard to imagine otherwise. He was a cockroach, hard to kill.

Walter said, "Call in the chopper."

Debra phoned.

They wanted to wait because the air here was still bad, because particulates could play havoc with the engine.

Walter said, "We can't just leave him down there."

"Much as we'd like to," Debra said.

Still, we waited, talking inflatable boat, talking remote cameras placed on clifftops, talking perp--perp, singular, because we'd seen just one inside the cabin--talking the state of mind of that perp who thought he'd accomplished what he'd come for, who might be seeing what we were seeing and realize he'd missed his target.

And then what?

Drive the boat out of the fog into Nameless Cove, storm the beach?

Debra was armed.

Yeah, and if *he* was armed he could shoot from the boat.

Yeah, but he didn't want us. He'd made sure we were high above the cataclysm--as witnesses--out of harm's way. He'd wanted Forster.

The perp would want him now.

On the other hand, it was equally likely he thought he'd gotten Forster and was headed home.

While we talked we started moving toward the sketchy path that led down from the promontory, not fully committed but getting into position to commit. By the time we reached the path, things had changed.

Forster was on his feet.

Bruised, bloodied. His ripped gold T-shirt had a red smear like a sash. The zip-tie cuff still clung to his wrist.

Debra yelled, "*Get behind that boulder.*"

He heard her. Turned. Looked up. Turned away.

"What the hell?" I said.

He started to walk, slowly picking his barefoot way through the pebbles and rock shards, heading east along the beach--that walk Walter and I had taken two days ago on our way to the mine.

That where Forster was headed?

Why?

Debra said, "Nobody's shooting at him."

There was no boat in the cove. Maybe there was a second perp, in position somewhere to take a shot at Gregory Forster, finish the job, and if so he had plenty of time. Forster was making excruciatingly slow progress. I thought I spotted a trail of blood in the sand. Hard to tell, at this distance. Could be just feathery red seaweed.

"I have to go after him," Debra said. "Shit."

Walter said, "Check on the chopper."

"Not putting it at risk."

She moved the short distance to the top of the sketchy path, and glanced at us. "This *is* the way? The way you two went down?"

I could only nod.

Walter said, "You know first aid, Debra?"

"Been a while."

"I got re-certified last month. And I have a kit."

There was no way I was allowing Walter and his first-aid kit to go down there without me.

The footing was just as tricky as I remembered. This time, though, my throat was raw from the dust. Breathing rough. Legs shaky. Balance shitty. The three of us descended with excruciating care, keeping our eyes on our feet until we reached the rocky sand.

And then we scanned the long expanse of Nameless Beach.

Forster was just passing through the gnarly boulder field. Then he came to that part where the beach cliffed out, to the mini-cove where Walter and I had stopped to remove our footwear. Forster didn't pause. He was already wet and barefoot. He waded into the water.

We set off.

By the time we reached the mini-cove, he'd already rounded the big-ass wedge of cliff.

We stopped, agonizing about footwear, because Forster's destination was surely the mine and if we needed to follow him inside we didn't want wet shoes. We removed our boots and tied them to the packs, Walter taking Debra's sneakers. We rolled up our pant legs.

Debra phoned her team, apprising them of our intention.

We plunged into the chill water and mucked through the squishy sand and when we rounded the cliff wedge Debra paused to stare--yeah, I remembered, that first sight of the windowed cliff that stops you in your tracks. Then we plunged ahead to catch up to Forster, who was just sloshing onto the beach. I'd expected him to head to the sea cave, but he'd chosen a site farther west. He stood staring up at the cliff at the far end of the beach. I wondered what he saw. My gut clenched. The perp up there, looking out a window?

We came ashore in time to hear him shout his daughter's name.

Stopped me wondering.

As Debra and Walter flanked Forster, I looked again. That end of the beach dead-ended in the cliff wedge and the only way past it was the way we'd just come. I studied the rough rock, which jutted out from the cliff, which made something of an L, enclosing the beach. I tipped my head back and saw an indentation in the rock where the wedge met the cliff, close to the bend of the L. The wedge was in shadow and it took me a moment to see that the indentation was another window. I couldn't tell if there was someone in there, and if there was, if that person was Jane Forster or the perp or just a fabrication of my tired trickster eyes.

Forster called her name again, voice thin as his shirt.

Walter said, "You're bleeding, Forster."

I looked. There was blood on his shirt and arms and legs. His bloodied head looked bloodier, up close.

Walter said, "I'll get the first-aid kit."

Forster started to move but Debra grabbed his arm and spun him around. She snapped, "We'll go look but not until you goddamn tell us who the perp is and where he's gone, because you're not in this alone anymore, *we're* here because of you, because you pissed somebody off so badly they brought down a cliff trying to bury you." She coughed, hacked, spat. "And you know what? This mine could be on your enemy's hit list, and we're in the shit along with you, and..."

Walter hissed, "*Stop.*"

She turned a murderous look on Walter, but she stopped.

He said, "Turn around."

Debra and Forster and I turned away from the window in the western cliff, to face the expanse of beach in the other direction.

There was a man in front of the sea cave pointing a gun at us.

My legs went soft, like sand.

We put our hands in the air.

He was several yards away but I recognized him immediately, by his balaclava, which he'd worn on the boat, which he wore still, now with big shades hiding the eye-holes. The mouth was a small black hole.

He must have been hiding in the sea cave when we waded our way here.

Where was his boat?

Didn't matter.

He was here. *He*, I decided, because of his size and bulk, although the bulk was in part the big chunky parka and the thick sweatpants. On his back was a bulky pack, and on his front was a black corded harness that looped his shoulders and circled his chest, and held a black cell phone. He moved our way. With his free hand, he tapped the phone, then nodded at us and gave a thumbs-down.

We hesitated a moment too long.

There was an explosion, a sharp crack, a gunshot, and the sand kicked up in front of us.

We got our phones and tossed them to the ground.

He tapped the gun with a forefinger, then pointed at Debra.

She got it quickly enough. She unholstered the pistol at her hip and tossed it. He waited. She took off her parka and spun around--no shoulder holster, no pistol tucked in the back of her pants. She lifted her pant legs. No ankle holster. She emptied her pockets--wallet, keys, small notebook, pen. She opened her palm--what else do you want from me?

Nothing. As she put on her parka and refilled her pockets, he aimed the gun at Walter and me.

We emptied our pockets. Wallets. Keys. Chapstick. A crum-pled receipt. We took off our packs, opened them, upended them, and dumped the contents on the sand. Our gear--warm hats and gloves, headlamps, water bottles, energy bars, first-aid kit, emergency foil blanket, maps and compass and pens and notebooks and the field kits--littered the ground. He waited. We opened the field kits. I was hyper-aware of the pointed-tip rock hammer, and the field knives. He lifted a hand and made a hammering gesture. Thumbs down. I removed it. I thought the knives were next. They weren't. He gestured for us to repack.

Rock hammer not okay. Knives okay. Whoa.

When we'd refilled our pockets and shouldered our packs, he gestured at our bare feet.

Walter and Debra and I dropped to the sand and retrieved our footwear and as we pulled on socks I glanced at Forster's bare feet and I thought any way you sliced and diced it there was nothing good about what was allowed, what was required, the only takeaway being the perp wanted us prepared, from here on out. And barefoot Forster be damned.

When we got to our feet, the perp turned the gun on Forster.

Forster, in damp shorts and torn T-shirt, clearly carried nothing. He stood shivering, facing the man who had already tried to kill him, bury him, obliterate him. Who could right now finish the job with a twitch of his trigger finger. Forster was rooted in place. Afraid to look away, or working himself up to something else.

It was something else. He bowed his head.

I thought *smart*, Forster.

But it wasn't. There was no space between the submission and the gunshot. Sand sprayed at Forster's bare feet. He stared at the sand then raised his head to face the perp, and for what seemed an impossibly long stretch of seconds, the two men faced one another.

I held my breath.

Forster turned away. Without a backward glance, he started

up the beach toward the wedge that led up to the far window near the bend of the L where it met the cliff, the tunnel stub cut off from the main tunnel. Where he believed his daughter waited.

We had no choice but to follow him.

I waited for another instruction by gunfire to change course, but it didn't come. We were headed where the perp wanted us to go. The last place I wanted to go.

Ahead, there was blood in the sand. Forster's bare feet. Up close, the droplets looked nothing like feathery red seaweed.

Walter and I fell in behind him, matching his halting pace.

Debra walked beside him. "Get an ID, in the boat?"

He shook his head.

I wondered how that mattered, right now. This was a guy who triggered explosions to bring down a landslide. This was a guy with a gun in one hand and the other weapon holstered on his chest, a cell phone that could send a trigger signal to an explosive initiator. That's what mattered.

There was sand in my socks, chafing my skin. I wanted to take off my shoes and dump it.

We gained the foot of the big wedge and Forster gestured at the crags in the rock and Debra took his arm and helped him start to climb.

Walter and I followed.

As we wound our way up I realized I would not have found this sketchy path on my own because it was all but hidden from the beach. One had to know the way. Forster, who'd explored this mine, clearly did.

When we neared the debris field below the window in the cliff, where past rockfalls had created something of a slanted ledge, we halted, piling up one behind the other. Forster was now in the lead. Above him was the window--its sill, for want of a better word, a low ragged rocky windowsill--was just above him. He slowly climbed up the ledge. It wasn't a difficult climb. I could have done it in moments. But I wore boots. I hadn't battled the sea and the waves swimming around the promontory. I hadn't dragged myself along Nameless Beach. If this was anyone else hauling themselves up the ledge, I would have felt admiration. What fortitude. But it was Forster. I felt only fury that we were about to climb into this window because of him.

This close, I could see that the window was partially collapsed, the opening no more than three feet high and maybe six feet long. It looked like an open mouth stretched wide, rimmed with broken teeth.

Forster reached the windowsill and took hold of the jagged edge. He leaned forward, then made a strangled sound.

Debra scrambled up the slanted ledge and stepped around Forster and shoved her sunglasses to the top of her head and bent to climb onto the sill, then stepped inside, disappearing into the dark. A moment later she appeared at the window and took Forster's hands to guide him inside.

I held my breath, waiting for one of them to speak. *Come ahead. Go back.*

I turned to look at the beach and saw the man still in place, aiming his weapon at Walter and me, the only ones still outside. I saw that the phones and the gun and my rock hammer were gone. I saw that the fog was coming in, blanketing the dusty air. I wondered, again, where his boat was. Next cove over, to the east? Cove after that? He anchors there and then clambers over some cliffy wedges, or just wades here. Then into the sea cave, to await us. Which meant he knew Forster was coming. Saw him swimming, or draped on Nameless Beach?

Walter all but pushed me up the ledge and over the windowsill. I landed inside in a crouch. Walter came down onto the rocky floor beside me.

It was murk in here.

I took off my sunglasses.

It took moments for my eyes to adjust. Light from outside filtered in but this room--for want of a better word--was deep enough that darkness swallowed the light at the back.

What I could see: Debra and Forster, vague shapes humped like boulders. Beyond them, another shape, but this one was slumped against a tall boulder, which was part of a debris pile, maybe waste rock from the original cutting of the window.

So she was here. Forster was right.

He called his daughter's name.

Debra said, "We need light."

Walter and I got our headlamps and fumbled them into place and switched them on.

In the light, we could see that Jane Forster was bound by a yellow rope, twice looped around her waist like a belt, the rope shoving her own belt and jeans lower on her hips. Our beams caught the end of the rope, where it circled behind the boulder, disappearing like a snake back into the debris that piled against the rough wall.

Debra said, "Somebody untie her."

Walter got there first, repositioning her so that he could get at the knot at her back. Her head swiveled, watching him.

Debra said, "Hurry, Walter."

"It's a constrictor knot," he said.

"What's a constrictor knot?"

"Pull on it, it tightens down. I need a knife."

I got my field knife and came over, remembering the last time Jane and I had faced one another, in the other tunnel, hostile Jane with her blue braid. Now, her hair was short and she was cringing away from my headlamp beam.

I shifted my light and gave the knife to Walter.

As he sawed at the yellow rope that linked Jane to the boulder, to the debris pile, to the wall, I took note of the plastic shopping bag on the ground, which spilled water bottles and snack bars. A plastic trowel was staked into a small pile of loose dirt, her toilet I supposed. The meager basics. No light--her headlamp was gone. Helmet gone too.

"*Jane*," Debra said, "there a bomb in here?"

She'd been watching Walter. She shifted her attention to Debra.

"No? Yes? You don't know?"

Her shoulders lifted.

"Bomb outside the window?"

Her shoulders lifted.

"Guy in disguise with a gun and cell phone strapped to his chest--he put you in here?"

She nodded.

Debra hissed, "*Hurry up*, Walter."

"Almost."

I knelt and stuffed the bottles and snack bars back into the shopping bag, and then added the trowel. Thinking, perp wanted to be sure we could cut Jane free. Left us our knives. And if we had none? I guessed Walter would have figured how to untie a constrictor knot. But Walter did have my knife, and the cut rope now fell to the ground, leaving a tag end like a tail at the knot, and Jane sagged away from the boulder, still wearing the yellow rope loops around her waist.

Forster caught her.

"*Jane*," Debra said, "there a tunnel back there that leads somewhere we can take shelter?"

She made a sound. A croak.

"*What?*" Debra snapped.

Forster answered. "She said yes."

"Then let's get the hell out of Dodge."

Walter and Forster got Jane around the waist and they moved toward the back of the room. Debra and I closed ranks behind them. My headlamp beam joined Walter's and lit the way to the tunnel beyond.

The tunnel branched off the room like a branch off a trunk, and we followed it a short distance and then it took a sharp bend to the left and I tried to map it as it had looked from outside--from the beach when I'd studied the far window where the rock wedge met the cliff at the bend of the L--that's where we were now, around that bend. And then we came to a small area where the tunnel pouched out, an alcove of sorts. Beyond that, as far as our beams reached, the tunnel continued. Further, it was swallowed in darkness.

"*Jane*," Debra said, "can we get out that way?"

She croaked, "Cave-in."

"Shit."

I agreed, growing colder than I'd already been. But cave-in ahead or not, it didn't matter because every step we put between ourselves and the window room--between us and whatever was on the receiving end of the perp's cell-phone signal--was a step in the right direction.

We continued, all of us trying to pick up our pace but the tunnel floor was rocky and uneven and none of us were at our best. As we snailed along I thought to turn my headlamp down to low power. Save the battery. Walter threw me a nod and had just reached to turn down his light when the blast came.

45

CACOPHONY. Thunder. Pain.

Pain in my ears. Covered them. Hit the ground. Hit a rock. More pain.

A yelp, from Forster.

I looked for Walter and found him on the ground beside me, hands over his ears.

Turned, found Debra. Same.

And then the tunnel filled with dust.

Yanked up my bandana, covered mouth and nose. Deja vu.

It must have been five minutes before we all sat up. Looking around. My headlamp lit the rock. The slice of tunnel I could see appeared intact. Didn't trust it, though.

I wanted to let everything settle. Whatever settling was going to occur.

Walter shut off his headlamp.

I kept mine on low power although its beam was dimmed by the dust.

We sat in the gloom saving batteries, waiting for the rocky sound of collapse.

Minutes passed. More. Who knew how many? We had no phones to time it.

Finally, Debra choked out, "Everybody okay?"

Forster said, "No." A small strangled sound.

I turned and my weak beam highlighted Forster. The wounds on his head and arms and legs and feet were still oozing. He was shaking so hard his feet knocked together. I couldn't tell if his T-shirt and shorts were still damp but they likely were because the weather outside had turned dank and foggy and the weather in here was even danker.

The man was on the way to hypothermia.

Walter already had his pack off and he stripped off his parka and put it around Forster's shoulders. In the end, Walter had to unclench Forster's hands and thread his arms through the sleeves. I got the emergency foil blanket from my pack and joined my partner to render aid, wrapping the blanket around Forster's legs.

The man was pitiable, now.

I didn't pity him.

Jane sat like her father, hugging her knees, but she wasn't shaking. She was warmly dressed. Best I could tell, she wore the same baggy blue parka and sweatshirt and jeans she'd worn two days ago, when she ambushed us. Kidnapped in those clothes. Or maybe she had another set. Maybe that was the extent of her wardrobe. Bottom line, they kept her alive in this dank place.

My heart squeezed for fierce Jane Forster.

My heart squeezed for us all.

Walter found the shopping bag I'd dropped. He withdrew a water bottle and held it to Forster's mouth.

Debra eyed the shopping bag.

I shook my head. Limited supply.

Let Walter hydrate Forster. Last thing we needed right now was to nurse an incapacitated Forster. Nobody spoke. We all understood--surely--how well and truly fucked we were in here. My heartbeat had been going a mile a minute ever since the blast. I took in a long Zen breath. My partner gave me a level look. No reassurance in that look, no pretense.

Finally, once Forster was stabilized, Debra said, "All right, since it looks like the rest of this place isn't coming down on our heads, I'm going to go find us a way out. And I could use some help."

I noticed--inconsequentially--that the sunglasses that had rested on top of her head were gone. I noticed that mine were crushed in my cargo pocket. I fished out the pieces and tossed them aside. No need for sunglasses in here, anyway. My heart started to race and my throat closed and I broke out in a sweat.

Walter cast a glance at Forster but Jane whispered, "Go."

Walter gave her his headlamp, raised his bandana, then looked at me.

Yeah. I steadied my breathing, tightened the bandana knot, shouldered my pack and turned my light to high power.

I left my field knife for the Forsters, to cut away the zip-tie handcuff and the yellow rope binding.

46

FIRST, we headed for the window room, moving on little cat feet, ears cocked for any sound of anything shifting.

Once we rounded the bend of the L, we slowed even more, studying the ceiling and the walls as I painted them with my light.

Dust was in the air.

The tunnel came to an end, branching into the window room.

There was no window. There was not much of a room. What remained was impassable, choked with debris.

"Perp knows his explosives," Debra said, words muffled by her parka-mask.

Yeah. Knew when he planted the explosives at Mile Rock Beach. Knew, here.

"Let's go," Walter said.

We carefully retraced our route and when we reached the Forsters, we uncovered our faces and Debra told them, "Still searching."

We kept going.

The tunnel got rougher. The walls looked undone, as if the

tunnel builders had run out of tools, or time. Rock bulged out here and there, forcing us to squeeze together, and then when we passed the obstructions we spread apart again.

The floor was rougher, as well. I mediated between playing my light along the floor ahead so we could assess our footing and aiming it straight ahead, toward that end point where light was swallowed.

The closer we got, the more my thin hope faded.

We knew before we reached the end.

Jane was right.

There was a cave-in.

The tunnel was as choked as the window room, although there was no dust here because the obstruction here had occurred in the past, and settled into permanence.

Hope died.

We stood numbed.

Then Debra said, "I guess we dig."

Walter grunted. "With what?"

I nearly laughed. Preferably, with a brick of the C4 or whatever explosive the perp carried in his pack. With a power drill. With tools left behind by the nineteenth-century tunnel builders. If we'd had my rock hammer with its sharp tip I'd have been willing to attack the pebbles and cobbles chinked in between the bigger cobbles and boulders, try to work those big bad boys free. But we didn't.

My heart raced.

"Jane had a trowel," Debra said.

It was a plastic trowel good for digging toilets and sand castles. I choked off a laugh before it turned into a scream. Before I fell to my knees and started digging at the pebbles and cobbles with bare fingers--because if that was the only way *out* then I was going to dig--Walter grabbed my hand and I realized I'd grabbed his shirt sleeve. His hand was shaking, in mine.

After an eternity, I whispered, "Trowel's better than nothing."

"All right." Debra cleared her throat. "All right, my people know we were heading for the mine. They'll figure this out. They'll go in through the sea cave. I assume that tunnel you two told me about will lead them to the other side of this rock pile. I assume they'll figure out we're here. So we'll go get that trowel, go get the supplies, go get the others, and we'll make camp here and take turns *doing something*. And when we hear my people on the other side of this rock pile, we'll shout until they hear us."

If they come.

Hear us through who-knows-how-many-feet of solid rock?

With however much air we have left to breathe, left to spare for shouting.

Motormouth Debra was wasting air, spouting her plan. But I nodded in agreement, because she didn't give up, and that gave me air.

My breathing steadied.

We turned our backs on the rock pile and headed downtunnel.

I switched from panic to numb. To automatic. I knew this drill, traversing old mine tunnels.

My boot caught on a rough patch and Walter took my arm and I steadied and nodded, and paid closer attention to my footing. We'd already traversed this tunnel, but the uneven floor was in a different orientation.

We moved slowly.

My heartbeat picked up, though.

My thoughts raced faster.

How long before the air cleared enough for Debra's chopper to fly?

How long before a ground team arrived?

Maybe Debra's people would indeed figure it out. As long as they didn't conclude we'd gone elsewhere. Question was, would that now-collapsed window look newly collapsed, from the beach? If one were looking? If one got to the beach before the fog grayed out everything. Before twilight set in.

We had gone about halfway when my light caught something on the floor, edged by a bulge in the tunnel wall. I stopped. Walter and Debra stopped. I cut around Debra--who flanked me on the tunnel's beach side. I knelt in front of the bulging rock, dipping my head so my lamp illuminated the ridges on the ground.

It took a long moment to read them. They were faint. Sketchy. Much of the sketch was missing.

If I hadn't seen their like before, I wouldn't have given these a glance.

But I had.

Holy shit.

I wished my headlamp had a mega-high-lumen setting because these faint ridges deserved the limelight. I wanted to showcase them. I wanted to light this place up. And then I didn't. My light was just enough. All we needed. The others crowded in and I wanted to hug them but instead I moved to give them room. Walter crouched beside me and looked at the ground. I swore I felt him grin. Debra, still standing, said, "*What?*"

I would have leaped up to drag her down for a close look but I couldn't tear my gaze from the gouges petrified in mudstone.

"Raccoon tracks," I said.

47

I STOOD and shut off my headlamp.

Before Debra could utter another *what*, we saw the glow.

It was high up on the tunnel wall, a faint halo that leaked from the edges of a rough slab of rock, which rested on a small outcrop and angled against the wall higher up.

We stared at the light for ages.

And then it was decided that one of us should try to climb up the knobby wall, and Debra decided it should be me, because I was younger and fitter than Walter--and it was decided that Debra should stand watch on the tunnel floor below me, because she was younger and fitter than Walter and able to catch me if I slipped. Although Debra didn't put it that way.

I gave Walter my headlamp so he could spot me.

It proceeded like a dream.

I found myself assessing the wall and locating hand- and foot-holds, the way I've assessed cliffs in the field that required climbing.

And then I was climbing. I climbed nose to rock, pausing with every couple of inches gained to assess, and reassess, and I slowly monkeyed my way up the wall, breathing in the sweet scent of old rock and fresh air. Air came down from above, with the light. I refused to expect anything more than a tiny source. I banked my hopes on that, a tiny opening in the tunnel wall that unsealed our tomb.

The climb was doable.

When I'd reached a spot that paralleled the outcrop upon which the slab rested, I gripped a knob of graywacke and turned my head to get the lay of the land.

Between the angled slab and the tunnel wall there was a space.

Bigger than tiny.

It was too small for a raccoon, though--at least the ones I'd ever seen. The raccoon that had made those tracks fossilized in the tunnel floor would have needed a bigger entrance. No doubt this opening had once been bigger. A window. And then erosion or settling or an earthquake or bad luck had partially collapsed it, breaking off the slab, which slipped down and came to rest on the little outcrop.

Leaving behind a gift.

Light and air came in through that small opening in the tunnel wall, and the light lasered inside like a flashlight beam and struck the slab, was deflected, and haloed around its edges.

It was a tiny glow. Had been subsumed by the light from my headlamp. We would have missed it entirely but for the prints of the long-gone raccoon.

A mercy.

I grinned.

I called down to my team, "I'm going to squeeze behind the rock slab."

Walter called, "Careful."

Debra called, "Go for it."

I went for it. Side-stepped over to the outcrop ledge. Side-stepped behind the slab. Found myself sandwiched between the slab and the tunnel wall. Between a rock and a hard place. A nightmare scenario, any other place, any other time. I braced for the adrenaline shot of claustrophobia but nothing came. The claustrophobia had been shocked out of me.

Above me, there was light and air.

I had to stand on tiptoe to reach the remnant of the raccoon's window. Only got to eye level. No worry. I kissed the tunnel rock and eyeballed the world outside.

It was a mostly gray world--fog blanketing the sea, heading for shore, the shore empty gray sand. My view was limited to a small empty slice of the western end of the beach.

It was a porthole to the world.

I didn't want to leave.

Back down on the tunnel floor, I reported.

After high-fives all around, it was decided that Walter and I would gather the others, and the meager supplies, and we'd set up camp here.

It was decided that Debra would climb up and take my place at the porthole, Debra being taller by several inches, nearly as tall as Walter--and Debra being skinnier than Walter, who muttered something about backing off desserts.

All in all, Debra was suited to get into position for the best viewpoint.

To keep watch.

48

WALTER and I sat facing the Forsters.

Jane wore Walter's headlamp, set at low power, dim as a dying campfire.

We spoke in whispers.

We'd gathered just uptunnel of the raccoon porthole--close enough to breathe its air, far enough to muffle our light and our voices because we didn't know what could be seen and heard from the beach below.

We had a view of Debra's right leg and foot, her black sneaker planted on the small outcrop ledge.

Plan was, if she spotted the perp she'd toss a small rock to the tunnel floor. An alarm, to alert us to shut off the light and shut ourselves up. Play dead. Don't alert him to our porthole. We didn't know if he had enough explosive left to blast the cliff and the porthole out of existence.

We assumed, hoped, he'd gotten what he wanted--seal us in here until we withered to husks, to bones. After all, he'd waited until we left the window room, until the light from our headlamps disappeared as we moved into the tunnel, until we were safely out of the way. And *then* he blew the window the hell up.

Question was, how long was he going to wait on the beach, savoring his revenge? At some point, he'd have to make his escape. Certainly before Debra's people arrived. Maybe he'd already left. Or maybe he was waiting for the fog to advance enough to cloak him while he made his way to his boat.

Either way, plan was that Debra would keep a lookout for our rescuers. When the air cleared enough for a chopper, or enough time passed for a ground team or a Zodiac team to arrive--she'd hear. See them. And then she'd shout *in here*, and flash a beam from my headlamp out the porthole. And--because Search and Rescue might be making so much noise they wouldn't hear Debra's shouts--she said we should hang a flag out the porthole.

We grew almost giddy. Debra called down from above, "How about white underwear? Mine's black and lacy, don't ask. Anybody wearing white?" Nobody was. She called down, "Then Forster's gold shirt." The shirt was by now dirt-gray. Screaming yellow would have been preferable but nobody in here dressed in neon.

The mood, though, flickered like neon, arcing from excitement to worry to expectation to caution.

It took us several minutes to settle down.

Walter's headlamp flickered, then steadied.

Giddiness evaporated.

Walter got to work, opening the first-aid kit and moving to tend the nasty cut on Forster's foot. Forster had stopped shaking, warmed in Walter's parka. I resented him for that. Walter wore a long-sleeve Capilene shirt and a wool hat but I still worried he'd get chilled.

Jane watched as Walter finished the foot and moved on to the head wound.

And then she whispered, "What happened to him?"

Forster grew a hopeful look that nearly got to me.

She ignored him. She appeared, I noticed, stronger. Sat straighter. And she'd just used more words than she'd spoken since we'd found her. It had been maybe half an hour since we'd climbed into the window and this was the first she'd shown interest in her father. They had, by necessity, cut off each other's bindings. Now, by necessity, they sat close to one another.

Walter answered her. "Someone took a dislike to your father."

"Who?"

"Guy outside."

She asked her father, "Revenge for Louis Swift?"

Forster jerked, and Walter stopped bandaging and said, "Stay *still*," and Forster went still as a small animal. He whispered, "I don't know anything about that. All I know is I'm sorry I lost you for so long."

She stared at him.

I wondered what he wanted. Her forgiveness? Something more? More likely he wanted her silence, no more questions about the Swifts. I wondered what she wanted. A reckoning? Reconcile the hurts of the daughter with the reality of the father? She watched him so carefully.

I glanced at the tunnel wall and saw Debra's sneaker move, a tiny side-step. She was hearing us, from up there.

Jane asked her father, "What'd the guy do to you?"

He began to shake. The memory of his ordeal, maybe. The chill in the tunnel, surely. Looking for sympathy, no doubt. Walter resettled the emergency blanket over Forster's legs and resumed bandaging his head.

Jane huddled more deeply into her parka.

The headlamp lit us like Halloween ghouls, all shadows and odd angles.

As the silence stretched, I began to tell Jane Forster the story of the landslide.

She listened closely.

When I got to the part where a battered Forster started down Nameless Beach, heading for the mine, I described the bloody trail in the sand, and she again looked at him, and I found myself thinking this is a tale to draw them together, and wondered why I was telling it that way. Why Gregory Forster deserved any softening of the story.

Survival, I guessed. All of us in here, in the same boat. Don't rock it.

I finished the tale. "Your dad led us here because he thought you were here." And led us all into peril.

She asked him, "How'd you know?"

Forster's words spilled out like sand. "He showed up at my back door masked and hooded, with a gun, forced me down the stairway to our little cove and I thought he was going to shoot me there but he had a boat and he forced me on board. Injected me with something. I get woozy. He zip-ties me to a rail in the cabin. Drives the boat to the beach here and points up at your window. I couldn't see you but I got the message. He wanted me to see you entombed. I tried to call out but I was so woozy..."

She just watched him.

Walter finished bandaging Forster's head wound and then wearily returned to sit beside me. I gave him a water bottle. He drank. I tried to assess the Forsters, in the dim light. They were each hugging their knees. Peas in a pod.

Forster turned to his daughter. "How did you..." He trailed off.

She looked away.

"Jane," Walter said, "we'd all like to know how you ended up in here."

She stared at her knees. "After I left you and Cassie in the other tunnel I came to the window in this tunnel to watch to be sure you got out okay." She added, still addressing her knees, "I'm sorry about the pepper spray."

"It's behind us," Walter said.

She didn't see me nod in grudging agreement. She only saw her knees.

"And then," she said, "the guy jumped me. He'd been hiding in this tunnel. He knocked me down and tied that rope. He waited until I guess you guys left, then he left. I didn't know if he'd come back, or what he wanted, or who he was. He wore a ski mask, and he never spoke. Later he did come back, with that." She nodded at the shopping bag. "He didn't gag me. I guess he thought nobody would come around and hear me yell. But I did, every day and night."

Two nights and two-plus days in here, I calculated. Until, finally, we came around.

"And he cut off my braid." She turned to her father. "He send it to you?"

"Something like that."

"And he took my phone. He made me unlock it."

I calculated. He took her phone the day before yesterday, and then yesterday afternoon he used it to send a text to Maxie Swift.

Walter cleared his throat. "Jane, I'm afraid I have some bad news."

As my partner began the story of the text and Maxie and us and the *Best Bay Tours* and Red Rock Island, I scooted to sit beside Jane, close enough to feel her start to shake, close enough to clap my hand over her mouth, should she cry out, and then close enough to wrap my arm around her.

Walter made no mention of suspects.

It was all about survival, in here.

Finally, Debra wearied and after some protest from Walter, I took her place.

It was decided that I could see enough of the slice of beach below our porthole to spot the perp, should he come our way.

He didn't.

I listened to the desultory talk down at the tunnel floor-- comments here and there, who wants water, who wants a snack bar, who's cold, what can anyone do about it anyway?

I watched the gray world outside. Fog licked the shoreline. Stay back, I told it. Debra's people need to see.

And then an hour or a half-hour or fifteen minutes passed and I thought I heard something and saw that the fog had thinned close to shore, a ghostly veil that filtered but did not hide. The gray inflatable boat came into view. Its squat blue cabin was unmistakable. Its scratched windscreen was familiar. Its pilot, obscured, was, by default, the perp in the balaclava.

I took the alarm rock from my pocket and dropped it.

Somebody gasped.

The light went out on the tunnel floor.

I shifted position so that my pale face was farther from the porthole.

And I watched, for fifteen or ten or five minutes while the boat squatted offshore, motor purring.

I watched until it revved up and did a showy turn and headed out to sea, deeper into the fog.

———

Debra was on watch sometime later when Search and Rescue arrived.

Down below in the tunnel we knew because she flashed my headlamp, which strobed the tunnel wall. There was a sharp intake of breath, nothing more, no cheers because we were conditioned to whispers, but we stumbled to our feet and stared up toward the raccoon porthole where hope had just squeezed through.

Then Jane put something in my hand and whispered, "She can use this."

It was the electric-blue belt, close enough to neon.

I moved to the wall and climbed up to the outcrop and tapped Debra's leg, and when she looked down I handed her the flag.

It took another day for the Department of Public Works excavation specialists to dig through the caved-in rock of the window room.

In the meantime, Search and Rescue rappelled down from the top of the cliff to pass water bottles and packaged food and headlamps and warm clothing and hand warmers through the porthole.

We slept, on and off.

When we awakened to voices inside the tunnel, I thought that it was a dream.

49

EVERYTHING WAS BRIGHTER.

Even now, two days after the exit from the mine, after our return to work in the familiar and weirdly unchanged lab, everything was brighter.

Blue sky.

White boats.

Green bay water.

Fiery sunlit warehouse windows.

Even those of us gathered at the marina's concrete berth looked different. Cleaner. Neater. Resurrected.

Brighter.

I squinted behind my sunglasses, watching Debra's people unlock the cabin of Gregory Forster's boat to examine the navigation system electronics.

He didn't look worried. He wore his shabby-chic ragged pants with a long-sleeve black T-shirt covering bruises and scabs and he stood with arms crossed, deck shoes planted wide, at ease, as though he was at the helm of the *Maverick* for a pleasure cruise rather than watching Debra's people execute a search warrant.

He hadn't been worried, either, about the search team at his Sea Cliff estate.

The warrant had been issued in response to the grains of manganese found in his doormats, which gave probable cause to search his laundry bin for pants with fresh manganese-oxide stains, to search the glove compartment of his car for a marine-grade fuel receipt, to search the entire premises for any possible proof that he had gone to Red Rock Island on the day Maxie Swift was shot.

He wasn't worried because he'd suddenly 'recalled' that he had, indeed, made a trip to that speck of rock, with his cousin-- over a month ago. And they'd no doubt wiped their feet when they got home. It had been a jaunt, so inconsequential he'd forgotten about it five days ago when Debra had asked if he'd ever gone boating there.

Now, when Debra's techs exited the boat cabin to report that the navigational electronics were fried, Forster said, "Damn system's been glitching for weeks."

The techs climbed off the boat and set the collection kit on the concrete, at Debra's feet.

Forster glanced at it.

I watched Jane. Her blue hair--chopped by the perp--was trimmed, evened out. It looked like Maxie's hairdo. Jane wore a thin blue T-shirt tucked into her jeans, which were cinched by the electric-blue belt, the reclaimed flag. She wore squared plastic sunglasses. The bright sun highlighted her long nose and the hollows in her cheeks--the way my headlamp had lit her in the tunnel the first time I saw her. And the second time. This time, though, I knew what fed that watchful expression.

Walter patted her arm.

She turned to him and I expected another of her stoic responses, a nod at most. But she elbowed Walter in response, like a kid.

Her father caught that, and frowned.

She stared him down.

Debra interceded, asking Jane, "Where, exactly?"

"Can I show you?"

"Be my guest."

Jane moved to the boat and stepped over the railing onto the deck.

Forster said, "What's this all about?"

"Wait," Debra said.

We watched Jane kneel in the middle of the padded vinyl bench in the stern. It was, actually, two benches with backrests fitted into a tight space, snugged up close. She worked a hand down into the rift where the two backrests met.

A bead of sweat slipped from my forehead to my cheek and then diverted to curl around my ear. Nerves. What if it was gone?

It wasn't. She withdrew her hand, fingers pinching a small black disk.

Forster's jaunty ease evaporated.

Jane moved to the railing and held out the disk.

It looked, I thought, like a puck from a table-hockey game.

Debra got an evidence bag from the collection kit, opened it, and held it out. Jane deposited the disk. Debra zipped the bag and stowed it.

Forster spoke. "*Again*, what's this about?"

Jane answered. "It's about our ancestors, Dad. And Maxie Swift's ancestors. It's about me and Maxie trying to get the *Dawn* story straight, going to Red Rock Island where it started. We got it straight. Our ancestors killed her ancestors."

"I know nothing about that." He added, gently, "Jane, you need to move on."

She held her ground on the boat. "You told me a long time ago, *Dad*, that we are not our ancestors. But you are. You're a killer. You killed Maxie. Was that revenge for Roger? Because a

Swift killed Roger, and that was because a Forster killed Louis Swift? Back and forth, the Forsters and the Swifts, it just keeps on?" She was breathing hard now, chest heaving, ruffling her thin blue T-shirt. "Whatever. My friend is dead."

Forster tore his gaze from his daughter. Looked around. Looked at me, at Walter, then finally at Debra. The two of them faced off, each in aviator shades. I suspected Debra's eyes were narrowed behind her shades. I suspected his were wild, looking for someplace to run. His hand went to his head, to the white bandage covering the patch where his white hair had been shaved. He steadied himself.

Walter had moved to the edge of the concrete berth. He held out a hand to Jane. "Would you like to get off the boat?"

She said, "I'd like to sink it." She accepted his hand and stepped over the railing, onto the concrete.

Walter and Jane and Debra and I stood in a half-circle facing Forster.

Debra took over. "Forster, surely you know what this is." She indicated the disk in the ziplock baggie.

He could not help looking at it.

"Oh," she added, "it might not be obvious. It's in dark mode. Your daughter is smart. When she hid it down in the crack between the backrests, she didn't want indicator lights casting a glow. Just in case your obsessive neatness meant you inspected your vessel every time you took it out." She wagged a finger. "Clearly you didn't, because you didn't find the unit--you would have removed it if you had."

Forster just shook his head.

"No? You *don't* know what this is? It's a GPS unit, made for boats! Waterproof. Motion sensitive--it turns on when the boat is traveling, stops recording when the boat isn't moving. In fact, that's why your daughter planted the thing. Back when she and Maxie started going to the island, she wanted to be sure she didn't run into you and Roger there. So she got the unit to monitor your boat. Did the job, as it turns out--the GPS tracked the *Maverick* five days ago."

He said, "I've had enough of this little show."

"Speaking of shows--we all saw one yesterday when we paid a visit to the website where the device sends its reporting. We watched the historical playback, as it's called, the animation of your boat's journey. Its location on a map. It shows that you motored from this marina to Red Rock Island, and parked your boat at the southwestern end. It gives the time frame--thirty-two minutes and nineteen seconds between the time you anchored, and the time you motored away. Correlating that with the time frame my geologists estimated, you arrived about ten minutes after Maxie Swift anchored the *Best Bay Tours* further north. Their location, on that long red beach, had no line of sight to your location. They had no idea you'd come."

"I hadn't come."

"GPS says otherwise." The detective shoved up her sunglasses to perch on top of her head--that raptor move of hers. "Here's a reasonable inference about what happened next. You knew the island, the history, so you made your own inference about what they were discussing. You grew agitated. The GPS time frame gives you plenty of opportunity to walk up the beach and get close enough to eavesdrop. Or maybe you just went directly to the top, climbing up that southern ridge. Plenty of time to choose your position, in hiding with a good angle for a shot. So we have you lying in wait, angry and armed and overwhelmed by events. Your cousin's murder. You daughter's kidnapping. You were pushed to the brink and looking for revenge." She paused, giving him time to protest. He was stone. She continued, "What I wonder is--what if they *didn't* come up top? You have a Plan B? What if they just hopped in the *Best Bay* and left the island? They'd have seen your boat, of course, but no crime in simply anchoring there. So, what next? You'd find another time, another place? Maybe, maybe not--I mean, could you have sustained that level of grievance? My take? I'd say yes. You have the devil in you, Forster."

His lip curled, as if to smile.

Her face hardened.

Hate, I thought. She wore a mask of hate.

And then she shook it off and resumed. "But you didn't need a Plan B. They *did* come up top. There *was* a crime. And after the shooting, you scrambled back down to your boat and headed out--GPS turning on again--and returned to the marina. And parked the *Maverick* right here." She swept a hand. "All clear, Forster? You understand what this means?"

"Nothing, as far as I'm concerned."

"Be concerned. This is sufficient evidence to charge you for the murder of Maxie Swift."

"This is bullshit."

Debra flicked aside her blazer and unhooked a pair of hand-cuffs from her belt.

Now Forster paid her heed. He said, "I've seen this movie before. Never thought I'd be in it. Let me give you the big twist-- the wrongly accused hero walks. And the vindictive detective loses her job."

"Wrong movie," she said.

"Then let's get real." He indicated the GPS. "All that says is my boat was at a certain place at a certain time. *I* say, looks like somebody stole my boat."

"*Somebody* didn't have your--and your ancestors'--history at Red Rock Island. *Somebody* didn't have your motive. *Somebody* didn't have reason to blame Maxie Swift. *You* had all that."

He said, "Your so-called evidence is circumstantial."

"You're right."

That took him aback. He eyed the cuffs. "Then you want to explain those?"

She grew a tight smile. "The vindictive detective is going to have to explain circumstantial evidence. Here's how *that* works, Forster. Many criminal convictions come entirely from circumstantial evidence--proof of a fact from which one can infer the fact in question. Fact: your boat the *Maverick* anchored at Red Rock Island, when the crime took place. From that, we can make a reasonable inference of the fact in question--you were the killer. Alternative explanations of the crime are easily ruled out--nonsensical, even. Such as, some random person stole your boat and drove it to that godforsaken island." She added, "All clear, Forster?"

He took a step backward. And then another.

I thought, another step or two and he was going to pitch right off the edge of the concrete berth into the oil-slicked marina water. He sensed that. Stopped. I thought, he's spent a lot of time on this concrete apron that shelters his boat. He knows where things are. But situational awareness wasn't going to help him, now. He'd pushed back hard against Debra, against the GPS evidence, against the circumstantial evidence, but he couldn't push any further. He'd been stopped. A line had been crossed and he wasn't going to find a way back to the other side.

Detective Talon opened the cuffs.

Walter and Jane and I stood outside the warehouse entrance.

Jane's car was a few yards away in the parking lot. Our trailer-lab was a few yards away, inside the warehouse.

We'd briefly discussed going across the street to Crossroads Cafe for a late lunch but none of us had an appetite. What we had was a chasm. Emptiness. As if we'd taken one of those roller-coaster San Francisco streets and on the steep downhill we'd gone weightless. At least, that's how it felt to me. I wanted to talk evidence with Walter, once we were alone in the lab. I wanted to talk about Maxie. I wanted to ask if my partner felt the evidence had sufficiently closed the circle--from Maxie's bloodstained sweatshirt to Forster's hands in cuffs. I wanted to talk about the chasm in which justice was feeling hollow.

But not in front of Jane.

Walter was asking how she was doing.

She lifted her hands, then dropped them.

"If there's anything we can do..."

"Find out what happened to Roger."

He said, "We will."

I regarded my partner, casting about for some way to amend that. We probably will. We'll do our damnedest. We'll do our job.

She started for her car.

I stopped her with a parting question. "What's next for you?"

"Next?"

"What I mean to say is, you've been through hell and I hope you're going to be okay."

"We've all been through hell."

"Right. So...just take care."

"Next for me," she answered, abruptly, "back to classes."

"Oh, good. Where..."

"San Francisco State."

"What are you studying?"

"Ecology."

"Great subject."

"So far."

I gave up.

She started for her car again. Then she paused and turned and said, "It is."

50

In the lab, Walter and I worked together to finish analyzing the mud samples from Roger Forster's boots.

We had interrupted the job when the Jane Forster case intervened.

And the gut-wrenching Maxie Swift case, after that.

Now, we resumed. Previously, mud from the deeply-recessed arch areas of the boots had given us a solid journey-history. Now--to be thorough--we looked at mud from other spatial areas of the soles, areas less likely to retain particle evidence.

Walter took the right boot and I took the left.

I took my time prying out each sediment plug, so as to keep them intact. Simply protocol, at this point, but I needed this, to ground myself. It was good to put my hand to the work. I pushed past the weariness I'd worn ever since we'd been pulled from the mine, and entered the rapt state in which nothing but grains of the earth filled my vision, in which the mug of coffee on my worktable went cold.

It was on the third plug that I uncovered something not of the earth, and stopped mid-dissection. Did a double-take. Used the high-power hand lens for a closer look. Put it under the scope for confirmation.

And then I whispered, "Oh no."

Walter came over and when I showed him what I'd found, he recoiled.

We talked it through. Up one side and down the other. Inside out.

When we ran out of talk, I took a break to stroll along the walkway bordering the warehouse, which I might have called a victory lap if it had felt at all victorious.

It felt like a gut punch.

51

WE ARRIVED at the mine in the morning when the tide was low enough to allow access. The sleek black SFPD inflatable nosed the beach. Debra shut off the motor and dropped anchor. We disembarked and sloshed to shore. No need to roll up pant legs and remove footwear. We all wore mesh water shoes.

Debra paused to point out to Captain Frank Heffernan the excavated window in the cliff at the western end of the beach.

Walter and I looked, as well. Impossible not to. Impossible not to see the shadow of Jane Forster in that window. Impossible not to take notice of the tiny raccoon hole through which I'd monitored the perp's squat inflatable, offshore in the fog. I blinked away the memory. Today, the windows were empty and the clifftop was chiseled against the sapphire sky and the only boat in sight was our inflatable. We had the place, truly, to ourselves. Yesterday at eight-forty p.m. an arrest had been made in Nevada. Here, this morning, there was no need to look over our shoulders.

Debra asked if the captain had any questions and he answered, testily, "Not yet."

When Walter and I had met with Debra and Frank the day

before yesterday at the department, he'd struck me as an impatient man. Fingers drumming the table, pointing as he asked questions, handclap like a shot to end the meeting. Fifties, weathered, red hair gone nearly to gray.

Now he impatiently moved toward the sea cave, Debra trailing.

Walter and I hung back a moment. He asked how I was doing, and I couldn't find the words. I asked how he was doing, and he said, "Still infuriated."

Yeah. Those words.

We moved, catching up to Debra and Frank.

Already did a stint in this hellhole mine--once more, today, and then never again.

Inside, our headlamps lit the gloom.

The captain took in the brawny brick tower wedged wall-to-wall, reaching nearly to the top of the cave.

He took out his cell phone, hit the video record button, spoke the time and date and location and names of persons present, then aimed the camera at Walter. "Go ahead."

My partner moved to the brick tower then turned his back on the decaying remains, facing Frank's camera, facing us. He appeared composed. I stole a glance at Debra, who appeared as composed as Walter.

"For the record," Walter began, "we're here in conclusion of the Roger Forster case. Evidence indicates that the victim took his final steps here. I will present three pieces of evidence to establish that. Firstly, the soil on the back of the victim's clothing is consistent with this cave--and I'll note that the soil right here is nearly indistinguishable from the beach sand just outside, which gets washed into the cave by high tides. Secondly, grains of brick were found in plugs of mud extracted from the victim's waffle boot soles, and the grains are consistent with the tower here. Note that the brick is crumbly, due to its porous nature, and to the pounding tides that wash into the cave."

The captain did a camera pan of the tower.

"Thirdly," Walter continued, "a new piece of evidence was found, three days ago. I'll note that my partner and I had previously interrupted the job when two other cases intervened. When we resumed examining Roger Forster's boots, we were taken by surprise." He paused.

For a moment I thought he was going to credit me with the finding. I didn't want the credit.

Debra said, "Finish it, Walter."

He shot her a look. "For the record, the new evidence was in a plug of mud extracted from the victim's left boot sole. In conjunction with two grains of brick, slivers of black-polished fingernail were found."

It turned so quiet in the cave that I thought I could hear the susurrous of low-tide waves outside.

Frank coughed.

Walter resumed. "Day before yesterday in the early morning my partner and I hiked to the cave, here, to look for the source. Tidal wash had removed any fingernail pieces that might have remained in the soil. So we turned our attention to the likely place where fingernails would have been chipped--this discolored section of brick here, near the entrance, where the surface is slightly abraded." Walter pointed; Frank filmed. "We'd noticed it on our previous field trip and thought the abrasion might have been caused by the edge of a pack, or some such. This time, we thought otherwise. The abrasion was caused, we believe, where fingernails scraped, and broke off. There was a tiny cavity where it appears a person used a sharp implement to dig something out. I was able to locate a particle of fingernail still lodged there.

Our belief is that the person returned at some point to recover the evidence, likely having noticed chipped fingernails." He added, "I'll note that it is devilishly difficult to remove a specimen from a cavity such as this without leaving a trace."

"The *person*?" Debra snorted. "That's evasive. I expected better of you, Walter."

He snapped, "I expected better of you, Detective."

Frank stopped the video. "Dr. Shaws."

"I apologize." Walter waited for the captain to resume recording. "The evidence led my partner and me to conclude that the victim Roger Forster stepped on fingernail chips that fell to the ground, in conjunction with freshly dislodged brick grains, which adhered to the mud in his left boot sole. The dislodgement, we believe, occurred during a struggle in which the victim was throttled from behind--asphyxiation being the cause of death determined by the medical examiner. It appears that, during the struggle, someone grabbed hold of the brick, breaking fingernails, and the logical explanation is that the person was off-balance." Walter stepped away from the brick tower.

Debra folded her arms. "You omitted something."

"No." Walter turned to her. "This video completes our geoforensics report. This documents the discovery history, the location, and the evidence identifying the person present at the time of the victim's death. For the record, I refer to Detective Debra Talon."

She said, "You omitted the name of the killer."

"We found no evidence identifying him. We didn't know his identity until you revealed it."

She gave a short laugh. "Credit where credit is due, huh? All right, for *this* record, I was called into my superior's office, day before yesterday, where my consultants Walter Shaws and Cassie Oldfield were already present. There, I was confronted with the incriminating evidence. I knew DNA could be extracted from fingernails so I attested to the ID. Further, knowing DNA could be used to establish relatives--and not wishing to have DNA techs poking around the remains of my loved ones--I identified Maxie Swift and Louis Swift as cousins, once removed, twice removed, the linkage doesn't matter, we were family. As for me, I'm a Swift on my mother's side. I'll note here that my geoforensics consultants were surprised when I named the golf-course greenskeeper Ned Cunningham, a cousin twice-removed, a Swift on his grandmother's side, as the perpetrator. Who was subsequently arrested, the next evening."

I said, "If you'd named him a hell of a lot earlier you could have prevented a hell of a lot of grief."

She ignored me. *"Further*--because I want this on the video record--an agreement was reached wherein Captain Heffernan will consider recommending a plea deal, if I give evidence against the perpetrator for Roger Forster's murder, and for subsequent crimes. I agreed, with the stipulation that I would document that *here*. Scene of the first crime. Context for Frank."

The captain stopped recording. "I'm *done* in here. We'll resume outside."

52

We emerged from the sea cave, swapping headlamps for sunglasses.

I watched Debra: the aviator shades, the buzz cut, the T-shirt and slacks, the sneakers. No blazer. Rather, a jacket with no logo. And on her belt no badge, of course, no gun.

I watched her take a seat on the sand facing the water, the best view. Fine. It was her show.

Walter and Frank and I sat facing the mine, facing her.

I shivered, chilled from the cave. The sun hadn't yet warmed the sand.

The captain resumed the video recording, speaking time and date and location and names of persons present. He aimed the phone at Debra.

She began. "It starts with the *Dawn*. For me, as a Swift, that resurrection was jarring. The family letters and stories come to life, the ugly past unburied. As the excavation started drawing crowds I wondered if there were Packington descendants and if so, if the publicity had reached them. That worried me because of my cousin Ned. The old stories had shaped him. He grew up angry and aggrieved--and a little paranoid. The ship's discovery reignited his paranoia." She shrugged. "We both stayed away."

I thought, not unduly paranoid.

"Maxie, though..." Debra's face tightened. "Maxie was curious and she haunted the dig. Turned out there *were* Packington descendants--now named Forster--and Maxie met one. They'd noticed one another, true Fencies, so Jane introduced herself, identifying her family. Maxie didn't have to ID herself--her last name told the story. When she told me, saying she wanted to befriend Jane, I asked her to keep quiet about Ned, and by exten- sion about me. She understood. We were close. She'd lost her parents years ago...and we became close." Debra shook her head. "It turned out to be a fucking useless attempt at containment. It was trying to herd cats. Roger was hanging around, Jane intro- duced him to Maxie, and then cousin Louis came to town to see the ship. Everybody meeting everybody. And Roger pitching that damn Sutro book. Louis the history nerd read it, got intrigued with the mine, and just had to go take a look."

Walter spoke. "Looking for gold?"

"No, he went for the Sutro history. Several trips. Conjecture here: Roger must have alerted Gregory that Louis Swift knew about the mine. In the Forster mindset, hidden gold was the only reason for a Swift to go poking around. More conjecture: on Louis's last trip, Forsters intercept him at the promontory. Confrontation. Louis takes a fall. And..." She paused.

Walter prompted. "And you Swifts blamed the Forsters."

She said, bitterly, "And Louis's death set off everything that followed."

"Set off Ned."

"Yes. Ned wasn't close to Louis, but Louis was blood, no matter how many once-removed places in the family tree. And now Ned's paranoia found focus. He wanted revenge. He started stalking the dig, looking for 'Packingtons'. What he found was Maxie--*his* blood--hanging out with Jane and Roger. He couldn't ID the hooded woman, but he did recognize Roger. He knew whose Sutro book Roger was pitching. And of course he knew the Sutro mine, where Louis had been going. So he came to me, worked up, and I filled in the blank. Maxie's new friend was Jane Forster. The Forsters--like the Swifts--were *Dawn* descendants. And that's how he learned the true identity of his old golf buddy Gregory Forster."

"Small world," Walter said.

"Small city."

I said, "*You* set off Ned."

"If I hadn't told him, he'd have asked Maxie. Better me than her."

"Nothing 'better' about it."

She folded her arms. "I tried to talk Ned down. Said I'd find out what happened to Louis. Roger was my best bet, I knew he used the dig as a PR opportunity, so..."

I cut her off, "So you posed as a reporter."

"Figured that out, did you Cassie?"

"The pretense. Not the who."

"The *pretense*," she said, "went like this. I waited for him near the dig entrance, in disguise--mousy brown wig, baseball cap, giant sunglasses. I was an eager reporter who wanted to see those *exciting* places in his cousin's Sutro book. The mine, in particular. I'd come prepared with helmets and headlamps. He was easily persuaded. I drove, rental car. Parked at the Lands End lot. We began our tour at the Baths--I wanted time to build cred, get him used to my questions. He was a cheery guide. Then, when we reached the promontory, I played nervous. Is it dangerous? No rails to prevent a fall! And he was suddenly in a big hurry to move on."

Walter said, evenly, "And what was your read, Detective? Was he involved in Louis's death?"

"You can drop the *detective*," she said, coldly. "My read? Could have been accidental. But wouldn't have happened without that interception, one or both Forsters involved."

"Then why ask Roger to continue to the mine?"

"To prove motive--that the Forsters believed there was hidden gold. Maxie had shared Jane's stories with me so I knew about the mining engineer. I tried to get Roger talking about that. Up in the tunnels, we talked coal, Sutro's folly. I used the words *black gold*. Asked how the mine was built. Flattered him. Asked about his interest. Used the word *ancestor*. That's when he got nervous, said time to go." She flashed a tight smile. "Turned out nerves were in order because when we got back down to the cave floor Ned was there waiting."

"How did Ned know you'd be there?"

"I *told* him, Walter. Beforehand. Gave him my whole damned itinerary. And it blew up in my face."

I thought, she talks like she's the victim.

"You know," she said, "I've interrogated suspects who talk about panicking at the scene. Now I believe it. Everything happened fast. Ned jumped Roger, got him in a throttle hold. I tried to pull him off, but he's a bulldozer, he threw *me* off, and I stumbled against the brick, chipping my nails, you got that right, you forensic geniuses." She saluted us. "When it was over, Ned laid him on the ground like a child. I was in shock. Ned was calm. Said he'd take care of it, dump the body at sea. It all went so damn smoothly. His boat was anchored close to shoreline. There was nobody in sight. Ned scooped up Roger and carried him like a child, wading to the boat. Dumped him on board, climbed in, and moved Roger into the cabin, out of sight. And then motored away."

"And you?" Walter asked.

"I was slow to think things through. I didn't know I'd broken my nails until I got back to the car and saw my hands on the wheel. I decided I'd return to the cave later to check for broken bits. It took a couple of days--the next morning I found out that Roger was *not* at the bottom of the sea. That Ned had dumped him at the dig. Later, he told me how he'd done it. So damn cocky. When he left the mine, he motored around the bay to the other side of the city, to a boat ramp he uses, got his truck, loaded the raft onto a trailer, and drove home. He lives in Dogpatch--that's a gritty area turning gentrified. Not Sea Cliff Forster gentrified, but affordable if you bought there early enough, which he did..."

Walter cut in, "We don't need a real estate description."

"Yes you do," she snapped. "Because Ned's real estate is walking distance to the dig. And he'd thought it through. He parked his truck and the boat trailer in the garage--it's huge, he works on junker boats. He left Roger in the boat, on his side, knees bent. That's where Roger's clothing picked up fibers--from the boat's floor mat, not a car trunk. Ned left him until the middle of the night when he was in full rigor and lividity was fixed. Ned understood postmortem changes."

"From you?" I asked.

"From TV cop shows. I never talked crime scenes with him."

I thought, right, no blood on your hands, *Detective*.

"He used a wheelchair," she continued. "Old injury, broken ankle, kept the chair. Which gave him the idea. He lifted Roger out of the boat and sat the body in the chair. Roger was still wearing the caving helmet. Ned swapped it for a wool hat. Then wrapped a blanket over him and took his 'ailing' friend for a late-night stroll. Nobody noticed--people avoid looking at people in wheelchairs. Twenty minutes to reach the dig, another ten to cut the padlock, wheel the chair down the ramp, tear out the security camera, and tip the chair to deposit Roger in that jammed-up position that suggested the body had been in a car trunk. Then he wheeled the chair home. Bagged his clothing and hat for disposal. And that was that."

"Not for you," Walter said.

"No. For me it was the beginning. There were two roads I could take. Cover it up. Or arrest Ned for murder and in the process get charged as an accessory. My problem was, he'd taken a photo of me in the sea cave staring at Roger's body--which made me look complicit."

Frank shut off the camera. Said, in a level tone, "Damn it to hell Debra, you *were* complicit. Ned was talking revenge. You told him you'd take Roger to Lands End, to find out what you could. You took him under false pretenses, to an isolated spot, which Ned was familiar with. And after the murder you were prepared to have Ned dump the victim at sea."

She'd flinched, when he started. She sat quietly, when he finished.

Walter said, "We have more to learn."

The captain resumed recording.

Debra raked her fingers through her buzz cut.

I stared at her French manicure. "Why didn't you cut your nails short? Skip the polish. Without that manicure, we wouldn't have thought of you when we found the nail chips in the boot mud."

She folded her hands in her lap. "It's my brand. My colleagues would have noticed."

"And Raptor? Why'd you tell us the nickname?"

"In case you heard somebody use it. I was owning it up front, trying to control the narrative."

"Wow, you thought it through."

"Yes I did, Cassie." She looked down at her hands, seeming to consult her mistake.

"Debra," Walter said.

She looked up. "After I returned from the mine, from searching for the fingernail chips, I drove a hundred miles south to a little town where nobody knew me and got a new manicure."

"And then?"

"And then you came to town. I'll tell you, Walter, if I could've gotten the B-team instead, I would have."

Nobody laughed.

She shrugged. "So now we had a crime scene, and I told Ned you'd be tracking the evidence. I told him to stay away. I was trying to control the scene, as if this job was normal." She gave a bitter laugh. "I couldn't even control Ned."

Nobody contradicted her.

"I thought he'd be satisfied with staging Roger's body at the dig. His revenge for Louis. His message to Gregory Forster--we will bury you. *We* being his message to *me*--we're doing this together. And he was just getting started." She spread her hands. "Everything that followed was Ned."

"Hang on," I said, "everything that followed was Ned *and* you. You had a choice."

"I did. I chose to protect myself. Don't ask me to justify it, because I won't."

"Then justify this--Maxie."

Debra flinched, again. "I tried to sequester her. Encouraged her to think Louis's fall was accidental, that Roger'd made enemies at the dig."

"You failed. She and Jane put it together."

"To my regret."

"And Red Rock Island?"

She snapped, "I'll get to it."

I started to respond but Frank pointed at me, shook his head, and addressed Debra. "Everything that followed. In order."

She snorted. "Everything, starting with my geologists' field trip." She addressed us. "Turns out that's exactly what Ned wanted, you finding your way from the dig to the mine. He wanted the story to come out--the murderous Forsters, past and present. The story gets unburied."

I said, "By us."

"For a start. He wanted to see you in action. He hiked in early and took up position in there," she pointed to the excavated window, "with its view of the sea cave entrance. And waited for you."

I recalled scanning the astonishing window eyes in the cliff when Walter and I arrived. Scanned right past that nearly indistinguishable half-closed eye in the western cliff.

"But he got a surprise," she continued, "when Jane showed up, and then a bigger surprise when she came out of the sea cave like a bat out of hell and headed straight for his stake-out. He retreated to that alcove, a little puzzled, a lot pumped up. And he concluded that Jane was useful. She'd be key to his takedown of her father. And he had the means at hand--he always carried spare boating shit in his pack, including a length of rope." Debra expelled a sharp breath. "You know what happened next. Jane told us about it, while we all waited to suffocate."

Yeah, we knew. And all that time in that hellhole mine we thought we knew that Detective Talon was on the level.

"Sooo," I said, "what don't we know about the takedown of Forster?"

"You were there, at the golf course. You saw it was Ned's territory, and Forster's. That's the one thing they had in common and it had been festering ever since Ned learned who his golf buddy was. You saw the ground crack and the grave--it really was an errant golf ball that led Ned to it. You saw me phone Burt Zhang about the grave, which brought him to us on the run. You saw Burt take Forster's head off about his cousin using the dig for PR. And then you damn well saw Burt lose his shit telling the history of the Forster ancestors at Lands End. You heard that Burt learned that shit from an anonymous email linking to an old newspaper article. Ned sent the email, the morning of. He wanted Burt riled up, wanted him to shove the sordid history in Forster's face, and most of all Ned wanted Burt to reveal the sad story of Mr. Li. Which had given Ned the idea for the cave. Which led us to the cave. Where you found the braid." She added, "*You* were there because Ned wanted you there, to make it believable to Forster."

I said, "You were pretty believable yourself.'

She sighed. "All right, Cassie, I got satisfaction provoking Forster. But I wasn't there by choice. Ned had that photo. He owned me. After he sent Forster the bury-you email--your daughter's missing, yada yada yada--he phoned me with the 'invitation' to meet up at the golf course and play my role. All I could do was try to contain the damage."

"Did you know Jane was in the mine?"

"All I knew was Ned stashed her somewhere supposedly safe. If I played my role, she'd stay safe. And by the way, the braid was never going to lead you to Jane. He'd learned enough about what you geologists could do with dirt, so after he cut off the braid in the mine, he 'washed' it in the sea."

Reflexively, I looked over my shoulder at that very sea, full of dissolved salts, which I'd found in the fanned-out blue hair on my worktable at the lab. I said, "Maxie saw it, you know. Jane's braid. At the lab. When she came to invite us to Red Rock Island. When she showed us the fake text Ned sent. Why did he want *us* at Red Rock?"

"To unbury the past. He wanted proof that Packingtons killed Swifts. He thought you could do it. He was at the dig--incognito, as he liked to put it--watching when Burt showed us that old boot. He saw Walter dig out those pebbles. And he saw Maxie and Jane watching. He thought once Maxie got you to the island you'd end up investigating that damn boot."

My skin crawled, thinking of Ned thinking of us. "He was right. She really did want to know if it came from her ancestor."

Debra gave a weary nod.

"But she didn't live long enough to find out."

Debra said, almost a whisper, "I thought she'd be safe. Ned wanted her safe--she was blood. When she got the fake text, she phoned me to ask what was going on. I told her about our morning at the golf course, at the cave, searching for kidnapped Jane. I expressed relief to hear that the kidnap was a hoax. I played my role. Maxie believed me. I gave her my blessing. Go get the geologists on the job--just keep my connection quiet. So she went to the lab to recruit you two, and when you phoned me, I played my role. Huge relief that Jane's safe, mixed with anger that she wasted our time. So I urged you to go to the island and meet up with her, get the job done. Ned wanted *you* safe, as well." She added, fiercely, "I thought you *all* would be safe."

I said, coldly, "You thought wrong."

"Maxie was mine, blood and heart. I never thought of Forster, I..."

Walter cut her off. "You should have thought."

"You don't have to tell me. That's *my* crime. On the record."

"And Ned?" Walter asked, relentless.

"And Ned still wanted revenge. Always, revenge."

"The slide."

"He'd been planning it ever since Louis. Ever since he set his sights on the Forsters."

"How did he get the idea?"

"He knew slides. Lands End was his turf, he was familiar with unstable cliffs. With earthquakes. You know that quake we had last year--that set off a little slide on the lower golf course.

He told me, at the time, bragging how he'd found it, got a geologist to come take a look, got an expert to regrade, got a pay raise. And then life went on. Until the Forsters came onto his radar and he found a new use for his turf. I assume he Googled--like you, Cassie--and learned what he needed. Maybe he even learned about Walter's pre-existing condition slide. One way or another, he educated himself."

"And you had no idea?"

"*None*, Cassie. By the day of, I was numb, just reacting. Even when he called me to Mile Rock Beach I thought he planned some kind of ambush. So I played my role, sent a team to Sea Cliff even though I knew Forster wasn't there. I cleared the beach, cleared trails, called an evac--because Ned said this was for Gregory Forster alone. I thought, good. I thought, even then, I could contain the damage."

Walter said, acidly, "Try to save Forster?"

"Try to keep myself out of prison."

"And we were?"

"Witnesses. You were part of his story by then. He told me to summon you. He wanted you, as geologists, to watch."

"You mean to figure out what was coming so we could get you up on the promontory, out of harm's way?"

"I didn't know about that, at the time. But yes, he wanted me safe. I'm blood. He watches out for blood."

I said, "Until he didn't."

"Until Gregory Forster got a twinge of parenting and went to save his daughter, and I got in the way."

"*We* got in the way."

She glanced at the excavated window. Then back at us. "I'm sorry for that."

"So it's blood," Walter said, "that you counted on? After Ned fled to Nevada, taking refuge with the shitty branch of the family. Or was it a simple quid-pro-quo? You two were locked in a standoff. If he names you, you name him, and vice-versa. So you kept quiet, and you figured he'd keep quiet. But then we find a chip of your fingernail in the boot soil, and you can no longer avoid accountability. And it's only then that you reveal the identity of the perpetrator."

She said, "You want contrition, Walter? You got it."

"It's not nearly enough."

Frank raised his palm. "That it, Debra?"

"That's it. The extent of my involvement."

"Then we're finished here."

"Actually," she said, "there's one more thing." She got to her feet and took off her shades and put on her headlamp.

53

ONCE MORE WE lit the sea cave with our headlamps.

Frank wasn't recording. Debra had asked that he wait. He provisionally agreed.

"This way," she said, heading to the far side of the gutted brick tower, ducking into the narrow corridor where the tower had pulled away from the rock wall. We followed, Walter assuring Frank that it was passable. When we reached the slot behind the tower--between the brick wall and the cave wall-- Frank looked up to the top of the cave where the walls narrowed and said, "Tight in here."

Oh yeah. Tighter climbing up but now there was no rope hanging down the brick wall; we weren't going to be climbing the 'footholds' up to the tunnel.

Rather, Debra moved on, halting near the end of the slot. She crooked a finger. "Crowd in." She leaned against the cave wall and pointed at the facing brick wall.

We crowded in.

Our headlamps lit the red brick.

She said, "When I returned to the cave to hunt for my broken nails, I also came back here. I'd remembered tearing my sleeve on a sharp edge of brick when I was watching Roger climb up to the tunnel. I found what I thought was the spot and then did a sweep of the whole damned dungeon without turning up so much as a thread. I found something else, though. You'll need to look at the underside of that one brick where it juts out, about three feet up from the ground."

Curious as a cat, Walter was the first to move. He hunched, tipping his head. His light washed the brick.

We couldn't see around him.

He took maybe half a minute, frozen in place, and then he let out a low whistle.

Frank and I jostled.

I got there first, crowding in beside Walter, and it would have taken me a half minute if Walter hadn't put his finger to the brick, next to a small lump. It was half grimed, half wiped clean, by Debra I assumed, looking for an incriminating piece of fabric.

Instead, she found gold.

It was small, barely a nugget, but under my light it was unmistakable, the rich deep yellow of the pure element.

I moved aside for Frank.

He took the half minute, as most anyone would, confronted with that color. Then he turned to Debra. "You want to explain?"

She said, "I want our geologists to explain."

I'd made the leap as soon as I saw it. I chose to leave the explaining to Walter.

He rubbed his chin. "Well," he said. "Well, I would have to do some research and I'd want to run a test in the lab but given the evidence staring at me, I'd say it's not out of the question that a mining engineer versed in chemistry would understand that gold is inert under a wide range of conditions. In which case he would know that grains and even small nuggets could be embedded into brick without creating points of weakness."

I regarded Debra. "This gold, hidden by the Forster engineer, was stolen from your ancestors. That's what you're saying?"

She lifted a hand, as if there was no other explanation for this tiny nugget embedded in the brick of a centuries-old half-built coal mine.

I sure couldn't come up with one. "Did you find more?"

"You better believe I looked. And no, I didn't."

We all turned to Walter.

"I would assume--emphasis on *assume*--that the engineer would emplace his 'doctored bricks' carefully, where they wouldn't be easily spotted. Also, erosion does its work. High tides flood in, erode, and take away."

She laughed.

"What's funny?"

"Forsters searching the mine for gold. Missing this."

Walter shook his head. "They'd need to know to look at the *brick*. I imagine they would have searched more obvious targets-- chinks in the cave rock, drilling marks in unlikely places, that sort of thing. If it were me, I'd search up in the tunnels where there would have been more room and privacy for someone to do their hiding."

She shrugged.

Frank gave her an assessing look. "Why'd you show us this? To prove your ancestors were robbed?"

She returned his look. "Another reason."

He turned wary.

"Context."

He was silent.

"Now's your chance to record, Frank."

He stiffened. He saw where this was going. "No need."

"Smart, Frank. You enter a gold nugget into the record and word gets around the department, you know how that goes, and then--*gold*--you're not going to keep that word contained. You're going to end up with a spotlight on the department and good luck then containing the scandal of your golden-haired detective."

"I don't need luck. I don't intend to enter your surprise into evidence."

"Just FYI, I have photos. And an Instagram account." She flicked him a smile. "Should you need persuading."

Again, he had to catch up and when he did, he said, thickly, like he was choking on the words, "I'll put in that plea-deal recommendation."

"I thought you might."

He was a pro, and his expression flattened into that deadpan cop face. But his fingers twitched. If there'd been a table in here, he would have drummed it. She watched him closely. She should have looked victorious, but she didn't. She looked like she had nowhere left to go.

A suffocating silence fell.

Walter suddenly unslung his pack and fished out the field kit and got the chisel and moved to the brick wall. He crouched and edged the chisel blade under the little nugget and then, with a practiced move, he popped it free. It fell to the rough ground.

We stared, our lights turning the nugget buttery gold.

Walter picked up the nugget and pocketed it.

Frank said, "What the hell?"

"It doesn't belong here. I'm half-tempted to give this little fellow the heave-ho into the sea. Gold is dense, heavy--it would find its way down into the sediment."

"But it's..."

"Worth something?" Walter nodded. "It certainly intoxicates. That's the predicament. This mine attracts the occasional explorer, who might grow curious about this decaying tower, wondering about its original purpose--a shaft lining, I suspect-- and who might be as sharp-eyed as Debra, or just lucky. Who might find this, should it be left in place. And then, as she put it, word gets around. *Gold*. In this case, the spotlight hits here. Lands End doesn't need treasure hunters tearing into this place."

"You plan on hunting down every grain of gold in here?"

"I plan on letting erosion do its work."

"What about the gold in your pocket?"

"It's dollar value? If nobody objects I'll take it to a precious-metal dealer, and then I believe I'll donate the proceeds to a housing-aid group."

I expected Debra to object but she was silent. No more revelations. She'd told her story on the beach, lamenting Maxie and admitting her guilt and then she'd led us in here and used this nugget to extract Frank's promise to push a plea deal, and now the only thing left was to bear the weight of her story. She was standing alone. Not a detective, not a colleague, not the motor-mouth case-runner. Left behind.

She noticed us quietly waiting. She rallied. She lifted her chin and said, "Don't forget that's Swift gold."

I responded more gently than I'd intended. "Not anymore."

54

DEBRA EDGED the Zodiac against the marina dock, dropping us off without a word.

In a daze, we trudged from the dock to the warehouse and into our trailer-lab.

For three days we'd participated in the downfall of Debra Talon, driven by raw anger. Seared, and then hollowed out.

Now, in the end, dazed.

Fluorescent lights turned our operating-room lab so bright I wanted to squint.

I wanted to sleep but it was midday.

Walter made coffee.

We set to work.

There was an outstanding item on our agenda: the analysis of pebbles collected from the sole of the old boot found on the *Dawn*, and the analysis of pebbles collected at Red Rock Island. Given that the island and its history indeed turned out to play a role in the Roger Forster case, we interpreted our contract to include that item.

It took long painstaking hours, because we were drained, and because we owed it to Maxie Swift to do a pinky-swear no-stone-unturned job. And we nailed it. Maxie had asked--on that long red beach--if that's where her ancestor Pegleg had acquired pebbles in his boot sole.

The answer was yes.

When we finished we emailed our report to Burt Zhang, as Walter had promised when the archaeologist allowed him to take the sample. We promised to return the sample the next morning on the way out of town because we were too damn tired to make the trip to the dig today. Within the hour Burt phoned to ask a dozen questions. We told him what we'd learned from Maxie, in regard to the pebbles, and the ship, and the island.

We told him nothing about the resolution of the Roger Forster case because it was now out of our hands and into the jurisdiction of Captain Frank Heffernan, who was keeping as tight a lid as he could on the whole damn mess. Because it was now his Debra Talon case.

Then we contacted Frank to arrange a time to vacate the lab and return the key.

And at the end of that long and trying day we picked up sandwiches and returned to our fancy apartment, on which we had an open-ended rental period with that steep discount. Grudging credit to Debra.

We were slumped in front of the TV in a stupor watching a replay of Shark Week when Burt phoned, again. Nine thirty-eight p.m. He wanted to postpone our return of the pebbles until late the next day.

And he told us what to wear.

And he needed a phone number.

55

WE SLEPT late and then had the entire day to wait for our meeting with Burt, so we filled the morning playing tourist, had lunch at a funky place in North Beach that Walter remembered from his Berkeley days, still in business and still funky, and then we spent the afternoon roaming the vast expanse of Golden Gate Park.

As the day drew to a close we made our way to the dig.

The crowds had thinned.

Work had concluded for the day.

We paused at the fence, looking down into the great pit, at the dig, at Burt Zhang guiding Jane Forster over the low edge of the chopped-down hull at the bow of the excavated ship.

Once aboard the *Dawn*, she glanced up and saw us at the fence.

She put up a hand. A wave, of sorts.

We grabbed helmets at the entrance and then took the ramp down to the floor of the pit. We tramped across the damp earth--

passing Roger Forster's final resting place, no longer an active crime scene--and came to the perimeter of the dig. Decidedly deja vu. We stepped over the ship's sheared edge, which still looked to me like a row of tree stumps, and walked the ghostly gut of the ship to join Burt and Jane at the stern.

Burt gave us a nod. Jane ignored us, her chin tipped, attention fixed on the inner hull where the silvery lead balls were still embedded. She was finally seeing it up close.

Since Walter and I had first been here, the entire hull had been thoroughly cleansed of mud.

The four of us stood in silence, giving due respect to the past.

Then Burt spoke. "The shooters were..."

"Packingtons," Jane interrupted, shifting her gaze to the archaeologist. "My ancestors."

I was next to Burt and her piercing gaze caught me, as well. No need for sunglasses down here in the pit, which was in deep shade. I took note that her eyes were golden-brown, same color as her father's. The tips of her blue hair showed beneath the white helmet. She wore her blue hoodie, hood down, and blue hiking pants.

Burt responded, "Acknowledged," and turned to lead the way out of the ship. He wore his red San Andreas Fault T-shirt, and dirt-brown hiking pants.

Walter and I wore our khaki field clothes.

All of us in quick-dry nylon that could be easily rolled up, and water shoes.

We were going to get wet.

Once more we boarded a boat at the marina beside the warehouse. It was a low-slung black speedboat, which Burt had rented yesterday after reading our report. He'd kept the boat on hire for today.

He'd had to time our trip after the day's work at the dig, adjusting for the tide level and the duration of daylight, and that brought us well into evening.

It was getting chilly, breezy, and we'd bundled up in parkas and wool hats.

We motored out of the marina, and then under the Bay Bridge, passing Yerba Buena and Treasure islands on our starboard side, and came parallel with the San Francisco waterfront on our port. From here, where Yerba Buena Cove had once existed, we'd be traveling the route of the *Dawn*, in reverse.

I wondered if Jane--seated on the starboard side next to Walter, facing the buried cove--was imagining her ancestors sailing that stolen ship from Red Rock Island to San Francisco. Or, she might have been thinking about the recent past, making this trip on the *Best Bay Tours* with Maxie.

I sure was.

We continued, the speedboat slicing through the green-gray bay water like a shark.

Nobody spoke.

Nobody called out the bridge or the prison island or any other landmark along the route.

When the rough crag of red rock came into view, I scanned the island looking for something new. The thing that Burt had found here yesterday, that made him want to bring us here today, was *best learned in person*, as he'd put it last night when he phoned and interrupted Shark Week.

I saw nothing out of the ordinary on that cursed island.

Burt turned the speedboat eastward toward the red beach and dropped anchor just offshore, where Maxie had parked the *Best Bay*.

The speedboat rocked in the strong breeze.

And then it was time to roll up our pant legs and climb over the side into the cold water and wade to the long red beach.

I could have done it in my sleep.

Ashore, Burt led us to the end of the red-stained beach where it gave way to rock, to a pile of big boulders that clogged the shoreline. We took a seat in the pebbly sand. The sun was setting and we wore headlamps, unlit, at the ready for the coming dark. The wind was fickle, gusting, dying back, gusting again. It was getting colder. I was focusing on wiggling my toes for warmth in my wet water shoes when I heard the whisper.

Walter cocked his head. Jane looked around.

There it came again, a definite whisper, louder this time. Then it fell away.

The wind.

"Your Maxie," Burt said, his canyon-deep voice drowning out by-products of the wind, "led me here last night."

I knew he meant our report, and our recounting of Maxie's story, but she wasn't anybody's Maxie now.

"My name is Burt Zhang," he continued, "but for this moment I am casting myself into a long-ago family of ship owners by the name of Swift. We were contracted by a family of greenhorns by the name of Packington to ferry them from Oregon to Sacramento, a jumping-off place to set out for the gold fields. We Swifts, having caught gold fever, accompanied the Packingtons to try our luck. We returned with gold in our pockets. Heading back, we stopped the ship here, to load ore for ballast, and to sell the manganese in Oregon. But it is gold, not manganese, that is on everyone's mind, and we fall into discord. Accusations fly, of theft, of chicanery, of greed. We escalate into a fight. During the melee I take a fall, my feet scrabbling in the pebbly sand, embedding pebbles into the worn sole of my boot. When I regain my footing I run for it, heading for the ship which is docked...just over there."

Burt abruptly rose from the sand and headed for the boulders that piled in the water at the edge of the shore.

He waded in.

There was no invitation to follow, no question that we would.

When we were all knee-deep, grouped around him like an audience, he pointed out two holes augered in a large flat-topped boulder. They were circular, nearly an inch in diameter. Embedded in one was a rusted iron rod, roughly sheared at the top.

"I run for it," Burt repeated, "and gain the dock here, its shore-end cribbed on these boulders. I run all the way along the planks to the end of the dock where the ship is moored. I run up the gangway and onto the deck, running for my life because there is a Packington coming after me with a Colt sixgun, and he fires, and fires again, and I'm hit, once in the boot sole without damage and once in the leg with grievous injury but I stagger onward, finding refuge in the bow behind a pile of crates. I yank off my boot and tear off my shirt to bandage my gunshot leg. And there I hide, listening to the shouts and the pounding of feet on the dock--Packingtons and Swifts, I can pick out their voices--and then they are all aboard, and there are gunshots and the thump of bodies hitting the wooden deck. Then, *then*, all of a sudden there is just one voice, roaring in terror. A Packington. I know the voice. Then it stops. There is silence, but for the wind. And in between the gusts I can hear what that Packington heard, a neck-tingling moan, coming from *somewhere*--back on the shore, or out in the water, or under the dock--and the remainder of the Packingtons now shout in terror, as well. They can't tell where the moaning comes from but they know what they *hear* and it's the sound of demons. The souls of the murdered Swifts, accusing. Now, from my hiding place behind the crates, I hear shooting start up again, a fusillade, the crack of sixguns firing, and firing, and firing, and firing."

When he paused I caught the whispers again, gusts taking them here and there, directionless, and now I thought they morphed into a faint moaning as if someone had lost their way, and I glanced at Walter and Jane, to see if they were looking around, if they were as suggestible as I was.

They were.

Burt was staring straight ahead, out to the end of the conjured dock where the *Dawn* was anchored in a past life.

I said, "What's that sound?"

He resumed. "The Packingtons don't know, they're afraid to look over the gunwale so they just fire straight into the hull at the stern because the sound is coming from that direction, from the island. *I* know, from my hiding place, because my family built this dock, because this is our island and we hear the sounds sometimes, particularly when the wind gusts and drives through fissures into the tunnel where we gather our ore, and causes the tunnel mouth to moan in complaint."

I looked toward shore, at the short steep hill that led up to the mine tunnel, its mouth sunk in darkness.

"I know," Burt continued, "how strongly sound gets amplified when it travels over water, and I know that because I've heard the tunnel sounds onshore, and on a boat well offshore--and the sounds heard offshore were always louder. I know all that but the Packingtons do not, because they are city-dwellers unfamiliar with the sounds of my island." The archaeologist turned to Jane. "Superstitious, even?"

"I don't know," she said. "I don't even know how they could've sailed the boat, if they were greenhorns."

"They didn't," Burt said. "They found me hiding behind the

crates and forced me to sail my ship, and along the way they threw the bodies of my family overboard, to be lost in the bay, and when we neared Yerba Buena Cove, thick with a thousand abandoned ships, I jumped overboard and swam to safety ashore. I assume the Packingtons jumped as well, losing themselves in the lawless waterfront of the Barbary Coast."

"But why go to San Francisco instead of back home to Oregon?"

"Long trip back home on a haunted ship."

Jane slowly nodded.

Burt added, "As nearly as I can deduce."

Walter said, "How did you deduce that there was a dock here?"

"Your Maxie said her ancestors gathered ore here, and built a dock. The site is obvious." Burt nodded toward shore, at the tunnel mouth. "The *Dawn* was a smallish brig with a shallow draft and so could be moored fairly close to shore. For ease of loading. The bathymetric map of the bay shows this island surrounded by deep water--from shore, the depth drops quickly. With those clues in mind, I found my way to this cluster of rocks and boulders below the mine, where the excavated rock was dumped. A cribbed dock was not uncommon in those days--a crib, a box of sorts, built of square-cut timber, assembled in opposing pairs, filled with rock to make a solid foundation. And this," he pointed to the iron rod sticking out of the hole in the boulder, "would have locked the wooden crib to the rock, and from here the dock would extend out over the water--the level of which would have been a good foot lower back then. As for the sound effects, I understand wind, and acoustics, and having pondered those fifty-one balls embedded in the hull of the ship, I made a visceral leap."

"Well," Walter said. "Well, that explains it."

Well, I thought, we have an archaeologist who knows his

stuff. And two geologists who know their stuff. And two hoodies who are, were, passionately devoted to learning the stories from their past, however agonizing.

As Walter pressed Burt on the mechanics of drilling a hole into hard rock with a hammer and auger, Jane turned and waded back toward shore.

Walter leaned close to me, whispering a suggestion, giving me a nudge.

Not sure I needed it. My feet were iced and my interest in hand-turned augers was vanishing and so I followed Jane to the red beach, which was turning deep coaly gray in the fading light. We sat companionably side-by-side, arms hugging drawn-up knees, huddled against the wind, and watched as the bay water edged toward inky black.

Walter and Burt were poking around the boulders at shore-line, their lights bobbing as they moved from rock to rock, no doubt hunting for artifacts. Their voices drifted our way, mixing with the tunnel's whispers, which now seemed to me like the island's own breathing.

Finally, I told Jane I had a story for her, if she wanted to hear it--the twisted saga of her cousin's murder. Officially, it wasn't mine to tell because it was part of an open case against Debra Talon. Unofficially, as Walter had just suggested, it was entirely Jane's to hear. When she nodded, I told it as Debra had told it on the beach, sparing no details, because Jane pressed for details.

I didn't tell her about the little nugget of stolen Swift gold nested into brick by a long-ago Forster engineer--her ancestor-- because it wouldn't make the story any kinder.

When I'd finished, we fell into silence.

Across the bay, lights appeared along the western shore. To the south, in the distance, San Francisco had lit itself up for the night, from waterfront to tower summits, the city a beacon.

I lifted my hand to switch on my headlamp.

Jane said, "Could we not have the light?"

I dropped my hand. Whatever you like, Jane Forster. That's your city over there, your bay out here, its ecology your subject. And this is your island--should you care to set foot here ever again.

We'll leave the light off and let the night fall.

THE END

FROM THE AUTHOR

Thank you for reading—I hope you enjoyed the story. You might also like other books in the series, all standalone novels that can be read in any order. See a complete list with descriptions on my **website**: tonidwiggins.com

NEW RELEASES
If you would like to be notified about new releases, you can sign up for my mailing list: http://eepurl.com/GtdZn

JOIN ME ON FACEBOOK
facebook.com/ToniDwigginsBooks

LEAVE A REVIEW
Reader word-of-mouth is pivotal to the life of a book. If you enjoyed reading this story, please consider leaving a review. It would be much appreciated.

ACKNOWLEDGMENTS

"Writing is easy. All you have to do is cross out the wrong words."
— Mark Twain

I had some help identifying the wrong words:

I want to thank the following experts in their fields for information, reading the book, and giving me terrific suggestions: G. Nelson Eby, Michael Foley, Jonathan Stock, Joy Walker. If there are factual or technical errors in Lands End, they are mine alone.

Thanks to Sierra Hartman for sharing his in-depth exploration of the Sutro mine. I made several modifications for purposes of the story. The nugget in the brick is pure fiction.

Thanks to Emily Williams for reading and commenting, and for the kayaktivist inspiration.

To Chuck Williams, for support, patience, and wisdom—thank you. Seven houses full.

No book is complete without a cover.

I'm fortunate to work with a talented cover designer—Shayne Rutherford at Wicked Good Book Covers. She has created extraordinarily wicked good covers for my books.

Many thanks, Shayne. I look forward to working with you on the cover for the next book in the series.

Made in the USA
Monee, IL
03 October 2025

31404366R10184